"Aren't you supposed to be at work?"

Penn's voice was rough, even though he cleared his throat.

Nadia lifted her head and blinked her eyes slowly open. Mesmerizing sky-blue eyes with long sleepy lashes. "I wanted to see you, make sure you'd recovered from Monday night," she said.

The shy grin she gave him didn't help his fight to ignore the heat that was building inside.

"Your back is better than the other night?"

"It's fine. I pushed too hard then."

Nadia shifted, moved her body, bringing her lips an inch from him and, *damn,* she had a way of setting him on fire. Her lashes lowered as she glanced down at his lips. Every muscle in his body tensed as he anticipated contact.

"I'm *not* going to kiss you," she whispered. "This time you have to kiss me."

D0725308

Dear Reader,

I've spent the past three years plus researching firefighting and firefighters for my Texas Firefighters series. One of the things that has made a big impression on me is the pride and love these men and women have for their noble career.

This made me wonder, as writers often do, what if? What if a firefighter who loves his career more than just about anything loses his ability to do the job? How does he handle that loss of identity as well as vocation?

Penn Griffin's story began to take shape in my mind. After a crushing on-the-job injury, he wrangles with these very questions himself. To complicate his quest, Nadia Hamlin, the woman whose insane dedication to her job was the indirect cause of his accident, is determined to assuage her guilt by being there for him. Penn doesn't want anyone to "be there," least of all Nadia.

I hope you enjoy the dynamics of Penn and Nadia as they try to overcome guilt, blame and their underlying attraction to each other.

If you'd like to learn more about my books and my writing life, please visit my website at www.amyknupp.com. I love to hear from readers directly, as well, so feel free to email me at amyknupp@amyknupp.com. Thank you for picking up *After the Storm*.

Happy reading,

Amy Knupp

After the Storm

AMY KNUPP

HARLEQUIN®
entertain, enrich, inspire™

If you purchased this book without a cover you should be aware
that this book is stolen property. It was reported as "unsold and
destroyed" to the publisher, and neither the author nor the
publisher has received any payment for this "stripped book."

Recycling programs
for this product may
not exist in your area.

ISBN-13: 978-0-373-60737-2

AFTER THE STORM

Copyright © 2012 by Amy Knupp

All rights reserved. Except for use in any review, the reproduction or
utilization of this work in whole or in part in any form by any electronic,
mechanical or other means, now known or hereafter invented, including
xerography, photocopying and recording, or in any information storage
or retrieval system, is forbidden without the written permission of the
publisher, Harlequin Enterprises Limited, 225 Duncan Mill Road,
Don Mills, Ontario, Canada M3B 3K9.

This is a work of fiction. Names, characters, places and incidents are
either the product of the author's imagination or are used fictitiously,
and any resemblance to actual persons, living or dead, business
establishments, events or locales is entirely coincidental.

This edition published by arrangement with Harlequin Books S.A.

For questions and comments about the quality of this book,
please contact us at CustomerService@Harlequin.com.

® and TM are trademarks of Harlequin Enterprises Limited or its
corporate affiliates. Trademarks indicated with ® are registered in the
United States Patent and Trademark Office, the Canadian Trade Marks
Office and in other countries.

www.Harlequin.com

Printed in U.S.A.

ABOUT THE AUTHOR

Amy Knupp lives in Wisconsin with her husband, two sons, five cats and a turtle named Scuttle. She graduated from the University of Kansas with degrees in French and journalism and feels lucky to use very little of either one in her writing career. She's a member of Romance Writers of America, Mad City Romance Writers and Wisconsin Romance Writers. In her spare time, she enjoys reading, college basketball and addictive computer games. To learn more about Amy and her stories, visit www.amyknupp.com.

Books by Amy Knupp

HARLEQUIN SUPERROMANCE

1342—UNEXPECTED COMPLICATION
1402—THE BOY NEXT DOOR
1463—DOCTOR IN HER HOUSE
1537—THE SECRET SHE KEPT
1646—PLAYING WITH FIRE*
1652—A LITTLE CONSEQUENCE*
1658—FULLY INVOLVED*
1702—BURNING AMBITION*
1748—BECAUSE OF THE LIST
1789—ISLAND HAVEN*

*The Texas Firefighters

Other titles by this author available in ebook format.

As always, I couldn't have written this book without help from others.

Huge thanks to Adam Best for his generosity, patience and thoroughness in answering my many (at times, odd) questions about back injuries. I'm sure I twisted some of what he told me in order to fit my story, but without him, I couldn't have done Penn's injury any justice.

Thank you once again to Jim Davies, who provided insight and answers to still more firefighting questions, sometimes the same questions I asked three years ago.

Eternal gratitude to the geniuses at Lakefront Brewery for creating New Grist gluten-free beer, without which I might not have survived writing this book.

Most of all, thank you to my husband and two boys for not banning me from the family, even when I was impossible to live with due to the overambitious deadline I set for myself.
Love you guys.

CHAPTER ONE

NADIA HAMLIN'S FRIENDS often said her job would be the death of her. Today, it seemed they might just be right.

Nadia stared outside, sweating and shivering at once, through the glass side door of the Silver Sands Hotel. She checked her watch, pointlessly, because she already knew she was running late for the mandatory evacuation of San Amaro Island.

Securing the files she'd grabbed from her office beneath her rain jacket, she squeezed her eyes shut and used all her weight and strength to force the door open against the wind.

She'd lived on the island for most of her twenty-seven years and never experienced a hurricane until now. Evacuations, yes, and she promised God and anyone who was listening she would never push it so close to the deadline again if she could just escape safely this time.

She'd left her BMW in the closest parking spot—it was the only vehicle in the entire lot— just twenty feet away, but it felt like twenty miles as she fought against the wind. Her hair was soaked before she was halfway there. Heart pounding, she swore out loud repeatedly. Not that anyone could have heard her over the roar of the storm. This might be only the early stages, but it was awe-inspiring, anyway—or fear-inspiring if, like Nadia, you flirted with being stranded.

When she reached the car, she let the wind press her into the side of it, the stack of folders between her body and the door, relieved to quit fighting for a few seconds. She fumbled in the pocket of her rain jacket for her keys, unable to see a thing because her long, wet hair was blowing everywhere, mostly in her face. Damn, she should have done this inside. At last, she pressed the unlock button and steeled herself for the effort of opening the door.

When she finally got the door open, she screamed as the wind whipped it outward. She fought to hold on, to prevent it from being ripped off her beloved car. It took all her strength to pull the door closed.

She sank into the driver's seat, exhaling shakily.

As she was about to start the engine, something crashed into the front of her car. Something *huge*. She swallowed, trying to get her heart out of her throat, and blinked back tears.

Her favorite swearword became her new mantra, the word steeped in disbelief and icy, paralyzing fear.

Now that she was out of the weather and her hair was out of her face, she could sort of see. And it wasn't good.

The something huge was…a sign? *For real?* A mangled commercial sign was lodged on the front section of her car. Seconds passed as Nadia stared, dumbfounded. She spotted the familiar coral and green of the sombrero from Ruiz's Restaurante, which was a good quarter of a mile up the beach from here.

That realization spurred her into action.

She twisted and fished her cell phone out of her pocket. Her fingers hovered over the numbers as she tried to figure out who to call for help. Not many options when you waited until the rest of the island population had already taken off, were there?

Nine-one-one, then.

She dialed it with her eyes closed tightly, hating that she had to call anyone. *Stupid, stupid, stupid.* But she really didn't care to die in the parking lot of her family's hotel—or anywhere, for that matter.

She half expected to get a lecture from the dispatcher about waiting too long to leave. Thankfully, the woman was business as usual and said a crew would be out to help her momentarily.

Momentarily seemed like eternity when you were stuck in a car during a hurricane.

Debris flew by, slamming into the side of the building and anything else in its path. Not knowing what else to do—and incapable of sitting here doing *nothing*—she turned the key, which she'd left in the ignition, to start the car. It hesitated, turned over a couple of times, and Nadia thought for sure it wasn't going to start. It'd always been reliable, but it was six years old and had a sign lodged in it. The engine caught on the second try, though, as if the hood wasn't partially crushed.

So now what? Of course she couldn't drive it— the chunk of sign was enormous, maybe eight feet across at its widest point, and from here it looked like it had melded with her car. Futilely, she turned the windshield wipers on to high.

Something hit her side window, making her jump. Pressing her hand to her chest, she yelled, as if that would do a bit of good. Whatever it was kept blowing past. She inspected the window, surprised it was still in one piece, without chips or cracks.

At a loss for what else to do, she turned around and went through the things in the backseat. Maybe she could use something there for…whatever. Maybe there was something she needed to take with her, besides the suitcase of clothes and toiletries she'd thrown in the trunk at the last minute. Dirty beach towel, box of business cards, convention-planning folder, Frisbee, old flatiron for her hair…

Maybe not.

As she turned back around, a man six feet from her door startled the breath out of her. A fire-fighter, she realized, registering the red truck behind him and the helmet that made him look top-heavy. The storm was raging so loudly she hadn't heard them approach. And this was the very beginning stages? Yeah, way past time to get out of Dodge.

Instinctively, she went for the handle and attempted to push the door open. The storm had other plans. Even leaning into it didn't make it budge.

The firefighter grabbed the handle and pulled, bracing himself against the back door. He managed to open it a few inches, and the noise and chaos of the weather intensified until he let it slam shut again.

Panicked, Nadia pushed the door from her side but the man, who she could barely see even though he was only two feet away, shook his head and held up his hand. Before she could question him, he made his way, obviously struggling to stay upright, around the back of the car to the passenger side. He opened that door more easily, climbed into the seat next to her and closed the door.

He'd been about to speak when he turned toward her, but as they made eye contact, they both froze in recognition.

"Penn?" Her relief at finding someone she knew was disproportionate and she attributed it to the storm. Any other time, in any other situation, she would likely barely say hi to Penn Griffin—because he wouldn't want her to.

He closed his green eyes and shook his head, exasperated. A moment later, he returned to strict professionalism. "Are you hurt, Nadia?"

"I'm fine. Well, scared to death, actually. I guess I kind of screwed up. I had to come in to get some files because who knows how long we'll be stuck off-site and unfortunately business won't stop in the rest of the world—"

"Nadia."

She took a breath, briefly closed her eyes, realizing she was babbling like a fool. In front of a man. A man she'd gone out with exactly once—or really it'd been more like half a date when you got down to it. Losing her cool in front of a good-looking guy wasn't normal for her. Again, she blamed the fact she was in the middle of a stinking hurricane.

"Let me get this straight. You're sitting in a potentially deadly storm because of some files. For your all-important job. Why am I not surprised?"

"I know. Not my best decision," she said more levelly. "I meant to be off the island an hour ago." She knew exactly what he was thinking. After their failed night out three months ago, there was little room for doubt.

"If you're not hurt, let's get you out of here ASAP. It's going to get bad."

"Going to?"

"This is only the beginning. The engine's running?"

"Yes, but I didn't think I should drive with…" She gestured to the front of the car.

"You did the right thing," Penn said. "By *calling*." He didn't have to clarify that stopping by the hotel before evacuating was not the right thing.

It hadn't seemed so risky at the time. If she had to spend a few days on the mainland, she needed to bring work with her, particularly the materials she needed to prepare for her upcoming conference. She hadn't counted on traffic being heavy this far north on the island, since most people had left hours ago. The streets had been bumper-to-bumper, though. And then, because all the other hotel employees were already gone, including her mom, Nadia had had to find the right key for the hotel, something she hadn't done in ages.

What should have been a fifteen-minute errand had taken more than an hour, and here she was.

Damn. She really hated messing up.

"What are we going to do?" she asked, reveling a little bit in Penn's reassurance.

"You are going to stay put while we get that thing off your car. I'll tell you when it's okay to go. Then I want you to drive straight to that bridge and get your rear as far inland as you can, understood?"

Nadia nodded but he didn't see her. He was already out the door. She noticed a second firefighter jogging toward Penn then. The two came together to the left of her car and she could see Penn gesturing and shouting to his colleague in order to be heard, pointing to the sign as he spoke. The other guy nodded and rushed back to the truck. Penn went to work on the sign. He peeled a couple of insignificant pieces away with more difficulty than Nadia would have expected.

As he bent over to get a better look at where part of the sign was embedded in the hood, things happened so fast, Nadia had a hard time making sense of them. A large chunk of debris blew into him and he went down, out of her line of sight. All she could see was his helmet, skittering across the pavement.

Nadia screamed and struggled to get the door open, black fear pulsing through her. As she fought against the wind, she watched for him to pop up, prayed that he would regain his footing and make another go at dislodging the sign. He didn't appear, though.

The door finally opened and the wind swung it out of Nadia's reach. No longer concerned about the car, she stepped out into the chaos just as the other firefighter ran to Penn. One more followed closely, the two of them yelling back and forth.

The wind overpowered her and she crouched close to the ground, bracing herself in a wide stance and waiting for Penn to move. Sheltering her face from the pelting rain, she watched the men scramble. She fought to see Penn's face, to ascertain whether he was conscious, but the firefighters blocked her view. One of them spoke into his radio. She couldn't make out a word he said.

Time seemed to slow down like a DVD player on half time, and she felt like she was watching from somewhere far removed.

An ambulance pulled up. The paramedic on the passenger side rushed out and yelled something at her she couldn't understand. The driver made a quick stop at the back of the ambulance and then ran toward Penn carrying a bag of equipment and a backboard.

A freaking backboard.

As the first paramedic reached her and ushered her toward the ambulance, the firefighters let the other paramedic get closer to Penn. The parts of him she could see remained motionless and she called out to him, desperate to see a reaction of any kind.

"They'll take care of him," the paramedic yelled, urging her forward. "Come on!"

Right before she was ushered inside the ambulance, she got a better view. Penn was lying on the concrete, looking…dead.

CHAPTER TWO

Consciousness was overrated.

Penn fought to stay asleep but the pain wouldn't allow it. It felt as if someone had jabbed the claw end of a hammer in the back of his left thigh and was raking it downward. And that was *with* narcotics, if he remembered right. Time had become meaningless. Immeasurable. Son of a bitch, he didn't know how much more he could take.

He glanced around the hospital room to make sure he was alone. In the two days since he'd been brought in, his colleagues had filtered in and out to check on him whenever they could. They'd attempted to keep the mood light, trading jokes about the state of Penn's concussed head and bringing him nonhospital food.

Rafe Sandoval and Paige Hegel, two of the paramedics on duty last night, had ducked in whenever they dropped off a patient. This was the nearest hospital to San Amaro Island and just far enough inland that it hadn't been evacuated or damaged by the storm. Penn's roommate and fellow firefighter, Cooper Flannagan, had hovered like a nervous mother hen so much yesterday that Penn was relieved as hell Coop had started a twenty-four this morning.

These people were like family. They meant well and he was thankful for them. But it was tough to keep pretending that he wasn't in agony. Hard to maintain civility.

Unable to stomach another doughnut or piece of candy, he pushed the wheeled table away with more force than he'd intended. It crashed into the metal heating unit under the window. Penn squeezed his eyes closed and trusted the nurses were on top of the morphine. He refused to ask for a stronger dose. Hated that he needed the drugs at all.

A knock on the partially closed door echoed through the room and Penn gritted his teeth, steeling himself against the pain. By the time the door creaked open, he'd pasted on his friendly face.

"Hey, there." Fire Captain Joe Mendoza ambled in. Behind him was Faith Peligni, Joe's gorgeous firefighter fiancée. "Mind some visitors?"

Penn did his best to not cringe. "Come on in. Not sure I'm very good company, though."

"We didn't wake you, did we?" Faith asked. Her dark hair fell across her face as she linked her arm with Joe's. He was decked out in a crisp San Amaro Island Fire Department T-shirt, and Faith wore clothes that gave no hint of her profession. Feminine, stylish clothes. It always tripped Penn out how she was such a girlie-girl outside of work.

"Nope. I was awake, just waiting for a visit from the department's eye candy."

Faith was well aware of the respect Penn had for her so he was one of the few who could get away with teasing her. He made sure to do it at every opportunity. She never failed to give it right back to him.

"You're lucky I'm too nice to punch you while you're down," she said, grinning as she walked around the bed toward the window. "I brought you a couple of paperbacks but it looks like the guys got you, uh, set up." She gestured to the stack of girlie magazines sitting conspicuously on the windowsill and set the books down next to them.

"That's Coop. Always has to be the funny guy. I'd tell you to throw them away but I think they're the only reason he visits."

"And he wonders why he's single," Joe said.

"How are you doing?" Faith hoisted herself up to the wide sill.

Penn hated that question with a passion, and every last person who came in to see him asked it. "Holding my own."

Translation: *I hurt like a mother but there's not*

a damn thing I can do about it so let's talk about something else.

"I hear the storm veered at the last minute," Penn said, endeavoring to get his mind off his discomfort. "What's the latest on the island?"

"Could've been a lot worse," Joe said.

"It's a mess," Faith said. "Palm trees and debris everywhere. A lot of beach erosion. It's hard to imagine how bad it would be with a direct hit. San Solana got the worst of it and it doesn't sound good."

"I'm surprised you're not out there working," Penn said.

"I had to force her to leave after thirty hours straight," the captain said protectively. "Couple of crews from central Texas and Louisiana showed up today to help out. We should be able to let residents back on the island late tomorrow, maybe early the day after." Joe sat in the plastic-upholstered chair in the corner, near Faith.

"Any new injuries reported?" Penn asked.

"No new ones. Surprisingly few overall. In general, people took Mother Nature seriously and got out like they were supposed to."

"Leave it to Nadia," Faith muttered.

Just the mention of her name had Penn tensing and his blood pressure crawling upward. He clamped down his jaw on the anger, not wanting his visitors to notice. Not wanting to think about

Nadia. He had enough anguish to deal with already.

He hadn't told anyone here that he knew the woman he'd tried to rescue. Knew…hell. She'd been haunting his dreams—totally against his will—for months, even after she'd embarrassed him by walking out on their date last summer. Just when the dreams would slow down, he'd see her again with Faith or at the Shell Shack and, sure enough, they'd start back up.

He'd managed to covertly find out she'd gotten off the island okay but had left it at that. "You spoke with her?" he asked in an attempt to avoid drawing attention to his reaction.

"She finally got a call through to my cell phone a couple of hours ago. Apparently she's been frantically trying to reach me, the hospital, anyone who could tell her how you're doing."

He grunted, sorry he'd asked.

"She feels horrible," Faith continued.

"She needs to get over it," Penn said evenly. "According to the doctor, the discs were probably weakened to start with," he explained halfheartedly. "Simple as that."

"Nadia's never been a simple girl. She's pretty hard on herself."

Joe chuckled. "Simple girl. Now there's an oxymoron for you."

"Got that right," Penn said.

Nadia was more complex than most. She'd grabbed his attention long ago with her looks, a body that wouldn't quit and a magnetism that tended to draw everybody in, male and female alike. But her devotion to her job had been a turn-off. Not only had she rushed out just after the entrées were served on their date, but she'd canceled an earlier date at the last minute, as well—both times because of her job at her family's hotel. He'd taken her inability to get through a single date with him as a sign to move on.

"Consider yourself warned," Faith said. "I have a feeling Nadia will be tripping over herself to make it up to you."

"Like I said, there's nothing to make up." He clenched his jaw.

"Even if I could convince her the injury wasn't her fault, I think she still regrets what happened when you two went out."

"Have you been warned about Nadia's two-date policy?" Joe asked.

"Joe." Faith leveled a look at him that promised trouble later, when they were alone. "You're not supposed to broadcast that."

Joe shook his head, only mildly chastised. "Guys have to stick together. If Nadia plans to prance around here apologizing…"

"Two-date policy?" Penn asked, disgusted. No

wonder she hadn't taken their plans seriously. "She actually said that?"

Faith smacked Joe's arm and looked at Penn. "Just her way of not letting things get serious with anyone. She won't let herself become more devoted to a guy than her job. I don't necessarily agree with it."

"Thanks for the tip, but there's no need. I got the message loud and clear three months ago. Moved on. Now..." He nodded toward his lower body. "I've got a hell of a lot bigger fish to fry."

That he wouldn't have those "fish" if not for Nadia's end-all devotion to her job... He shook his head. Not going there.

"Agreed. You need to focus on healing. What's the latest?" Joe asked, leaning forward on the chair, propping his elbows on his thighs. "What kind of news are you getting from the doctor?"

"She's recommending surgery. *Strongly recommending* were her exact words. Because of the loss of mobility and the level of pain, she doesn't believe waiting it out is an option."

Faith grimaced sympathetically.

"How soon can they get you in?" the captain asked.

"Not until Thursday." Five more days. Penn had asked if they could knock him out for the duration, only half joking.

"And how long will recovery be?"

"Joe," Faith chided. "You sound like you're pressuring him to hurry back to work."

"Not at all," Joe said. "I'm asking out of concern, not as an officer. Your job will be there. They do expect you to be able to return?"

Penn swallowed hard, fought off the worry that hovered over him like a swarm of bees waiting for the right moment to attack. "Doctor won't say just yet. A week or two after the surgery, we'll know more."

"Not knowing is rough," Joe said. "You do what you need to. No worrying about work allowed."

"We'll cross our fingers for you," Faith said. "Let us know what we can do."

"Thanks. There's not much of anything but sitting around and waiting. Or lying around, as the case may be."

And that was the bitch of it. He was stuck here for hours on end, wondering what his future held. Flipping out about whether the career that defined him was going to be permanently yanked away. Wondering what he would do without it. Trying to imagine who the hell he could be if not a firefighter.

Penn closed his eyes in frustration. Faith and Joe must have taken it as fatigue, because they wasted no time in saying their goodbyes.

Penn managed to wait until they disappeared down the hallway before he hit the call button for the nurse. Though he'd refused an increase in painkillers this long, there was nothing he wanted more right now than to be as out of it as possible.

CHAPTER THREE

OVER THE PAST EIGHT DAYS, Nadia had thought if she could just see Penn with her own eyes, she'd feel better.

She realized now, as she peeked through the partially open door into his hospital room, that she'd been wrong.

He looked like he was asleep. But more than that, he looked…not like the Penn she knew. Though their dating attempt had been an epic fail, she'd hung out with him as part of a group numerous times at the bar the island's firefighters frequented, whenever she went out with her BFFs, Faith and Mercedes. Normally, Penn exuded warmth and friendliness, which, in combination with his physical wowness, had caught her attention in the first place. Today he seemed pale and weak.

For a good thirty seconds, she strongly considered walking away. That wouldn't solve anything, though.

Knocking lightly as she crossed the threshold, she waited for him to turn his head and look at her.

"Hello? Okay if I come in?" Doubt had her second-guessing her decision to visit. "Penn?"

Okay, then. She could keep busy until he woke up. She'd come not only to reassure herself but to apologize, and if she left now, she'd just have to squeeze another visit into her unrelenting schedule.

Her heels clicked on the tile floor as she rounded the bed to the only chair in the private room. The oversize bag she used as a catch-all purse clunked to the floor as she sat down.

She looked at Penn, who still didn't stir. Now that she could see him more clearly, his bed angled up just slightly, it struck her that he wasn't sleeping peacefully. His features were drawn, jaw clenched tightly. Angrily? His tan had faded considerably. She'd never seen him with so much as a five-o'clock shadow, but now the lower part of his face was covered with scruff, somewhere between stubble and an actual beard. His expression was anything but relaxed or calm and she wondered how anyone could sleep in that state.

He wore an old black tee that definitely wasn't hospital-issue. The sheets were pulled up to his waist and she studied the outline of his solid thighs....

"What are you doing here, Nadia?"

She jerked her gaze to his face, noting that

he sounded less than friendly. He studied her through partially open, half-alert eyes.

"You weren't asleep."

He exhaled loudly. "Nope. Just wish I was."

"How are you doing?" she asked. Faith had explained the severity of his injury but it'd been three days since that conversation and Nadia had been itching for an update, hoping for some better news.

"Really learning to dislike that question."

He shifted a little as if he was going to sit up, cringed and stilled.

"Does it hurt a lot?"

He closed his eyes and was quiet for several seconds. "Only when I move."

"Surgery should relieve that, though, right?"

"I had surgery yesterday. This *is* relief." There was definitely anger underlining his words.

Nadia stood abruptly and walked to the side of his bed. "Penn, I am *so* sorry. I've been out of my mind worrying about you." She grasped the hem of her silky camisole to keep from touching him, recognizing that there was nothing inviting about his body language—and besides, she didn't want to risk hurting him more somehow. She'd done enough harm as it was.

His gaze followed her hand to her camisole and then he studied her, seeming to take in every inch from her thighs up. When he didn't acknowledge her apology, she started fidgeting with her other hand, feeling self-conscious at his overt perusal.

"I know," she said, looking down and realizing how he must see her—a complete and utter mess. "I look like I've been through a war. I spent the night in the Chicago airport because my flight was canceled. Then the guy next to me on the plane today spilled his Bloody Mary on my jacket, so I had to take it off or smell like a bar. I can't wait to get out of these clothes—" She paused awkwardly. "Into some clean, unwrinkled ones."

"What were you doing in Chicago?"

"I had a meeting planners' conference. I flew out directly from Dallas. Had to change my flight after the hurricane evacuation."

"You've been out of town since before the storm?"

"Well…" She frowned. "*During* the storm is probably more accurate. But yes, I just got back into Brownsville. Rented a car and drove directly here. My car should be ready at the repair shop but I haven't picked it up yet. Penn." Without thought, she sat on the edge of the bed next to his knees. "I mean it. I feel horrible."

His brows dipped and she inwardly flinched. "Don't waste your energy. My job is full of risk."

"If I'd known—"

"Seriously, Nadia. Let it go."

Feeling like a little kid who'd been scolded, she stood, put space between herself and his bed. Letting it go wasn't an option. According to Faith's last report, the best-case scenario was that Penn would be struggling with his injury for months. He'd probably always have some negative effects. But the worst possibility of all...

She turned away and pretended to look out the window to hide her raw, too-strong emotions. Her career meant everything to her. *Everything*. It was part of who she was, and if it was ever taken from her, she would be devastated. And because of her, that was exactly what Penn might be facing.

She couldn't bring herself to ask whether his doctor had made a prediction or a formal prognosis regarding his firefighting career.

Someone entered the room behind her and she swallowed hard, forcing the softball-size lump of guilt down.

"Hey, Mr. Fireman."

Nadia turned around to see a tall African-American woman dressed in cartoon-character-print scrubs walk up to the opposite side of Penn's bed.

"Hey, Mrs. Nurse." Penn's tone was warmer than it had been with Nadia, though still a little strained.

"That's *Miss*. And I don't intend to change that anytime soon. Hi, there, hon," she said to Nadia.

Nadia put on her meeting-people face and returned the greeting.

"Got good news for your firefighter here," the nurse, Chantelle, according to her name tag, said. "He's behaved himself enough to go home."

"He'd argue about being called *my* firefighter, but that's excellent news."

"Maybe for you," Chantelle told her. "The nurses here are going to cry. The *other* nurses." She shot Nadia a conspiratorial look.

Penn cracked a slow half grin, the first hint of anything besides anger that Nadia had seen from him yet. "I'll be sure to come back and visit them."

"Not for a long time. You're not coming back until you have an appointment. You're going to take it easy, mister." The nurse handed him several pages stapled together. "This is the information we went over earlier. If you get home and figure out you were spaced out because of the meds, it's all here in writing. You're clear on everything for now?"

"Yes, ma'am."

"You're to start out walking two to three times a day. Just a little bit, to begin with. Three to five minutes." She reached over and turned his stack to a different page and tapped it. "Walking is important, Penn. But don't overdo it."

"Got it."

"When you get out of bed, you use the log roll like we showed you. No lying on the floor or the sofa, no recliners. You need to sit several times a day on a straight-back chair. Bathing instructions are here." She flipped pages and pointed again. "No tub baths for ten days and no shower until Sunday." Chantelle eyed Nadia, obviously suspecting she and Penn were involved and might want to get naked together. "You have any questions?"

"Back to work next week, right?"

"If you're trying to be funny, you have a twisted sense of humor," Chantelle scolded. "No bending. No lifting. No driving. No—"

"Yeah, I got it. No nothing."

"You here to take him home?" Chantelle asked Nadia.

"I'm calling my roommate," Penn snapped before Nadia could respond.

"I can take you home, Penn."

Penn bit down and tried to hide the pain as he twisted too much reaching for the phone on the side table.

"You're going to hurt yourself." Chantelle handed it to him.

"Thanks," he muttered, sidetracked.

No way in this lifetime was Nadia going to be here when he did the fricking log roll. No one needed to see him moving like a ninety-year-old man, but especially not Nadia. God, he hated this.

"Cooper's expecting me to call." He paused, trying to remember Coop's number, then punched it in. The call went straight to voice mail. "Or so he said."

"It's no trouble," Nadia said, appealing to Chantelle. "I'm here. Offering. Willing."

"Go back to your job," Penn mumbled as he dialed the number for the station. "Vickie, it's Penn."

"Hey, it's good to hear your voice," Vickie said. "How are you?"

"I'm doing okay. Surgery went well." Blah, blah, blah. "Listen, can you track down Cooper for me? The punk turned his phone off."

"He's not here. They had a call," she told him. "A house fire. The engine and truck both left about twenty minutes ago."

The pang of excitement that shot through him at the mention of a fire was as ingrained as the need for three large meals a day. "Where is it?" he asked. "Was anybody in the house? Did they lay a line?"

"Slow down, ace. I don't know much about it. You'd have to talk to Lorraine but she's keeping kind of busy at the moment."

If the dispatcher was busy, then the fire was the

real deal. He'd have to wait to get the lowdown from his roommate when he got off duty.

"You want me to tell Cooper you called?"

Penn eyed Nadia, who stood with her arms crossed, watching him expectantly. He was *not* getting a ride home from her—he'd rather hang out in this hellhole for a few extra hours. And it could definitely be hours if the fire was a big one.

"You do that, Vickie. Thanks," Penn said before ending the call.

"Oh, dear." Chantelle was looking down at her pager as she rushed toward the door. "I'll be back."

"Penn, I really don't mind driving you home," Nadia said once they were alone again. "It's the least I can do."

He looked away from her, out into the hallway at nothing, clenching his teeth so tightly it was a wonder he didn't crack his jaw. Two weeks ago he'd been playing football with the guys at the station. Hitting the bars on his nights off. Helping his team win the Shell Shack Beach Volleyball Championship. Now he couldn't even drive a damn car.

He was thirty-one years old. In the prime of his life, supposedly. And he was now dependent on help to get anywhere. Humiliating.

"One of the guys will take me home," he said

as forcefully as he could. He didn't want this to turn into a big deal.

"Do you have any family you could call?"

"My family lives eight hundred miles away." And there was also the small detail that he hadn't yet told them about his injury. "I'd like to be by myself right now, Nadia."

She studied him for several seconds.

"Really," he assured her. "This isn't your problem."

Nadia breathed in audibly and shot him a sympathetic look. "Okay, I'll give up this time. But I'm bringing you dinner. Tomorrow night. I'll be there at six."

"Thanks, but there's no need."

"Say no all you want—I'm still showing up. I want to do this, Penn."

Yeah, well, he wanted peace, but because of her hard head, it didn't seem he was going to get it. Maybe if he agreed to it, she'd get over her guilt or whatever was driving her and that would be that. "Fine," he said tiredly. "Six o'clock."

CHAPTER FOUR

NADIA WAS A MASTER JUGGLER. As the director of events and marketing at one of the largest hotels on the island, she had to be. The first day back after a business trip was always something akin to nearly contained chaos, but throw in a hurricane, too, and all bets were off.

She was pretty sure she was on the verge of dropping a ball.

"Mark, we're missing three tables in Coquina. And leave enough room along the back wall for the servers this time, even if you have to move the other tables closer together."

"You got it."

"Wasn't the group in Sand Dollar supposed to be done at four o'clock?" Cheryl, one of Nadia's assistants and a good part of the reason she retained any sanity, asked as Nadia rushed by.

Nadia stopped in the second-floor hallway outside the smaller of two ballrooms and checked her watch. It was twelve after. She referred to the master scheduling bible. "Yep. They're cutting into our setup time for the Senior Golf Association dinner reception."

Muffled applause came from behind the closed doors and Nadia breathed a tiny bit easier at the signal that they were finishing their seminar.

"You guys will just have to hustle times two. As soon as this group starts clearing out, you can begin working at the front of the room. Subtly, of course. I'd help you if I didn't have a meeting."

"We've got it covered," Cheryl said. "No worries."

"Bless you," Nadia said as she hurried toward the trio of small meeting rooms to make sure everything was going smoothly.

In truth, the three different groups holding conventions at the hotel would most likely be a little more forgiving than usual because of the storm last week, but Nadia didn't want to bank on that. Two of them were new business for the hotel, and she desperately needed them to rebook for next year. Having everything go perfectly, especially right after Hurricane Jezebel ripped through so nearby, would go a long way toward making that happen.

"There you are, Nadia."

Her mother's voice made her stop and turn around. She threw her arms around the older woman as soon as she was close enough.

"Hey, Mom." She hugged her extratight. They

hadn't seen each other since the day before the
mandatory evacuation, over a week ago. Though
they lived together, Nadia had checked in to work
so late yesterday afternoon after her trip that she'd
ended up crashing in the hotel room she had per-
petually reserved for herself for such occasions.

"You look good," her mom said as they pulled
apart.

Nadia wished she could return the compliment,
but the bags under her mom's eyes were deep and
dark, her hair dull and brittle-looking. She knew
her mom's stress was snowballing because of the
financial troubles the hotel had been suffering,
and it killed Nadia that she couldn't seem to work
hard enough to turn things around.

Her family had been running the Silver Sands
for twenty or so years and had owned it for fourteen of those. After a few years of dynamic growth
and financial success, they were definitely feeling
the effects of the poor national economy. Though
many in the industry had similar woes, that fact
did little to comfort Nadia. Not when she'd lived
through rock bottom with her parents before and
still had haunting memories of what it had done
to her mother.

"How was Chicago?" her mom asked.

"I made some good contacts. The planners
for a national accountants' association booked
an appointment to see the property in a couple

of weeks. Their annual conference is usually a little over a thousand people. I need to check on Starfish to make sure everything's okay. Walk with me?"

Her mom fell into step with her toward the meeting rooms, her arms crossed. "Good going on the contacts. You got my email, right?"

"About the roof damage?" Nadia asked. "Sounds like it could have been worse." Thank God for insurance.

"Without a doubt. The Beachcomber had to close temporarily. Winona doesn't know for how long. It took five days to get the insurance people out there."

"Ouch." Nadia stole a long look at her mom. Joyce Hamlin was trying hard to hide her worry. She'd taken time to apply makeup today, something she didn't do very often. When she noticed Nadia staring, she looked away.

"Why are you handling *this,* Nadia?" She swept her hand toward the meeting rooms looming in front of them. "You have people to see to the details and the day-to-day."

"Just making double sure everything's okay since these groups made a point of not canceling so soon after the storm."

"You haven't even started the process to replace Simon yet, have you?" Her mother pegged her with a look of disapproval.

"I haven't had time," Nadia hedged.

In truth, she'd purposely put off hiring a new events manager. Though she wasn't naive or egotistical enough to think she could do both jobs at once, her hope had been that she and a couple others could cover the manager's duties for a few months. But all of them were working extra hours and still not handling it well. No surprise. Simon had been a rock star and overseen, well, a lot. More than three normal people could do. Nadia had just wanted to save a little money by putting off hiring. With more than one national chain having shown an interest in buying their property, every dollar counted.

"I want you to line up interviews this week," her mom said, slipping into the take-charge, accept-no-excuses tone that got things done in every department of the hotel.

"I'll see if I can get that organized."

"Nadia, I mean it. You can't continue to work sixty-hour weeks. Get it done."

Seventy-hour, not that Nadia was counting. Her social life had taken a hit the past couple of months, but that was okay. She'd cut out the casual dating she'd loved but still made a point of seeing her friends regularly. That was the nature of her career. She didn't remember the last time she'd worked a mere forty hours a week, and she was 99 percent sure her mother never had.

The doors of the meeting room on the far left were open so Nadia and her mother ducked their heads in. The room was laid out exactly as diagrammed in the bible. The refreshment table looked well stocked and everything seemed under control. They checked the other two rooms and confirmed that the staff was on top of everything, then headed back down the hall.

"I need to run back to my office," Nadia said, again checking her watch and then swearing. "I hope she's not early."

"Who are you meeting with?" her mom asked.

"Lily Herzinger and her mother. Lily's the one whose wedding was supposed to take place right when the eye of the hurricane was predicted to hit."

"Ah, yes. So they're going to reschedule, right?" Her mom's voice was hopeful as they walked in the direction of the corporate offices. The soft pink and ecru of the decor that Nadia had once found soothing now barely registered.

"I hope so," Nadia said, faking a wide grin. "They've chosen their new date. The twenty-eighth."

Her mom stopped in her tracks. "Of what month?"

"This one."

"The twenty-eighth of October," her mom repeated.

"That's the one."

"Ten days away. In the middle of the Nature's Paint convention."

"Yes, ma'am. We're meeting today so that I can convince her that we can indeed still accommodate her very large, very lucrative-to-us wedding. Because she's been calling around to every other place on the island again to see what else is available."

Nadia had no idea how Simon had regularly dealt with bridezilla customers like Lily, but he'd had a talent for soothing them and earning their trust. Lily had been a challenge even for him, though, by taking weeks to commit to holding her reception at Silver Sands, and then changing every decision she'd made along the way at least a handful of times. It was enough to make Nadia pull her own hair out.

At her mom's silence, Nadia glanced over and could swear she had paled. Damn. She hadn't wanted to give her mother any additional stress, but this was one that couldn't be kept under wraps. If she could convince the Herzinger-Caldwells to stay with her, it would take lots of juggling to pull off the wedding during one of the biggest conventions they hosted every year. For-

tunately, Nadia had never been put off by challenges—in fact, she thrived on them.

"After your meeting, we need to get together.
It's not our usual dinner night but I could really
use your opinion on some pressing budget issues,"
her mom said, frowning. "We can grab something
from the kitchen."

Getting each other's perspectives had been
something Nadia's parents had always done, for
as long as she could remember. When her dad
had died, her mother began talking issues through
with Nadia over the phone, even before Nadia
had finished college and officially taken a job
with the hotel. To her thinking, that was part of
what made it a "family" business. They worked
together, even though they both had their specific responsibilities. When one of them needed
a sounding board, they dropped just about everything.

"Sounds good," Nadia said, and as the words
came out of her mouth, she remembered her
plans with Penn. Crap. "Don't order me anything, though. I should be done with my meeting
by five. Five-fifteen at the latest." She could let
Penn know she'd be a half hour late and squeeze
in everything.

"Ohh? Are you going out?" Her mother got
that tone.

"No. Not that kind of out. I'm taking dinner

to a back-surgery patient who can barely move." Wasn't that a roundabout way of describing Penn Griffin?

She'd gone to a questionably large amount of trouble to arrange a carryout gourmet dinner for two from the Bay City Grill, the very location of their failed date. They'd missed out on the excellent food that night. The least she could do was make up for that.

"Who's that?"

"It's a firefighter," Nadia admitted as they approached her office. "A friend of Faith's. He was injured during the storm. There's Lily." Thank God. Saved by the nightmare client waiting in the hallway. Or maybe the indecisive, commitment-phobic woman had technically slipped back into *potential* client status—*for now.* "I have to run."

Nadia turned away before her mother could see that her cheeks were burning. She'd never been good at hiding things from her mom, never had a lot of reason to. She shouldn't be now, but she hadn't told her about her own stupidity at evacuation time. Hadn't found the nerve to confess her rotten decision that had ultimately led to Penn's injury. The truth was that the files she'd risked Penn's life for hadn't ended up being vital, after all.

The whole thing had been eating away at her, and even after Penn's rejection yesterday and his

decidedly cool attitude toward her, she was determined to do whatever she could to help him.
She knew she could never make up for what she'd
done, but that didn't mean she wasn't going to try.

CHAPTER FIVE

PENN WAS GOING TO BE pissed.

Nadia knew that, had known it even as she and her mom had continued discussing a possible restructure of the hotel's management staff, but there wasn't a lot she could do about it. It wasn't as if she could just walk out on her mom, aka the hotel's general manager and her boss.

She'd texted Penn that she was running late and he'd never responded. And now it was ten till seven. She was double late.

She knocked on his door, steeling herself. In the few months she'd known him, she'd done nothing but screw up with him. He had no reason to be friendly and she couldn't even blame him.

The door opened and Penn's roommate, Cooper, who Nadia had met through Faith, smiled at her. "The infamous Nadia. What are you doing here?"

Infamous? That didn't sound good.

"Hi, Cooper. I brought Penn dinner, as I promised. He's probably annoyed that I'm late."

"He hasn't said anything." A look crossed Cooper's face—something she couldn't quite read, but it was safe to say it wasn't a happy look. "You're sure he knew you were coming?"

"He knew," she replied quietly as Cooper let her in the door. "Is that the kitchen?" She nodded toward a darkened room to her right.

"Help yourself."

Nadia went in and lifted the bag up to the counter. Cooper followed her and looked curiously at the bag.

"He's here, right?" she said, doubt starting to take over.

"In his room. First left in the hall. Not real active today, but you can go back and see if you can drag him out."

"Is he…okay?"

Cooper chuckled dryly and shook his head, his shaggy dirty-blond hair shifting with the movement. "Okay? Griff can hardly walk. Not a lot of okay about it."

She closed her eyes for a moment. "I meant…" She shook her head. "Never mind." Brushing past him, she went to find Penn's room.

When she reached the doorway between the kitchen and living room, Cooper spoke up. "I'm concerned about him."

She stopped and faced him to answer. "I am, too. I barely sleep at night from worrying."

He sized her up some more as if trying to decide whether she meant it. His features softened noticeably and he boosted himself up to sit on the counter. "Between you and me, he's too quiet," he said. "Beyond what I'd expect under the circumstances. Hasn't been out of bed all day."

"Could his pain medications be making him sleepy?"

Cooper shrugged. "Could be, I guess. I don't know... Maybe you can get through to him."

A knot tightened in her stomach as she walked away.

Penn's bedroom was dark, the door mostly closed. Without hesitating, she pushed it open and peeked inside.

"Hello, Penn." She stepped into the small darkened room, able to just barely make out his shape from the light that filtered in from the hallway.

He was a silent lump on his bed, and again seeing him so uncharacteristically motionless made her falter. If she tried hard enough, she could almost make herself believe he was still fine, that he was just taking a nap and would soon hop out of bed and go about his normal life. His blankets stopped low on his hips showcasing a rock-hard abdomen. She had to remind herself to swallow. She'd seen him in swim trunks on the beach months ago and was well aware of his amazing body, but that didn't stop her from thanking God his eyes remained closed as she stared.

"Pretend you're asleep all you want. I'm not leaving until you talk to me."

He turned his head toward her. "What do you want, Nadia?"

"I told you I was bringing you dinner tonight." She brazenly turned on the lamp on the nightstand.

"I'm not hungry." He reached up slowly and put his hand behind his head, making his arm muscles flex in a distracting way.

Even recovering from a serious injury, he made one heck of a pretty picture, Nadia thought. Except for the anger etched on his face.

His dark hair was short and coarse, and she'd bet if he ever let it get longer it would be curly. His nose was narrow and straight, and the bone structure of his face was model perfect. Not like the metrosexual guys in clothing ads, more like a younger version of the Marlboro Man without the cigarette. His skin, though paler than she remembered, was still somewhat tanned all over, or as all over as she could see. She refused to think about the parts out of her view.

"It's from Bay City Grill. I owe you another apology," she said, coming up next to his twin bed. "For screwing up our date."

"That was a lifetime ago."

"I know. But I never apologized, not after I ran out." She'd said she was sorry several times before she'd left to handle the emergency at work, but she should have faced him afterward. Instead, she'd guessed he was pissed, so she'd taken the easy way out—avoidance. "I'm sorry I had to leave early that night."

"It's fine," he said, but he didn't sound fine. "Ancient history. Forget about it."

"When was the last time you ate?"

"Beats me."

"How much walking have you done today?" she asked.

"That'd be a goose egg." His tone was becoming defiant.

Alarm shot through her. "The nurse said you're supposed to walk several times a day, Penn."

"Haven't felt like getting up just yet, *Nadia*."

"Come on. We can walk and you can eat. Hurry up before your roommate gets all the good food."

"You don't listen well, do you?" he asked.

"Don't you want to heal? As fully as possible?"

He eyed her but didn't respond.

A radio message burst into the momentary silence, startling Nadia.

"What was that?" she asked.

"Emergency services scanner. Better company than a lot of people," he said pointedly.

Nadia bit her lip and scowled, frustration pulsing through her. "How can you just lie there when your future depends on getting your butt out of bed and working your muscles?"

The continuing silence pushed her until she hit a point where she couldn't *not* take action. Anger fueling her boldness, she stepped forward and whipped the blankets back, throwing them to the foot of the bed, relieved he wasn't naked below them. Though the nylon running shorts that left little to the imagination weren't much better.

"Like what you see?" His tone was as hard as his muscles.

"Come on, Penn. You're walking. Three minutes. I refuse to stand by and have it on my conscience when you don't make a full recovery. Do you want to get your career back or not?"

His jaw stiffened. "Maybe it *should* be on your conscience."

"I've got that covered, thanks," Nadia snapped back. She worked to tamp down her irritation. That was what he was going for, she realized, but it didn't make it easy to ignore. "You're only hurting yourself."

"Too bad the hurricane name wasn't due to start with the letter *N,*" he muttered through a clenched jaw. "Hurricane Nadia has a certain ring…."

"There's still time this season to get to *N.*" She crossed her arms and waited. "Come on, Penn. You're starting to piss me off."

"I'm starting to piss *you* off?" he yelled. "I'm stuck here in my flipping bed, barely able to get up to take a whiz, I have a goddamn grandma-chair in my shower, all because you couldn't follow evacuation orders, and *you're* mad?"

She closed her eyes as acid churned in her gut. Taking a few steps back, she considered walking away from his abuse. Except…she deserved every last bit of it. Her eyes burned with tears. Dabbing the corners of them with her fingers, she swallowed and straightened, reminding herself that no matter how much this sucked for her, it was ten times worse for him. She inhaled slowly to steel herself and faced him again.

"Okay," she said. "This is doable. Three minutes of walking at a time, right?" She paused but he didn't move a muscle. "Three little minutes. One hundred and eighty seconds. And then food… You need to eat so you can heal, and you have some of the best food on the island out there waiting for you. Just getting out of this bed, this room, would probably help your mental state—"

Penn pounded the mattress beside him and swore, making Nadia jump. He breathed hard several times, raging silently.

"Get out of my room," he said in a low, measured voice. "Get out of my condo and go home. When I need your rah-rah crap I'll be sure to call you."

She narrowed her eyes at him, any desire to help him clouded over. She stared, waiting to see if he'd realize what a jerk he was being, take back his words. He turned his head away from her and stared angrily at nothing.

"Okay." She feigned a tone that said she wasn't bothered in the least. "Go ahead and rot in your bed for all I care. I'm sure your roommate will appreciate some extra dinner."

She marched out of his room, her pulse hammering. When she reached the front door, she glanced toward the kitchen to see Cooper staring back at her from the doorway. His eyebrows rose in question.

Ensuring that Penn hadn't followed her out—not that he could move that quickly, anyway—Nadia walked to the kitchen and let out a frustrated grunt.

"No go?" Cooper asked.

"Didn't you hear him?"

"Yeah." His eyes were sympathetic. "Everyone in the building could have heard him."

"Maybe I pushed him too hard."

"Maybe he needs to be pushed."

The food was still untouched. "There's dinner for two in here," she said, unzipping the insulated bag and removing numerous containers. "Sirloin, salmon and shrimp something or other, red potatoes, veggies. Help yourself to whatever you want."

Cooper wasn't shy about opening each container to check it out and then claiming the seafood. "Thanks, Nadia."

She nodded distractedly. "Am I the only one who's dropped by to see him since he got home?"

Cooper shook his head as he got silverware out of a drawer on the other side of the kitchen island. "Several of the guys have been here, some around lunchtime, a couple this afternoon."

So Penn hadn't had been stewing by himself all day. "Has…has he been like this to everyone?" she asked, waving a hand in the general direction of Penn's room.

Cooper jabbed a piece of shrimp directly from the foil container and shook his head. "He's been okay, acted upbeat when the guys were here. But they were all bullshitting. Keeping it light."

"I've tried to apologize but…that doesn't help, does it?" she said.

"Who knows what he's going through, Nadia." Cooper set the food aside on the counter. "You've got to realize he's a guy who's always been active. As firefighters, we define ourselves by our strength and conditioning as much as anything. Penn's never been one to lie around much and now he can barely sit upright."

A bad taste rose in her throat from the overwhelming guilt. She attempted to swallow it again and not make this about her. She must have failed to keep her feelings hidden, though, because Cooper stepped closer, concern on his face.

"Don't beat yourself up. Danger is a part of our job. We face risk every single time we answer a call. Penn's luck just ran out."

"Because of a poor decision I made."

"Let him adjust to things. This is huge for anyone, but especially for a guy like him."

Nadia nodded, knowing Cooper was right. Whether Penn would admit it or not, he had to be reeling on so many levels. "So…what? I just leave him be? I'm not sure I can do that. I want to do whatever I can for him."

"Even if he makes it clear he doesn't want your help?" Cooper asked gently.

Nadia considered the question. Reran the exchange with Penn just minutes ago. Hiding away in her cozy little world while Penn dealt with his life-changing injury—whether that change was temporary or permanent—wasn't an option. She might be consumed by her career for most of her waking hours and some of her sleeping ones, but she couldn't just forget about his circumstances. Couldn't blow off what had happened because of her.

She raised her chin slightly and met Cooper's

gaze. "I can take a lot more than what he gave today."

Cooper smirked in approval. "Then I say have at it. You've got to do what you've got to do."

She'd give Penn space, but she wasn't going to desert him. He was going to need someone in his corner, and though it would be hard for her to take much time off work what with the usual load plus annual budgets due in less than a month, it seemed the least she could do was be that person.

If he wouldn't let her do it for his sake, then she was going to do it for hers.

CHAPTER SIX

ANGER WAS WHAT FINALLY got Penn to move.

After Nadia had left, he'd continued to work himself up, rationalizing that he had every right to blow up at her. So what if he was normally the nice guy? There was nothing normal about being incapable of just about everything. Nothing status quo about feeling worthless and helpless, like an invalid instead of a guy people depended on in the worst of situations.

News flash: three freaking minutes was an eternity to walk when you had an incision in your back that was swollen and sore and muscles that had no interest in doing what you'd always taken for granted.

Food was slightly more motivating. The smell of whatever Nadia had brought had wafted back to his room. He'd ignored it while she was here, not in the mood to give in to bribery or even a simple friendly gesture. But yelling apparently worked up an appetite, and he'd be damned if he was going to let Coop have all the grub.

Cussing himself through the dread of moving,

he carefully rolled to his left side, then lowered his feet to the floor as he sat up. He gritted his teeth at the pain and realized what an idiot move skipping his meds had been just two days after surgery. After he caught his breath, he held on to the footboard and gradually stood up.

He took several seconds to get his bearings and try to convince himself it didn't hurt as bad as it did. Pain was an illusion, right?

Like hell.

He glanced down at his red running shorts and decided they'd have to do, as dressing himself had recently become an ordeal. He was supposed to lie down to pull any pants on and the heck if he was getting back in that bed right away. He took three slow steps to his closet to hunt for a shirt.

"Who the hell in their right mind under the age of sixty owns button-down shirts?" he muttered as he bypassed the sloppy stack of T-shirts on the top shelf. Getting into his shirt yesterday at the hospital had required the nurse's humiliating assistance, and even worse, Coop had had to help him get it back off when he got home. Not even being half out of it from his meds had dimmed that kind of embarrassment.

He whisked the hangers from one side to the other, futilely searching for something other than jeans and the very few dress clothes he owned. When he got to the last hanger, the one that had been hidden away by everything else he owned since the beginning of time, he snorted. "Finally I have a use for this butt-ugly thing." He took out the god-awful blue-and-purple-flowered shirt Coop had brought him from Hawaii and pulled it on one arm at a time, leaving it unbuttoned, then made his slow way to the kitchen, holding on to the wall.

"Holy aloha!" Cooper cackled from one of the bar stools when Penn entered the room. "The red shorts make the outfit, dude."

Penn succinctly told his roommate where to go.

"Glad you made it out of bed," Coop said more seriously. "I was about to start in on dinner number two."

"What'd she bring?"

"*She,* meaning the highly attractive, thoughtful blonde that you just yelled at, brought steak and seafood, some veggies, potatoes, all kinds of good stuff my body probably won't recognize. I left you the sirloin and anything resembling vegetables. Have a seat."

Penn eyed the set of bar stools along the kitchen island bar and scoffed. "Remind me again why we don't have a real dining table with chairs?"

"Because we're bachelors who eat in front of the television the nights we're home and at the Shell Shack all the others."

Penn's stomach rumbled and he took a plate

from the cabinet. He carried the covered foil container with his dinner in it to the lower counter next to the sink.

"Where are you going to sit?" Coop asked.

"I'm not." He opened the drawer for a knife and fork and went to work on the steak.

"So what was that, blowing up and sending a woman who wants to nurse you back to health out the door?"

"Just trying to get some peace." Even before the accident, whenever Nadia was around, he'd felt anything but peaceful. Now that was amplified about a hundred times. She put him in a rage.

"Seems like she genuinely feels awful about what happened to you."

"Don't we all," Penn muttered. He took a bite of tender, medium-rare steak and closed his eyes. He hadn't realized how hungry he'd been but now he didn't know if he would ever stop eating. He turned slightly toward Coop and felt the movement in his back. Yeah, he'd stop. He wasn't going to be able to stay on his feet for much longer. He picked up speed, sawing the meat and shoving it in his mouth.

"What's really going on here, Griff?"

"Making up for not eating all day." He knew he was playing stupid and Coop knew it, too, but the fact of the matter was he didn't *know* what was going on or why he was responding to Nadia the way he was. Didn't care to analyze it. Rationally, he knew she didn't deserve his anger. He couldn't seem to hold on to that when she was in the room, though.

"If it'd been a stranger on the other end of that rescue call, you wouldn't hold it against them."

"Nope."

Cooper stared critically at him from the side, his arms crossed. Penn concentrated on scooping food in so he could go back to bed. Maybe finding those pain meds would be worthwhile, as well.

"What happened between you two? She deserted you on a date a few months back, right? Was there more?"

Penn set his knife loudly on the edge of his plate. He speared another bite of steak. Stuck it in his mouth, took his sweet time chewing it. He had another bite halfway to his mouth when he saw his roommate shaking his head at him as if he was the biggest wuss on the island. Without lowering his fork, he made an effort not to grit his teeth and explained. "We were supposed to go out the week before our infamous half date. That time, she texted me at 4:00 p.m. to cancel our seven o'clock date. Work again, in case you're keeping track."

"Ouch."

"I was a dumbass to try a second time."

"But you liked her enough to try."

Yes, he goddamn liked her enough to try. That was the bitch of it. Out loud, he admitted to nothing.

Cooper set two smaller to-go boxes next to him. Penn popped the lids off them and jabbed several green beans from one. "Nadia is a workaholic. I don't care how much I'm attracted to a woman—if she can't set aside three hours for a first date…" He shook his head. "The whole reason she was nearly stranded on the island during the hurricane was she couldn't evacuate without some precious files from work."

"Thing is," Cooper said, stealing a bite of red potato, "she seems to have a thing for you."

Penn stared straight ahead at the walnut cabinet. "Yeah, and that thing is called guilt."

"It's a safe bet that's part of it. So you going to keep making her pay?"

"If it makes me feel better, yeah." Penn shoved the empty plate aside. Fought to hide a grimace at the increasing pain in his lower back. "I need to get off my feet."

"I got this," Cooper said, gesturing to the dinner remains. "Go relax."

Relax. Yeah, right. He nodded his thanks to his roommate and shuffled toward the bathroom in search of his pills. Nothing quite like settling in with a good old dose of resentment while waiting for oblivion to take over.

CHAPTER SEVEN

IT TURNED OUT PENN wasn't much for lying around in bed all day doing nothing. Not that he'd ever thought he was, but up until this morning, hiding from reality was the only thing he wanted to do, and bed seemed like the place to do that. Today he still had no interest in reality but he couldn't stand staring at his bedroom ceiling for another minute.

He'd walked his three minutes. Twice. Wasn't he a good patient?

Damn. He rubbed his hand over his face from forehead to chin. The wait for his follow-up doctor appointment was killing him, as that was when the doctor would give him word on whether he'd be able to return to his career. It was tough to be positive when there was a big question mark hanging over your head.

Penn walked into the kitchen and went directly to the fridge. As usual there wasn't much in it besides beer and summer sausage, Cooper's main nourishment. If his roommate died tomorrow, an autopsy would probably find only beer and sausage in his veins.

It took him a moment to locate the leftovers of what Nadia had delivered yesterday. Coop had stashed them on the bottom shelf beneath the lunch-meat drawer. Penn started to bend for them, swore and remembered he wasn't supposed to bend for *anything*. Knowing Coop and food, he'd probably hidden everything down low for that very reason. Penn bent his knees to get hold of the green beans and red potatoes he hadn't finished last night before he'd needed to get horizontal.

"Don't hurt yourself," Coop said as he breezed into the kitchen with a fast-food bag in his hand.

"Don't put stuff on the bottom shelf," Penn shot back as he slowly straightened. "I'll forgive you if there's something in that bag for me."

"Might've gotten you a couple ketchup packets."

A knock at the door prevented Penn from telling his roommate what he thought about that. "I'll get it."

Cooper had started toward the living room and stopped, giving Penn a questioning look.

"I got it," Penn repeated, irritated. Answering the door was a normal thing to do, and since he was already upright and longing for any semblance of normalcy…

He opened the door and felt his jaw drop at the sight of the little sister he hadn't seen for a couple of years. "Zoe?"

"Mom is one seriously ticked-off woman, Penn Griffin. And insane." She stepped across the threshold. "Oh, and hi."

Penn grinned for the first time in days. "Come here, you." He held his arms out to hug her. She stepped toward him and hesitated before wrapping her arms around him cautiously. "I'm fine as long as you move slow," he told her.

She gave him a quick, gentle hug and stepped back, looking him over critically.

"Mom really sent you down here to check on me?"

"What did you expect? You called us three days *after* major back surgery to tell us you'd been injured almost two weeks before?" Zoe shook her head, her chin-length brown hair swinging with the motion. "I'm the first to agree she's hard-core, but really, you kind of deserve it this time."

Penn, wearing the god-awful Hawaiian shirt again, looked away. He had no argument that his mom, or even his sister, would accept.

"So she bought you a last-minute plane ticket? Isn't that a little overkill?"

"It's the only way we could be sure you're okay. That you're taking care of yourself. Seriously, Penn, we didn't even know if you could walk!"

She hauled in a hefty duffel bag he hadn't noticed sitting on the outdoor walkway. It landed against the wall next to the front door with a substantial thud.

"I'm okay. Walking just fine." *At this particular moment, anyway.* He went toward the kitchen as he spoke.

"And I'm babysitting him," Cooper said, perched on the counter and craning his neck to see around Penn. "What more could a guy need besides twenty pieces of chickenlike bliss with dipping sauce?"

Uh-oh. Penn cringed even before Zoe replied.

"Some food with a little health value, maybe?"

"Ah. I get it." Coop hopped down. "You're one of *those.*"

"Coop," Penn said, trying to convey an unspoken warning to his blockhead friend. "This is my sister, Zoe. Zoe, my roommate and junkfood zealot, Cooper Flannagan."

Cooper crossed the space and offered his hand. Zoe, who'd been too serious since her first breath, hesitated a moment as she assessed him, then shook it.

"Nice to meet you," Coop said.

"Same." She dropped her hand and stepped back.

Penn made the mistake of thinking she'd let Coop's previous comment pass.

"I'm one of what, by the way?" his sister asked.

"Health freak. Which is cool. But you have to understand, bachelors have different standards. Especially when they have a physical job. Our priority when it comes to mealtime is quantity. How many burgers can I get for my buck?"

"I'll keep that in mind." Instead of launching into one of her value-of-nutrients speeches, Zoe inspected the kitchen and wandered back to the living room doorway. "So this is your secret hide-out."

"Nothing secret about it." Penn followed her into the room and watched as she spun around slowly, then went to the window to check out the view of the community swimming pool. He started to lean against the doorjamb out of habit but stopped himself at the first jab of pain.

Zoe raised one brow at him, an expression that had always bugged him, mostly because he couldn't master it himself. "How long have you lived here?" she asked.

He shrugged. "Three, three and a half years."

"And I've never been here."

"You could have visited."

"You never invited me."

"Since when do you need an invitation? You showed up today without one."

"I showed up today with a decree from Mom."

"You're twenty-four—"

"Twenty-five," she corrected. "And until I finish my doctorate, I'm living in Mom's house. I value peace, so when she has a grand idea like having me check up on my dear, derelict brother, I usually go along with it. Especially when it includes a free trip to an island."

"Martyr," Penn said dryly. "So you've checked on me. I bet Coop can give you a ride back to the airport." Though he didn't mind Zoe in general, he wasn't in the mood for houseguests. At all.

"Nice." Zoe strode past him, back into the kitchen. "I've confirmed that you're alive and mobile—"

"You hit at a banner moment for that," Cooper said, watching her with amusement as she waltzed around the kitchen and checked out all the cabinets. Wasn't much to see in there except for cheap dinnerware, some pans and a few likely expired dry goods. "He's up right now for food, but he spends most of his time in his room, on his back."

Penn glared at his traitorous roommate. He bit down on a sarcastic comment, though, fully aware that Coop had gone out of his way so far to make things easier for him. He was under no obligation to do that, and there were times, like now, that getting a meal would be a lot harder for Penn to manage without his roommate.

"That's what I suspected. And then there's the problem of your kitchen."

Penn joined Cooper by the far counter, out of his sister-with-a-mission's way, and helped himself to the chicken nuggets his roommate offered.

"This kitchen is spotless," Cooper said defensively.

"Not hard to keep an empty room clean," Zoe said. She exhausted her search, turning to face them and crossing her arms over her chest. "In all seriousness, what on earth do you guys eat? There's not enough in here to feed a dieting mouse."

"Don't ask a question unless you can handle the answer," Penn said.

"We eat a balanced diet," Cooper insisted.

There was no way this was going to end well. As soon as Penn devoured his food, he was going straight back to his room to take cover.

Zoe looked doubtfully at them both.

"Mexican, Chinese, American, seafood," Coop continued. "See? Lots of balance."

"Maybe I've never told you," Penn said to his roommate. "My sister is getting her PhD in nutrition. You aren't going to win this battle."

"There's no battle," Zoe said quietly. "I'm here to ensure my brother gets the best possible nutrition so his body can heal. If you want to kill yourself slowly by eating garbage, that's none of my business."

In response, Cooper took out the remaining large order of French fries and handed it to a grateful Penn.

"It's all we've got," Penn said to his sister. "You can reform me later, but right now I'm starving." He shoved a couple of fries in his mouth. "So where are you staying and how long will you be in town?"

She looked up from the smartphone she'd whipped out. "I'd hoped I could stay here on your couch?"

"I guess so." Penn thought twice and looked at Coop. "Okay with you?" It was Cooper's condo, after all. His parents had left it to him when they'd died. Penn paid a token amount of rent each month to live here.

"As long as she doesn't try to reform me."

"Get her started cooking," Penn said, "and you may not want her to leave."

"Yeah? If she promises not to hide veggies in my spaghetti sauce, we'll give it a go."

"Funny," Zoe said, smiling.

"He's serious," Penn told her. "He and vegetables don't get along real well."

"How old are you?" she asked Cooper, mimicking Penn's earlier words and tone.

"Thirty-three years of a vegetable-free life-style."

"It's a miracle you guys survive on your own. This is why God created marriage."

"God or Satan," Penn said. "One of the two."

"Your sister might have a point. Nothing wrong with having a woman around to take care of you. If it's the right sort of woman."

"And what's the right sort of woman, O wise guy?" Penn opened his mouth and dumped the last of the fry crumbs in.

"The one you sent packing seemed like a good start."

Zoe was reaching into the upper cabinet behind her for a glass. She turned and eyed the two of them curiously.

"Nadia?" Penn said in disbelief. He'd thought Coop was over that rant.

"My brother had a girlfriend?"

"Nah, he screwed it up too early for that. She brought him a gourmet dinner from one of the island's best restaurants. He sent her away practically in tears."

"She wasn't in tears," Penn said.

"What did you do to her?" Zoe asked, filling her glass from the tap.

Penn had been trying to forget about it, forget about Nadia.

"He yelled at her."

"You're lucky I can't take a swing at you right now," Penn told Coop. "I didn't yell."

"They could hear you all the way at the station. She's a beautiful girl," Coop said to Zoe matter-of-factly. "Seems nice, too. She visited him in the hospital, offered to give him a ride home when he was released. Do you think he took it?"

"I'm guessing no?" Zoe said, taking a few steps toward them.

"Hell, no. The moron waited around another six hours before I could get there and drive him home. I'm a pretty all-around awesome guy and all, but I'm not nearly as hot as Nadia is. You need to quit blaming her for your injury, dude."

"Don't you think I'm trying?" Penn demanded, his volume increasing.

"Why would you blame her?" Zoe asked, looking from one to the other.

Cooper gave her a brief blow-by-blow of what had happened. Handy, since Penn wasn't about to do it.

"Ooh," Zoe said. "She must feel awful. I'm sure that's why she brought you food. And then you still made her cry."

"She didn't cry."

"You need to apologize to her, Penn. I've been on the receiving end of your mean side."

"At least thank her for the grub," Coop said.

"She spent a big chunk of change on it. Can't remember the last time I ate so well."

"Okay, okay," Penn said grumpily, feeling more and more like crap and not just because he'd been standing for too long. "I'll tell her I'm sorry if it'll get you two off my back. I'm sure she's fine, though."

"Fine like your senior prom date?" Zoe asked like the little smart aleck with the infallible memory that she was.

Cooper checked his watch. "I'd love to stay and discuss Penn's screwing-up-with-girls history but I've got to run."

"Where are you going?" Penn asked, hoping Zoe could find something to do because he was talked out, stood out, everythinged out.

"Shell Shack. Two-dollar Sandblasters tonight."

A fact that was as ingrained in everyone's head at the fire department as CPR and house fire protocol. "I have a back injury, not a brain one, jackass." Yeah, he was pissed he couldn't join them. "Drink one for me. Or two."

"You got it," Coop said on his way out. "Nice to meet you, food chick."

"Um, yeah," Zoe said, frowning. "Same."

Penn spoke up before she could launch any complaints about Cooper. "You never said how long you were staying."

"My flight home is Friday."

"Three days? Are you sure you can stand us for that long?"

"I'm a little out of practice, but yeah. It's good to see you, Penn. You don't look quite as bad as I'd imagined."

"Thanks, I think. I'll be fine. You really don't have to stay."

"You want me to leave?"

"I didn't say that. But I'm not good for much tour guiding. I need to go back to bed. Hope you don't mind entertaining yourself."

"If you consider working on my dissertation self-entertainment, I'm good to go. I have a lot to get done while I'm here. As soon as I go pick up some dinner ingredients and feed you a proper meal. Mind if I borrow your car?"

"If you're getting food, you can borrow whatever you want."

"While I'm gone, you're going to call Nadia, right?"

"Wasn't planning on it."

"Come on, Penn. You're a firefighter. What happened to being noble and heroic? I know you're in a really bad state right now but...she didn't do anything intentional."

"I told you I'd apologize," he snapped. "But I'll do it when I'm damn good and ready."

He made his way to his room for his keys and some cash, knowing full well that his sister was right, which just pissed him off even more.

CHAPTER EIGHT

NADIA HAD A GOOD FEELING about this guy. Well, these people, technically, but there was no question that Dr. Gene Morris was the one who called the shots.

He was the president of a regional association of podiatrists and his group was scrambling to reschedule their annual conference. In Nadia's experience, it was rare that he was taking such an active part in it—most busy professionals left the organizing to paid planners. His planner was with him, but because the storm had forced their last-minute venue change, he wanted to personally see to it that they booked a facility that could offer a well-run conference. That, of course, was where Nadia came in.

She opened the door to the Sea Grass patio of the hotel and let Dr. Morris and Stacy, the planner, pass through ahead of her. "This is another possibility for a dinner setting if you prefer something outdoors," Nadia said. "We can place heaters throughout the area if the temperature's a little cool, always a possibility in February, and you still have the amazing view."

Their timing couldn't have been better tonight. Because the doctor wasn't able to get away until after office hours, they'd set this appointment for the evening. As they walked outside, the sun had dipped low behind them and cast a particularly stunning show of oranges and reds over the water. Nadia couldn't have paid for better advertising.

"I see. Fantastic." Dr. Morris turned to Stacy. "This would be nice for Saturday night, don't you think?"

"Absolutely." Stacy typed something on the electronic tablet she'd toted around for the entire tour. "Are all the usual options available out here? Buffet, sit-down…"

"Anything you want," Nadia said.

Though the storm had caused the hotel's events department all kinds of chaos, this possibility of new business was an upside. The conference for podiatrists had been booked for two years on San Solana, the island north of San Amaro. Unfortunately, the hotel they'd planned to use was all but destroyed. While Nadia truly felt for the hotel owners—like Silver Sands, it was one of the few family-owned operations left in the area—she wasn't about to turn down the extra business.

Every little bit helped, and a conference with an anticipated four hundred and fifty attendees was more than a little bit.

As Dr. Morris wandered across the large concrete area toward the beach, Stacy shot several questions at Nadia and noted the answers on her tablet. She nodded slowly as she typed. "We'd definitely want our final dinner out here. It's beautiful. So what's—"

"There you are, Nadia!"

Nadia frowned and turned to see her mother walk purposefully out the door. When Joyce realized Nadia wasn't alone, she faltered.

"Oh. I'm sorry," her mom said, smiling at Stacy. "I didn't realize you were with someone. Come find me later."

"It's okay, Mom. This is Stacy Keller. She's working on rescheduling a conference that was misplaced by the storm. Stacy, this is Joyce Hamlin, our general manager and my mother."

Dr. Morris rejoined them, looking eager for an introduction so Nadia did the formalities again. He complimented her mother on how well maintained the property was and what a calming atmosphere it had. If only he could see behind the scenes, where there were never enough minutes in the day. Calm on the outside was what they strived for, though, and her mother beamed at the praise.

"Why don't we sit down and talk more specifically about what your group needs and what you have in mind," Nadia said.

"Is it okay if I join you?" her mom asked. A vague alarm went off in Nadia's head—her mom trusted her implicitly and wasn't one to check up on her, so the request was...odd.

"Of course." Nadia's mind returned to the business at hand as she silently reviewed the information Stacy and Dr. Morris had offered so far. "The most direct route to my office is this way." Nadia led them across the patio, with Stacy falling in next to her and her mom and the doctor following. "If your attendees bring family members, we have a long list of activities to keep them busy. We have two pools, two hot tubs, a workout room, sauna, tennis court, basketball, surf lessons, beach volleyball...."

Her phone buzzed with a message and she absently pulled it out as she walked. "Our restaurant serves everything from salads and sandwiches to steaks and seafood. There's a breakfast and coffee cart daily. The bar is open until—"

She made the mistake of glancing at the screen of her phone. The text message was from a local number she didn't recognize and her eyes skirted over it to the actual message.

Nadia, it's Penn.

"Uhhh…" She struggled to remember what she'd been saying.

"The bar," her mom prompted. "It's open till midnight on weeknights."

"And two on weekends."

Why was Penn texting her? He'd made it clear he didn't want to talk to her when she'd brought him dinner. Better yet, why did a text from him have her instantly rattled?

Business, she reminded herself. Potential clients.

Bar hours, restaurant, what else did she need to tell these people? "Oh, and we have a top-notch full-service spa."

"Now you're talking," Stacy said. "I haven't had a massage for years."

Nadia barely heard her, and thankfully her mother joined in about the excellent skills of their spa staff.

It was a bad idea but Nadia stole another peek at the text message.

Sorry for yelling the other day. You didn't deserve that. Dinner rocked, even cold. Thx.

She slipped the phone back in her jacket pocket and tried to play it cool. Attempted to tune back into the conversation that had taken on a more casual tone.

Penn had gone out of his way to apologize. She hadn't thought she'd hear from him again.

As the four of them sat down around the table in her office, her mom caught her attention with a curious glance that said, *What the heck is going on?*

Nadia shook her head minutely and tried to get her mind on this meeting. This very important meeting that could mean a chunk of unanticipated revenue.

When Dr. Morris and his planner left almost an hour later, Nadia exchanged a confident smile with her mom.

"It looks good," Nadia said quietly.

Her mom shot a quick look at the doctor's backside; he was at the other end of the hall, about to turn out of their line of sight. "Yes, it does," she agreed emphatically.

"Mom! He's nice but he's…old."

Her mom laughed. "Hate to tell you this but he's not more than about five years older than me, dear daughter."

"Oh. But he's a client. Or *will be* soon, anyway."

"Stop," Joyce said, still smiling. "I'm not going

to have a fling or anything. I merely said he looks good. And I agree, they're going to sign. Nice job, once you recovered from…whatever that was. Who texted you?"

Nadia sighed, on the verge of blowing off the question. But she and her mom didn't hide much from each other. Not telling her about Penn made it seem as if there was something going on. There wasn't. Nothing but an unexpected apology. She briefly explained what had happened the other night.

"This is the back-injury patient?" Joyce asked.

"Right."

"Penn? Didn't you go out on a date with a Penn?"

Crap. She needed to start hiding *more* from her mom. "Kind of."

"There aren't many Penns around," her mom said knowingly.

"Same guy. But the dating part is over."

"Well, something doesn't sound exactly over if you're bringing him food and he's texting you."

"His meds must have worn off or something, but believe me, he doesn't like me. Did you not hear the part about him blaming me for his accident? And dinner was the least I could do since it *was* my fault."

Her mother shot her a doubtful look but Nadia didn't give it much thought. She needed to catch

Cheryl before she left for the day to make sure she'd worked out some last-minute solutions for an event tomorrow.

"Did you text him back?" her mom asked, waiting for her at the door.

"Not yet." Nadia grabbed her copy of the events bible and hurried into the hallway.

"Don't leave the poor guy hanging."

"I won't, Mom. I'll respond to him. Soon."

CHAPTER NINE

PENN THOUGHT ALL HE NEEDED was a drink of water.

As soon as Zoe and Coop went out the front door on another grocery run, Penn talked himself into getting off the edge of the bed where he'd been perched, just about paralyzed by the storm of a hundred different emotions going through him.

He'd been through what felt like dozens of appointments and consultations that afternoon. Zoe had been a saint to go with him because he couldn't have handled the news alone. She'd hesitated to leave him by himself now but he'd managed to persuade her that they all needed to eat.

As if he had any kind of appetite.

Slowly, wearily, he made his way to the kitchen for a glass. When he grabbed one from the bottom shelf, he fumbled with it and it fell to the counter. The crash rattled his already thinly stretched nerves and he swore. Pounded the counter next to it, making the glass jump.

Without thinking, he picked up the glass and flung it across the room as hard as he could, ignoring the pang in his lower back and receiving momentary satisfaction as the glass shattered against the wall. Rage shoved the satisfaction aside in no time, and Penn reached for another glass. Hurled it at the same spot on the wall. Without twisting, he turned to get another and another, ranting and cussing at the top of his lungs.

He'd lost count by the time the shelf was empty and eyed the one above. The fight drained from him and he was suddenly too tired to even get the drink he'd set out for before losing it. He stood there, ramrod straight, holding on to the counter, not sure he trusted himself to do anything else.

When someone knocked on the door, he ignored it. No doubt it was a neighbor who'd heard all the glasses being smashed and his incoherent tirade. They'd just have to assume he was dead in here because he wasn't answering the goddamn door.

He stared at the wood grain on the cabinet at eye level, tracing the curves of it with his eyes, feeling blessedly numb. His breathing once again evened out. When the knocking came again, he barely noticed it.

He realized his mistake as the front door opened but he had a hard time summoning up any anger at Cooper for leaving it unlocked. He'd worked all the mad out of himself and had nothing left.

"Penn?"

Not even Nadia's voice pulled him out of his stupor. He listened to her footsteps ease into the condo as she hollered again. She headed to his bedroom. Moments later, he heard her gasp when she reached the doorway to the kitchen.

"Oh, my God, are you okay, Penn?"

He turned around to face her and caught sight of the impressive pile of glass on the opposite end of the kitchen floor. "Better now."

"What happened?" She carefully made her way toward him, avoiding the shards of glass.

Penn merely shook his head, deciding it was pretty damn obvious what had happened and if she couldn't figure it out, that wasn't his problem. He watched her approach, waiting for the now-familiar surge of anger. It was only a ripple instead of the tidal wave she usually created in him, and didn't that say a shit-ton about his mental state?

The fear in her eyes finally compelled him to speak. "Had a bit of a temper tantrum, I guess."

She again glanced at the glass pile. "I guess. Where's your dustpan and broom?"

"You're not cleaning it up."

"And how are you going to get down on the floor to do it?" she asked gently.

Excellent point he hadn't yet thought of.

Nadia set a white paper sack on the counter, brushed past him and opened the cabinet beneath the sink. She pulled out a whisk broom but apparently couldn't find a dustpan. When she looked at him again in question, he said, "That's Coop's department."

She stood and looked around the kitchen, her gaze settling on the mail that Coop had evidently thrown on the bar. She picked up a sturdy sales flyer from the grocery store. Bending down, she began sweeping glass onto it and systematically dumping it into the trash can. Penn tried to think of what he could do to help her, but short of bending down and doing it himself, all he could come up with was moving the trash can closer as she worked her way across the floor in silence.

"Coop could do this when he gets home," he said tiredly.

"Did something happen to set you off today?" she asked.

"Please, Nadia. Stop."

She stood and dumped more glass into the trash. She gazed up at him and, in spite of everything—the insanity and tragedy of his day, the ugly animosity he normally didn't hesitate to throw her way—he got caught up in the blue of her eyes. Just a little bit. She was so damn pretty. And unreasonably patient with him.

"You look awful. Why don't you go lie down?"

No response came to him. He wasn't about to go back to bed with her still in the place, but he needed to get off his feet. Physical exhaustion had set in long ago and his adrenaline from the glass incident stopped pumping. Sitting down was preferable to falling on his ass. He went to the living room without a word.

All he wanted to do was to flop down onto the saggy brown couch that was almost as good as comfort food. But he couldn't. Couldn't even lower himself carefully onto it, because he might not be able to get back up without excruciating pain. No cushions for him.

He took the straight-back dining chair Coop had lifted from the station and turned it around in front of the window. Straddling it, he faced the view of the deserted swimming pool.

Sounds from the kitchen were rhythmic and regular: the sweeping of more glass, the lid going up on the trash can, glass clinking in, lid going down. When there was a long break in the beat, he waited for the cycle to start again. Instead, he heard Nadia approaching him from behind.

Without a word, she leaned against the window, her hands on the low sill supporting her weight. She studied him with a question in her eyes.

The least he could do was explain.

Seconds ticked by, turned into minutes, as Penn willed himself to put the doctor's prognosis into words. He needed to say it, to get used to saying it.

He rose from the chair, slowly, in the way he'd learned to move in the past few days to avoid a shot of pain in his lower back. He took several steps away from her.

"My firefighting career is over."

A sound came from behind him, a quiet gasp as if someone had died. Not far from true. His career was as dead as a skunk in the road.

He waited for her to speak. Silently dared her to deny his news. When he finally turned around to face her, he saw the last thing he'd ever expected. Nadia's eyes were closed, her face distorted as if she was the one in pain, and tears ran down her cheeks.

Hell. He hated to see a woman cry. Something inside him stirred to life, breaking through the ice that'd kept him numb since the last glass had been flung.

He closed the space between them, stopping a few inches in front of her and waiting for her to look at him. Instead, she moved into him, covering her eyes with her hands, and buried her face in his chest.

Her hair tickled his chin and the scent of it teased his nostrils. Berries and sweet vanilla. He lifted his arms, hesitating, then tentatively rested them on her sides, at the curve of her waist. He held her like that while seconds ticked into minutes, only vaguely aware that he should be the one in need of comforting.

He felt her inhale deeply, felt it in the way her middle shifted beneath his hands, and before he knew it, she'd straightened and taken a step back from him.

"I'm sorry, Penn. That's terrible news. What are you going to do?" she asked, backing up to the window again.

Penn retook his position on the chair, again straddling the seat, resting his arms on the back of it. "Do?" He shrugged. Question of the decade. "Go to therapy when they tell me to, work my butt off to regain as much strength and agility as I can."

She didn't comment. Seemed even less satisfied with his answer than he was.

This exact scenario—being told his career was over—had been on his mind since he'd first woken up after the injury and been in such excruciating pain. He'd been unsettled for almost three weeks, imagining what might become of his future. Now he knew. Hated every bit of it, but he knew.

Nadia wove their fingers together, grasping his hand and squeezing. He let her. Was too tired to make a fuss over anything, and if he was honest, the contact felt good, minimal though it was.

"I wish I knew what to say to make it easier, Penn."

Her sky-blue eyes didn't waver from his and the air between them changed. Sparked with an awareness that buried all the ugly things he'd felt toward her lately and made him regret they'd never really gotten the chance to explore the attraction between them. She moistened her lips, drawing his attention to her mouth, making his heart speed up.

Before he could register what was happening, Nadia leaned forward and kissed him. The touch was brief, as if this were just a friendly gesture, but her mouth hovered a breath away from him and their eyes met again. As her lids lowered, she pressed her lips back to his and there was nothing friendly about it this time. She tilted her head and teased his lips with her tongue. Penn instinctively cradled the back of her head with his free hand as the kiss deepened, needing the contact, the distraction, as much as he needed oxygen. She tasted of sugar, a heaven of sweetness he couldn't get enough of.

He was vaguely aware of her taking his face in her hands, of the rumble that came from his throat as they tried to ignore the oddness of their position. He could touch more of her if he stood up and pulled her body into him, but to do so in his condition would mean stopping, if only temporarily. Stopping was not an option.

He dropped his hand to her waist, pulled her closer. Nadia stumbled when her foot rammed into the leg of the chair. The contact of their lips ended abruptly as she reached out for his shoulder to regain her balance. Penn steadied her with his hand at her middle.

She tried to laugh, embarrassed. Straightened. "Awkward."

Awkward was an understatement. If he could move like a normal person, none of that would have happened. He got a taste of the anger that had been absent since his kitchen rampage. He stood again.

"Why did you come over today, Nadia?" His words had a way of turning the sensual tension between them into something altogether more unpleasant.

She narrowed her eyes at him, letting him know she hadn't missed the change in his tone. "I meant to text you back days ago. After you apologized. I brought cookies for you. My great-grandmother's chocolate chip recipe, sold exclusively at Silver Sands. I don't take them to just anybody."

The bag she'd set on the counter, he realized. He nodded. "Thanks. You shouldn't have come over. As you may have noticed, I'm not in my right mind."

"Yeah, I kind of gathered that. Lucky for you, I need to go, anyway."

"Let me guess. Back to work?"

"As a matter of fact, I'm having dinner at Faith's."

The front door burst open at that moment and Cooper and Zoe destroyed the mood.

"I can't believe you made me take him," Zoe said when she saw Penn sitting there. "How do you two even stand upright with all the crap you put into your bodies? You should be dead."

"Got your Dew, dude." Cooper came in behind Zoe, rolling his eyes as he shut the door. "Whoops. Are we interrupting something?"

"Not a thing," Penn said, relieved that Nadia was moving toward the door.

"Hi," his nosy sister said to Nadia. She set down her two grocery bags and extended her hand. "I'm Zoe. Penn's sister."

"Nadia Hamlin."

The look on Zoe's face at hearing Nadia's name was easy for Penn to read. It was nosy and knowing. One hundred percent smart-ass sister.

"Nice to meet you," Zoe said. "Too bad you can't stay."

"I just brought some cookies over for Penn. Sorry to have to run."

"Cookies?" Coop asked.

"In the kitchen. Help yourself." Penn went to the door and opened it wider, hoping to hurry Nadia along so he could retreat to his bedroom.

His roommate went after the cookies. Zoe picked up her bags again and followed Coop into the kitchen.

He cleared his throat, trying to force down his renewed annoyance—at who knew what, Nadia, life, the cheeriness of his sister and roommate, you name it—and worked hard to get out what he knew he needed to say. "Thank you for taking care of the mess."

Nadia nodded, walking past him without slowing down. "See you later, Penn."

Well, goody for him. He'd managed to erase the effects of Nadia's kiss in record time.

CHAPTER TEN

NADIA HAD HAD to pull over and sit in her car for a few minutes after leaving Penn's condo. She'd told Cooper she could take whatever Penn dished out but today's sample had been unreal.

His subtle coldness after she'd made the mistake of kissing him still lingered with her, even when she pulled up outside Faith's house. And while it might have been easier to feel anger toward him and nothing else, that wasn't to be. Because she knew how much he was hurting. Could imagine how staggering it was to lose one's career.

She relaxed her tense shoulders and told herself to set all the Penn stuff aside for a few hours while she had dinner with her two best friends in the world. She climbed out of her car and walked up the flight of stairs to Faith's front door.

"Hey, about time you showed up, busy girl," Faith said as she let her in. She picked up the gray, nearly full-grown cat winding its way around her feet. "Long day at work?"

Once Nadia was inside, Faith closed the door and set the purring cat down.

Faith looked a little worse for the wear, but then she'd been sick for the past week. Her long, dark hair was pulled into a ponytail and her face was free of makeup. She normally wore cute clothes, even when the three of them—she, Nadia and Mercedes—were staying in, but today she had on old cutoff jean shorts and a stretched-out lavender T-shirt. Nadia had tried to convince her to put off dinner, but Faith insisted she needed a mellow girls' night.

"Are you feeling better?" Nadia said, ignoring the question.

"Mostly. Not contagious, though. Come on in. Mercedes is making the salad. Lasagna is in the oven."

Joe, Faith's fiancé, came down the stairs then and picked up his cell phone and keys from one of the end tables.

"Our power corporate girl finally made it. How're you doing, Nadia?"

"Late as usual," she said, grinning. "I brought cookies."

"You're forgiven." Joe came over and took the bag, identical to the one she'd delivered to Penn, opened it and helped himself.

"Hey," Faith said, swatting him lightly and taking the bag away. "Girls' night, girls' cookies. Aren't you leaving?"

"If I have to." Joe pulled Faith into him and kissed her, so tenderly, lingering for a moment afterward. A scene like that could make any single girl ache, even one who avoided relationships with every fiber of her being. "Take care of yourself," he said in a private voice. "Don't overdo it."

"Go. Have fun at the Shack. Eat some seviche for me."

"You're going to the Shell Shack?" Nadia asked, well aware that the bar scene wasn't Joe's favorite thing.

"Long enough to give you women some girl time and to wish Nate a happy birthday."

"I meant to get him a card," Faith said. "You know, since none of the twenty men in the department will think of that."

"You've had other things on your mind. I'll buy him a drink on your behalf. He'll like that better. Behave yourselves, ladies."

Joe was out the door and the sound of vegetable chopping echoed from the next room. Nadia followed Faith into the kitchen and greeted Mercedes with a side hug.

"I miss you girls," Nadia said. "You're always busy with your men now."

"Ironic, isn't it?" Mercedes said, setting aside the knife and washing her hands. "Now that Faith and I are both in relationships, you've stopped the frantic dating thing. You're never going to find your man by working till midnight every night."

"There is no 'my man' and I'm fine with that." Nadia popped a cherry tomato in her mouth. Ever since the summer, she'd dated less—okay, *none*—and at times she missed having a social life, whether with her girlfriends or the man of the week. "I do, however, think I need to get out more."

"What do you call this?" Faith said. "Home-made lasagna, two of the best girls around, casual clothes, no makeup required…"

"I call it perfect."

"Who ruined you on dating?" Faith joked.

"My last date was the disaster with Penn. That's when I rededicated my life to my job."

"So has work slowed down at all?" Mercedes asked, pushing her wavy hair behind her shoulder and tossing the salad.

Nadia laughed. "My events manager quit six weeks ago, we're deep into developing our spring marketing campaign, and then throw in a hurricane that screwed up all kinds of events…all of that at budget time." She intercepted Faith on the way to the table and took the stack of plates and salad bowls from her. Busied herself setting them at the three places. "Hasn't slowed down a bit."

Faith added a basket of garlic bread to the table next to the salad. "Ready to dig in?"

The three of them sat and began serving up food that smelled amazing.

Nadia scooted her chair back. "You must be slipping, Faith. Where's the wine?"

"Scandal!" Mercedes said, grinning. "Maybe she's been sicker than she let on. Or maybe she and Joe have been staying in all day drinking wine and eating strawberries in bed."

"I completely forgot. Check the wine rack over there. There should be a red you guys can open."

"You're not joining in?"

Faith shook her head. "My stomach is still iffy."

Without checking the label, Nadia took out a bottle of red and set it on the table. To her, wine was wine. It was all good.

They caught up on Mercedes's boyfriend, Scott, and his new job teaching EMTs and paramedics, on Mercedes's grandmother, who lived with her, Faith's parents, who were renewing their vows for their anniversary, and any number of other topics. By the time they stopped talking for a moment, half the pan of lasagna was gone, they'd devoured the bread, and most of the salad was history, as well.

"Wow. We *ate,*" Nadia said.

"We're not done yet." Faith went to the refrigerator and took out a homemade cheesecake and fresh strawberries.

"You baked?" Mercedes asked. "I thought you'd been sick."

"Yeah." Faith sliced the cake and transferred a huge slab of calories and sugar to a dessert plate. "About that…the cheesecake is to butter you two up."

"Fatten us up is more like it. I need to look good without my clothes on, you know." Mercedes grinned wickedly.

Nadia laughed and took the plate. "No one sees me naked. Where's the whipped cream?"

Without her permission, her thoughts veered back to Penn. To the high of breathing in his scent, of tasting him, feeling the warmth of his mouth. The very first touch of his lips had sent a jolt to her center, made her feel things, physical things, she hadn't let herself feel for a long time. If ever. Though she used to date plenty, it'd been a couple of years since she'd had sex. All part of her strategy for not getting too involved. For a second, though, she'd wanted to get involved, in every way possible.

"What are you buttering us up for?" Mercedes asked Faith.

Nadia and Mercedes exchanged a curious look and watched Faith cut another large piece in maddening silence. Once she'd set the slice on the plate, she licked her thumb and set down the knife. Sat back in her chair. "Girls, I need your help planning a shotgun wedding."

Nadia dropped her fork, and the bite of cheesecake on it, to her plate with a clatter. She stared at her friend, waiting for the punch line.

"You and Joe are getting married next spring," Mercedes said, looking as dumbfounded as Nadia felt.

"That was the plan. Things changed."

"You're pregnant?" Nadia forgot about cheesecake, forgot about everything else.

If there was one person who was vigilant about birth control, it was Faith, who lived for being a firefighter. Until she'd met Joe, her job had been her number-one priority in life. And pregnant people couldn't fight fires.

"Yep," Faith said, stretching out the single syllable.

Now that Nadia studied her, she saw fatigue and worry that went beyond a virus or a cold.

"That's why you haven't worked all week," she said. "You weren't sick."

"Well…I was. I've been puking my brains out every morning. But like I said earlier, it's nothing contagious. We haven't told anyone at work yet. I've been trying to accept it myself first."

"Are you going to quit?" Mercedes voiced the question that was burning in Nadia's mind.

Faith stared at the cheesecake intently, but Nadia would bet she wasn't seeing it. Faith shook her head slowly, clearly at a loss. "I don't know." She finally met their concerned gazes. "Not right now. I mean I'm obviously out for the duration of the pregnancy. Effective immediately. That's all I know. I can't think about…after the baby's born."

"I don't know what to say," Nadia said. Offering congratulations seemed insensitive. And yet condolences didn't seem right, either.

Faith forced a smile. "Say yes to helping me pull this off. We want to have the wedding within a month. Hopefully before I start showing."

"Of course," Nadia said.

"You know we're in." Mercedes patted Faith's hand sympathetically. "You'll be the best parents ever."

"With such short notice, the yacht idea we were planning is out. We can have the wedding in the church my family belongs to but the most pressing thing is a reception site."

"Lucky for you, you happen to be friends with the owners of the Silver Sands. I need to check our schedule to be sure, but if you're interested, we can make it happen there." Even if the ballrooms were full, Nadia would find a solution. The Sea Grass deck, maybe.

"I'm interested. Enough to work around the hotel's schedule if I need to. Will you let me know what's available the next time you're at your office?"

"I'll call you later tonight." She'd be back at the office after this, anyway.

"Bless you. You guys are the best." Faith sat up straighter and cut herself a sliver of cheesecake about half the size of what she'd given Nadia and Mercedes. "It's going to be okay, right?" she said, summoning up a cheerful tone as if she was trying to convince herself. "I'm marrying the best guy in the world. In a month."

"Joe's perfect. Your child will be beautiful," Nadia said. "And adored."

"And spoiled by his or her auntie-wannabes," Mercedes added.

"I can't even…" Faith bowed her head so they couldn't see her eyes but they didn't need to to understand she was reeling. "I know I should be grateful but I feel like my career was just starting to roll. The guys in the department were finally starting to accept me and now…"

Now it was over, just like that. Just like Penn's career.

"You should talk to Penn," Nadia said. "I'm sure he's going through some of the same things."

Faith zeroed in on Nadia. "Did he get bad news from his doctor?"

Nadia didn't answer. Penn needed to notify the fire department that he wasn't coming back himself. Though Faith wouldn't spread the news if Nadia asked her not to, it wasn't fair to ask her to keep Penn's prognosis from Joe, who was one of the officers. "You'll have to ask him yourself."

Both women stared at her and Mercedes nodded. "She knows something."

"You went to Penn's again? After you took him dinner?"

"I… Yeah. I took him cookies before I came over here."

"The way to a man's heart," Mercedes said.

"It's not like that," Nadia told them. *Nothing like that at all.*

"If it wasn't like that, I'm thinking you would have fessed up to going over there right away." Faith's eyes had a disturbing twinkle to them that had nothing to do with a pregnant glow.

"You definitely look guilty," Mercedes said.

Nadia stuffed her mouth full of cheesecake to give herself time to come up with a response. "He blames me for the accident. Believe me when I say there's no love lost."

"Maybe I'll go see him soon. After he talks to the chief," Faith said. "Hopefully by then I'll be in a better place mentally. It's a lot to swallow but…everything will work out. For both of us."

Everything would work out, Nadia did believe that. But Faith's career…it was such a part of who she was, just like Nadia's. And just like Penn's…

She took another bite in silence, deeply concerned about Faith, and even more so about Penn.
At least Faith had a husband-to-be, and the possibility of going back to her career in a year or
so. Because of fate and some help from Nadia,
Penn had nothing.

She set down her fork and shoved the plate
away, her appetite gone.

CHAPTER ELEVEN

A COUPLE OF HOURS AFTER Nadia left, Cooper and Zoe were still—or maybe once again—making noise in the kitchen as Penn emerged from his room and went to join them.

He'd gone to bed to avoid them and then crashed hard, probably because of his state of mind when Nadia had left. Hard enough that he should feel a lot more refreshed. Instead, it felt as if cobwebs had taken over his brain and a pile of stones was weighing down his shoulders with every step.

"He stirs," Zoe said cheerfully as he entered the room. She stood in front of the sink. Coop was sitting at the island, sharpening one of the kitchen knives.

"Guy's gotta eat, like it or not," Penn muttered, heading for the refrigerator.

"Don't you dare," his sister said. "No snacking. I'm going all out for my last night here. We're having shrimp creole."

"She's a bossy one," Cooper said. "Obviously you got all the 'laid-back' in the Griffin family."

"I only boss when it's necessary. It just happens to be abundantly necessary where you two are concerned."

"Amazing we've survived so long without your guidance, Queen Zoe." Coop grinned and paused his sharpening to take a swallow of beer.

Zoe, who was peeling and deveining shrimp, zinged a piece of raw shellfish in his direction, missing only because Coop veered sideways at the last second. He turned to locate the shrimp on the floor, then shook his head in mock exasperation at Penn.

"She stopped being my problem years ago," Penn said, deciding a beer was exactly what he needed, whether he was supposed to have alcohol or not. He helped himself to the twelve-pack in the fridge.

Coop retrieved the piece of shrimp and sauntered to Zoe's side. Holding it out to her, he said, "I believe you dropped this, shrimp."

Zoe faced away from Penn so he couldn't see her expression as she stared up at his roommate, but something in her stance, the set of her jaw, caught his attention. These two had gone back and forth, teasing and disagreeing about more than just health food for the entire time she'd been in town. But now, Penn wondered if there was more there. Zoe looked sassy and flirty. Shy Zoe who normally only did "sassy" to her brother.

"You're lucky I don't like to waste good food or I'd peg you from close range," Zoe said.

Coop still held the now-sharpened knife in the hand away from her. He raised that hand slowly and presented it, handle first, to her. "Your weapon, madam. Use it wisely."

Penn narrowed his eyes at the pair. Their words were mundane enough, but Penn could practically see the tension arcing between them. He cleared his throat to remind them they weren't alone and wondered where the hell he'd been while *that* was going on. Of course, the answer was easy. He'd been in a stupor, induced by either narcotics or depression depending on the moment.

"So," he said, still trying to wrap his head around the thought of his roommate and sister having anything in common. "How long does shrimp creole take? I'm weak with hunger."

Zoe seemed to snap out of her daydream and rinsed her hands. She took a cutting board from one of the lower cabinets, placed it on the counter to the right of the sink and set three peppers— green, orange and red—on top of it. "The sooner you get chopping, the sooner we all get to eat."

"Ask and you shall receive a task," Coop said, amused.

"And you," Zoe continued, "can start the brown rice on the stove. It'll need forty-five minutes to cook, at least."

"We have instant rice," Cooper said. "Five minutes, no sweat."

Zoe shuddered and started to glare at him, then figured out he was intentionally egging her on. "Feel free to make that fake food for yourself but put some real stuff on for Penn and me."

"The woman doesn't joke about food," Penn said, trying to smile.

"But she loves it when I do." Cooper rummaged through the now-full cabinet and took out a bag of rice. He tried to covertly read the directions on the back.

Penn took a drink of his beer to keep from laughing aloud. He was no kitchen wizard himself, but he could cook rice. His roommate, on the other hand, had never learned to make anything and seemed perfectly content to grab a bag of chips and a hunk of summer sausage to fill his gut.

Penn sliced into the orange pepper as Cooper found a pot and added rice and water, muttering to himself about pushy women and the glory of takeout.

"Would you like me to run out and get a bottle of wine?" Coop asked.

"Oh, good idea," Zoe said enthusiastically. "A nice, mellow cabernet-Shiraz blend would be perfect."

Coop glanced at Penn as if to ask if she was for real, and then laughed. "Beer guy here. I wouldn't know a mellow cabernet from an irritable one."

"Cabernet-Shiraz," Zoe said, clearly in her

kitchen-autopilot mode. Then she looked up at Cooper. "I'll write down a couple possibilities, and if the liquor store doesn't have those you can ask them for something similar."

Coop raised his brows at her, unable to prevent a grin.

Zoe scribbled some names on a paper towel and handed it to him. "Thank you, Coop. You're a thoughtful guy."

He nodded as if satisfied and grabbed his keys from the counter where he'd thrown them. "Remember that," he said as he left.

"He just wanted to get out of food prep, you know," Penn said.

"Oh, I know. Poor guy is really anti-kitchen, isn't he?"

"Not everyone's like you, Zo. What's going on between you two?"

"Going on?"

"I may have my head up my ass these days, but even I couldn't miss that."

She set the bowl of peeled shrimp next to the stove and eyed him. "I don't know what it is. Well, it's technically nothing. I'm leaving tomorrow."

She looked thoughtful for a moment, then shrugged. Returned to busying herself with ingredients. "It's just as well. I need to catch up on my research. I haven't gotten as much done here as I'd planned."

"Spending your time carting me around to appointments didn't help."

"What?" Zoe stopped in the middle of rummaging through one of the drawers. "Penn, that's what I'm here for."

"You're here because Mom forced you."

"No. I could have refused. All I had to do was tell her I was behind on my research and she wouldn't have pushed it."

Penn nodded. "Nothing's changed, huh? School and achievements are still her top priority."

"I don't know that she'd agree with you on that," Zoe said. "But she does have a boatload of money invested in my education. And we weren't sure how serious things were down here."

"I'm sorry, Zo. Last thing I want to do is screw up your studies. You should have left two days ago."

"I'm crushed you don't like my company." Zoe poured cooking oil into a skillet, then gave Penn her full attention again. "I'm glad I was here. You're trying to be all manly and act like you can handle everything on your own but you don't have to be that way with me."

"I'm not being any way. I take care of myself." Or he always had in the past. Zoe had been an angel but he couldn't get used to it.

"No one with a serious back injury takes care of himself. I'm worried about you."

"Nothing to worry about. I'll be fine. Coop's around if I absolutely need something. I'll be driving in no time. I've got nothing to do *but* take care of myself."

"And that's exactly what concerns me. What are you going to do, Penn?"

Before he could answer, she noticed he'd finished chopping the peppers. She slid a fat onion in front of him and he began slicing, grateful for something else to focus on.

"Well?" she prompted.

"Well?"

"I know you're reeling, Penn. Who wouldn't be?"

"I'll…adjust. Eventually." Maybe by the year 2030. "I don't know what I'll do yet but I'll find something. Nothing to lose sleep over," he lied. He hadn't given his professional future any serious thought. Refused to.

"I know you will but in the meantime…" She stared at him from the side and he gave all his attention to the onion. "Smaller pieces," she suggested. "You're down, Penn. You have to watch that."

"Of course I'm down! I just lost my entire career." Cutting off anything else that might slip out, he rested the knife on the counter between slices. "Sorry. Yeah, I'm frustrated. I'll get over it."

Zoe took the bowl full of chopped vegetables.

She added them to the pan on the stove, and the air was filled with the hiss of hot oil.

"I could come back in a few weeks," she said. "You'll be out and about more and you can show me around. Give me the tourist treatment."

Something she'd had very little of since arriving, he realized. "You should have gone out and explored this time."

"That wasn't why I was here." She sighed. "We're going in circles now. What about Thanksgiving? I could come visit then and make you and Coop a turkey, then we could go whale watching or whatever it is you do here. Whales are cool."

A ghost of a smile crossed his face. "You're a nut. We have dolphins here."

"Better yet."

He walked over to her at the stove. Wrapped an arm around her neck and squeezed affectionately. "Don't come back, Zo. It'll only make me feel like crap, because I'll know you're taking time away from school to check up on me."

She pretended to look devastated. "I see how you are."

"I'm grateful to you for being here this week. Incredibly so. But coming back next month isn't going to help."

When she still looked doubtful, he added, "We can talk about possibilities for Christmas. Will that get you off my case?"

She grinned and squeezed his middle in a bear hug. "For now. Only because I have veggies cooking."

He yanked a strand of her hair and directed her back to the stove. The truth was, Zoe couldn't help him. No one could. Doctors and therapists might be able to put his body back together to a degree, but he was on his own for what the hell to do with the rest of his life.

PENN HAD NEVER REALIZED the night could be so damn dark.

Even when he was on the clock at the station, falling asleep had never been a problem. When he was ready to catch some z's, usually all he had to do was find a pillow and put his head on it. Apparently now he was joining the ranks of insomniacs.

His brain wouldn't give it up. Wouldn't stop obsessing over the doctor's verdict and how that affected the rest of his life. *Affected* was such a mild word, really, when what losing his career really did was screw him all to hell.

He'd never realized how much of his life revolved around being a firefighter. His friends were all firefighters. His roommate was. His favorite bar was owned by a firefighter and his wife and was the main hangout of, what else, off-duty firefighters. He spent a massive chunk of his time with people involved with the fire department.

And now he wasn't a firefighter anymore.

He couldn't fathom it. Didn't even want to begin to imagine how he would earn a living once he was able to work. He had no skills except for fighting fires, truly. One semester of failing grades in college had done nothing for him but piss off his mom. He'd gotten through his fire sciences classes after that only by sheer will, because he'd so single-mindedly wanted to become a firefighter. Even in high school, the only job he'd had was stocking shelves at a grocery store. Not exactly something he could pay the rent with these days or see himself doing till the end of time.

If he wasn't a firefighter, he was nothing.

He started to roll over and swore, the twinge in his lower back reminding him for the hundredth time that casually changing position wasn't an option.

The longer he lay there, the more he was climbing the walls, racking his brain for an escape. Previously, he could have gotten up and taken a run. Now? The best he could do was a slow walk to the parking lot. Couldn't even drive once he got there.

Penn had never been a fan of self-pity and he was starting to get on his own nerves. Sitting up slowly at the edge of the bed, he funneled the pity into the now-familiar anger. Grabbed his pillow and punched it once, which did nothing to relieve any of the blackness that'd been building up inside him all day.

His cell phone buzzed and lit up on his nightstand. He scowled at it, figuring it was a wrong-number text or one of the guys out at the bar screwing with him. He picked it up and raised his brows. Nadia.

Got cookies?

Penn scoffed and wondered why she would even want to contact him after the way he'd treated her earlier.

Carefully positioning himself against the headboard, using a pillow for back support, he considered his options. To reply or not to reply? It was 1:17 a.m. Easy to get away with feigning sleep. But the message wasn't going away and he'd have to acknowledge it eventually.

What the hell. At the very least, he could kill some time and maybe distract himself from his depressing thoughts.

He finally replied: Cookies made awesome midnight snack.

Did I wake you?

Penn scowled. A little late to worry about that.

Some people turn their phone off when they sleep. ;)

I was awake, he admitted. Not really sleeping much. You?

Working. I know. Shock. So...

Curious, he prompted her. So?

There was a pause. Maybe she was typing and maybe she wasn't, but Penn leaned his head back and allowed his mind to veer back to earlier today. That kiss. There was definite chemistry between them. Just remembering how she'd felt, how she'd responded to him, made him hard now. Good to know parts down south still functioned. Not that he was in any position to use them, now or in the near future.

Another message popped up from her. I imagine news from doctor is crushing.

Crushing. That was one word for it. Pretty damn good word.

Rather not talk about it.

Understandable. There's something I'd rather not talk about but need to say...

He stared at the screen, waiting for her to continue. Curious as all get-out but unwilling to prompt her to spill it.

Finally, another message appeared. Kiss was a bad move on my part.

So. Add "direct" to Nadia's list of qualities. And thankfully, not a hopeless romantic.

He weighed his reply carefully. So many wrong things he could say without even meaning to.

He settled for: Not a big deal.

I know you've got way more important things on your mind.

Every last one of which sucked. None of which he cared to spend his time thinking about. Before he could figure out a response, his phone buzzed again.

Won't happen again. Not that I don't like you. Just that we both seem overwhelmed right now. Me with work, you with your back. Did you know it's possible to babble via text message? ;)

Ignoring her question, he typed: Heard about your two-date policy.

Going to kill Faith. I did away with that policy anyway. Instituted no-date policy.

I've got the same. Guess we're even.

It's almost 2:00 a.m., only crazy people and drunk people stay up this late.

Penn chuckled quietly. And insomniacs and workaholics.

There is that. I'll let you try to sleep now. Glad we talked.

He set his phone on his thighs and realized he was smiling into the dark.

He blanked his face and shrugged. So she'd distracted him. Made him relax for a few minutes. No big thing. After trying so hard to keep Nadia out of his life, he had to admit that tonight she'd been just what he needed, when he'd needed it.

Even after he'd been an asshole to her. Repeatedly.

He knew blaming her for his injury or directing any of his anger toward her wasn't right. Maybe it was high time he tried to put that into action. First, he owed her an apology. Then he needed to figure out how not to let the blame sneak in again.

CHAPTER TWELVE

THE FIRST THING THAT struck Nadia two days later as she walked toward her mother was the odd look on Joyce's facc. Undeniable happiness, yes. A wide smile that had been absent of late. But beyond that she looked…flirtatious?

Her mom?

Was it a full moon? Had her mother lost her mind?

As Nadia approached the table in the hotel's restaurant where her mom was sitting, she zeroed in on the man in the opposite seat. His back was to Nadia, his dark gray hair the only feature she could see. He wore a white dress shirt with the sleeves rolled up and rested his arms on the table casually, confidently.

Nadia veered around a table, changing her angle just enough that recognition flickered. Dr. Gene Morris, the podiatrist who'd toured the property last week. Neither of them noticed her until she stood right in front of the table.

"Nadia!" Joyce straightened. "You remember Dr. Morris?"

The man stood and shook her hand.

"Of course." Nadia looked between them, baffled, waiting for them to explain what they were doing there. "Am I late for a meeting I don't remember?" she finally asked.

"No, no." Dr. Morris pulled out the chair next to him. "Join us, please. I wanted to sample what your kitchen is capable of. Not an official visit." There was a mostly empty dinner plate in front of each of them.

"We were just discussing the best things on the catering menu," her mom said. "Marcel is checking to see if he can track down some of Joan's almond-pear torte so Gene can have a taste."

Gene? First-name basis? While it was natural to be more casual with a meeting planner by using his or her first name, it seemed a liberty with a physician.

What was her mother trying to do? Like Nadia, she rarely dated. Both of them were too busy with work, and both of them had always preferred it that way.

Nadia pulled the chair out the rest of the way and sat, endeavoring to hide her irritation. Selling the hotel's events services was supposed to be her job. Well, not even hers, really—the events manager's, but since she hadn't yet hired one, it fell under her umbrella of responsibility. Not her mother's.

"It's to die for," Nadia told him. "If you like pears, of course. But we have so many other good choices, like our triple-chocolate mousse, the chocolate avalanche, Joan's carrot-zucchini cake.... Normally, we set it up so you can have samples of each when you're planning your menus."

"I'll definitely have to join Stacy for an official menu-planning session," Dr. Morris said. "We'll consider the torte an extra treat. Maybe Marcel will come back with two pieces and you can indulge along with us."

The torte was always amazing but Nadia had homed in on his first comment. "Setting up an official menu-planning session...does that mean you've decided to hold the conference here at Silver Sands?"

"I have, young lady. I'm most impressed with your facilities and the food is excellent. The general manager's not bad, either." He winked at her mother.

Winked at her mother.

So wrong for Nadia to have to witness the flirting.

"That's the best news I've had all day," Nadia said, pushing the personal ick-factor out of her mind and focusing instead on the welcome promise of the boost to the hotel. "So Stacy will still be helping you out?"

"She will, indeed. In fact, she'll be handling most of it now that we've agreed on a site. Except for the dessert tasting, of course."

Marcel, the restaurant manager, appeared at the table then. "Bad news," he said. "There's not a piece of almond-pear torte to be found. I even looked in Joan's secret stashing spot. No luck. However, tonight we do have five other fabulous desserts for you to choose from."

Dr. Morris shook his head graciously. "Honestly, I've been trying to figure out how I was going to fit in the torte. I'll take it as a sign. Dessert was not meant to be this evening."

"Are you sure?" Joyce said. "I don't want you to go away wanting."

Oh, God, was the double entendre intended?

"I'm very satisfied, but thank you, Marcel. I've been assured by this young lady I'll be exposed to a variety of Joan's masterpieces later on."

"Absolutely," Nadia said.

"Tonight's dinner is on the house," her mother said.

Joyce and the doctor debated the tab for several uncomfortable seconds before Nadia broke in to try to end it.

"I'm going to weigh in on my mom's side this time. Two against one." That made it more business than personal, didn't it?

He finally accepted, and the three of them

walked out into the hotel lobby together. Maybe Nadia should have bowed out to let them say goodbye privately, but this *was* business. She ignored the little voice in her head that asked why she was being so adamant about that.

After Nadia agreed to contact Stacy to arrange a meeting and they all said good-night, she and her mom headed toward the executive offices.

"Was that a date?" Nadia asked as soon as they were around the corner. She'd meant to sound nonchalant, not curt or nosy, but she could tell from the look her mom gave her, she'd missed her mark.

"I…" Joyce glanced over her shoulder. "I don't know, to be honest. I was going over some spreadsheets in my office just after five and was called to the front desk. There he was. He invited me to join him."

"That's a date."

"He was legitimately testing the food. Why does it matter, anyway, Nadia?" They'd reached Nadia's office and her mom followed her in. "Do you have a problem with Dr. Morris?"

Why did it matter, indeed? Nadia collapsed into her chair, suddenly so tired she might seriously consider sleeping at her desk tonight. Her mother sat in one of the visitor chairs opposite her and crossed her arms.

"If it was business, I should have been in on it from the beginning," Nadia finally said.

"We didn't talk business for most of the dinner."

"Then it was a date."

"Okay, then. A spontaneous date."

They stared each other down.

Joyce spoke first. "Apparently you have a problem with that."

"That depends. Was it a onetime thing?"

Her mother chuckled. "Well, I really don't know, since my daughter chaperoned our goodbye. I have no idea if he'll call or invite me out again."

"Do you like him?"

"Of course I—"

"You know what I mean, Mom."

Joyce leaned back in her chair and draped her arms over the metal sides. "Yes. I like him." She stared Nadia directly in the eyes as she said it, as if challenging her to object.

Nadia leaned her elbows on the desk, running her hands over her face. What was wrong with her? She was irritated to no end, but she couldn't say why.

"It's just that we've never gotten involved with the people we do business with, I guess." Even Nadia herself didn't believe that objection.

Her mom laughed again. "Not many opportunities for me to do so, when you get down to it. But hey, we landed the business, right? Win-win."

"What happens if you two get involved and something goes sour between now and February?"

"Then I'll handle it. Really, Nadia? You're worried because he's a client?"

Nadia exhaled noisily. "The hotel needs all our attention right now, wouldn't you say? The timing just seems rotten."

"It was one dinner, honey. He seems like a nice man but we're not getting married or running away to Tahiti."

Nadia met her mother's gaze and nodded. "I know. I'm overreacting and I'm sorry. Have your fun." She attempted to smile. "Now we should both get back to work."

"I'm actually going to go home for the evening," her mom said as she stood. "My momentum is gone and I could use a full night's sleep for once. Don't work too late, honey."

Nadia wasn't able to respond before her mother waltzed out the door, seeming energized instead of tired. She glanced at her watch. Just after seven. Home? Her mother?

She tried to shrug it off and clicked her mouse, waking up her desktop computer. Her mother might not feel the need to work but there were still things that needed to be done.

CHAPTER THIRTEEN

BETWEEN THE INTENSE physical therapy session earlier today—his third—and now a long walk, Penn figured maybe he had a chance of sleeping tonight.

Coop was working, and since Zoe had left, the condo had become deathly quiet like he'd never noticed before. Sitting became hugely uncomfortable after a few minutes. Going back to bed was out of the question, for his sanity's sake, until there was no doubt he'd be able to drift off. When he was closed up inside by himself, it was harder to put his uncertain future out of his mind, and he couldn't bring himself to think seriously about it. Not yet.

Walking out of the condo had been a relief.

He made his way toward the beach on the gulf side of the island, even though their condo was closer to the bay. The drama of the waves appealed a lot more than the calm quiet tonight. He'd had enough quiet lately.

As the sun dropped in the sky behind him, Penn walked down the public path between two hotels toward the sand. He moved out to the waterline and relished the spray on his legs and the incessant roar of the waves.

The gulf and the beach were the main reasons he'd relocated to San Amaro when he'd left Boulder. But he'd learned to take them for granted, he realized now. The fire station was on the beach, as were most of the restaurants and bars he frequented. It wasn't until he'd become laid up in a stuffy room blocks away that it hit him how good he'd had it.

He watched the waves rise, curl and spill over, again and again, as the last light faded from the sky. The urge to kick off his shoes and wade out up to his knees was overpowering, but one thing stopped him. One ridiculous thing. Because bending at the waist was off-limits, putting his shoes on was an ordeal. It'd taken him an embarrassingly long time and some awkward contortions to do it at home. He sure as hell was *not* going to go through that in public.

Without thought, he turned to the right and gazed down the shore toward the fire station. Though it was a good mile and a half south, he could pick it out easily from the bright-as-noon lights shining out from the windows of the common room. The outside world was quiet right now, but inside the station, it'd be anything but peaceful. The guys—and Faith, if she was on duty—

would be sitting around the table shooting the shit after dinner, or maybe by now they'd be in front of the TV arguing over what game to watch. Or maybe they'd be out on a run.

Penn wanted so much to be in on it, just to have a normal damn night, working, jawing with his buddies, that he could practically taste it.

He could walk down there, just stop by. Maybe see if there were any leftovers from dinner. His stomach growled at the thought. It was out of the question if he wanted to be able to make it home on foot. He'd been walking a lot more and had increased his endurance, but he was close to his limit for the night already. He refused to stoop to asking one of his coworkers for a ride because he couldn't make it a couple of miles.

He turned away from the station and took a few steps north. Watched a family of five, probably tourists, packing up picnic supplies and getting ready to head back to whatever hotel they were staying at.

The distinctive coral color of the Silver Sands Hotel, about a block and a half away, captured his attention. He wondered if Nadia was still there. It'd been several days since she'd texted him in the middle of the night. Since he'd promised himself he'd apologize to her. He hadn't done a thing about that promise yet but now seemed as good a time as any. He pulled his phone out to send her a message.

Got cookies?

The mere mention of them made his mouth water and it hit him that he'd forgotten about dinner. Zoe had left the kitchen well stocked, but none of it was convenience food. If he wanted to eat, he was going to have to break down and cook something. Which, no doubt, had been his sister's objective.

As the seconds ticked by, he became more and more convinced Nadia wasn't going to respond. Telling himself it didn't matter, he strolled farther in from the water to find a suitable place to sit and rest before heading back to his suffocating condo.

His phone buzzed. Just checked. Front desk is out! On way to kitchen.

He half smiled and typed his response, still standing. That's excellent service.

Only the best at Silver Sands. How'd you know I was working?

Superspidey senses.

Funny. You're in luck. Found cookies. Want me to bring them over?

Penn tried not to let her offer get to him. You'd do that?

Home deliveries only for the injured.

Guess I shouldn't tell you I'm staring at hotel, then.

You're here?

Down the beach. Near Lambert's.

The ice cream shop held no temptation for him when it was a choice between that and Nadia's chocolate chip cookies.

On my way with emergency cookie stash.

Penn ignored the surge of anticipation. Will meet you by your hotel.

Where he hoped like hell there was a decent place to sit.

He made his way toward the building and came to the conclusion that even in athletic shoes, walking in the sand was harder on the body. Maybe it should have been obvious, but apparently this was yet another thing he hadn't noticed until he couldn't do it anymore.

When he was three-quarters of the way to the hotel, he spotted a woman coming toward him.

Her blond hair looked almost white in the moonlight and he knew it was Nadia before he could see her face. His heart did its usual picking-up-speed thing at the sight of her.

"Hey," Nadia said once they were close enough. "What are you doing out here, anyway? I thought you couldn't drive for a month."

"I can't. But I can walk." In theory. He was beginning to wonder how he would make it home. Resting first should do the trick. "I came out to breathe in some fresh sea air."

She looked at the gulf and inhaled deeply, causing her chest to rise and catch his notice. She wore a dark skirt that hit her at midthigh and a thin pink camisole that looked like it belonged beneath a suit jacket. One hand cradled a white paper bag and the other held her shoes, dark-colored sandals, with stiletto-looking heels that could be used as a weapon.

"Fresh air helps everything. I think I needed some, too," she said. "Want to sit out here and devour cookies?"

"Thought you'd never ask."

Nadia looked around, as if trying to find a good spot on the sand. When she turned to him, though, she frowned. "You need a solid place to sit, don't you?"

"A handicapped space," he said, trying to smile. Irritation bubbled up that he was no longer just a normal guy who could sit on the beach with a woman. He fought it off before he could take it out on Nadia, as he seemed to do on a regular basis.

His attention was captured by the thin strap of her camisole, or rather, the sliver of delicate lace that was exposed beneath when it shifted on her shoulder. Though he tried to resist, his eyes wandered downward to see if he could glimpse the lingerie through the lightweight material in front. Sure enough, the detail of the floral lace texture was just discernable as it stretched over the curves of her breasts.

"There are some pretty supportive chairs on the patio back there." She gestured over her shoulder toward the hotel.

Penn snapped his gaze back to her face. "Is it crowded?" he asked, ignoring the image of her slipping off that camisole and revealing the bra that intrigued him so. He couldn't say why. Women's underwear had never particularly enthralled him before. Normally, it was just another layer to get out of the way. But there was something about the contrast between the unflappable, steamrolling woman and the delicate femininity of the lace…

"Not this time of year."

They headed in the direction she'd come from. In spite of the beautiful woman walking next to him, Penn was absorbed by the growing discom-

fort in his back and legs. Maybe he'd overesti-
mated what he could handle after that PT session.
He couldn't wait to sit down.

Nadia led him to a small wrought-iron table
for two with straight-back, cushioned chairs. It
was on the outer edge of the patio, closest to the
beach, partially secluded by palms.

"I haven't been in your hotel for years," Penn
said, looking around with interest now that he
knew one of the women behind the business.
"How long has your family owned it?"

"We moved here when I was in first grade but
my parents only managed the hotel back then.
They were able to purchase it about fourteen
years ago."

"And they still oversee day-to-day operations?"

"My dad died a few years ago but my mom is
the general manager." She opened the paper sack
as she talked and handed him a cookie. "This place
kind of rules our lives, mostly in a good way."

Not exactly headline news. He bit into his
cookie and realized he was scowling. "You seem
to like it that way."

"Silver Sands is in my blood, I guess."

Nadia broke off a bite-size piece of her own
cookie and paused. "We should probably talk about
something different. My job is a sore subject."

"I never said that."

"You didn't have to." She rustled in the sack

for seconds for both of them. "It's true that this place doesn't leave me much time for a personal life, but it's a conscious decision."

This was where he was supposed to apologize and yet…she was right. Her job did set his teeth on edge. Especially given what her dedication had cost him. He gave himself credit just for remaining calm. That was progress.

An uncomfortable silence arose and he shifted his attention to the view, the dessert, anything besides that one topic that kept coming between them.

"We're doing this all wrong. We need drinks," Nadia said. She tilted her head and her camisole strap shifted, again revealing a hint of distracting lace. "What would you like?"

A shot of tequila would dim the pain shooting down his leg, but it wouldn't go well with the best cookies on the planet. "What are you having?"

"Milk, of course. There are eight more cookies in the bag to dunk."

"You can't eat six of these things." They weren't small cookies, and Nadia's body showed no evidence that she overindulged in sweets. Not that he was looking.

"Watch me," Nadia said. "I haven't had anything since lunch. Milk for you, too?"

He shrugged. Nadia went over to a house phone he hadn't noticed on the exterior wall closest to their table, picked it up and spoke softly enough he couldn't hear. With bare feet and wind-tousled hair, she looked less like an executive who ran this hotel and more like a teenage girl calling her mom to ask to break curfew. Which should have discouraged him from checking out her legs, from noticing she had just the right amount of tone to them, that her hips curved out to give her an hourglass shape.

He positioned his chair to face the beach so she was out of his line of sight.

She returned and took her seat, smiling at him, seemingly oblivious to his turmoil. Did her job obsession make him want to smash something? Did he want to kiss her again? Blame her? Sympathize with her?

The answer to all was yes.

"Milk is on its way," she said.

"I could get used to this kind of service. Now I understand the real reason you spend so much time here."

"It has its perks."

"Pool? Gym? Cook?" He nodded. "Not bad at all."

"I always intend to use the fitness center more often than I do. My dad would disown my mother and me if he could see how seldom we take advantage of it. It was his favorite part. He worked out seven days a week, no matter how busy he was."

"What happened to your dad?" Penn asked hesitantly.

"He had a heart attack in his sleep." She seemed to forget about her cookie, lowering her sad gaze. "So ironic. He was so active and did have a lot of stress but it wasn't until he was resting peacefully that…" She shook her head.

Aggravated or not, Penn was moved by her story. He touched the back of her hand, unsure whether he should have asked.

"It definitely brought my mom and me closer. This brings us closer." She gestured to the building beside them. "It's kind of our last connection to him, as well." She laughed sadly. "Doesn't make a lot of sense, probably."

"Kind of does." Penn couldn't really relate to the family ties. He and his sister had gotten along well enough while she was in town but he couldn't imagine them working together. And as for his mom… No way, no how, never.

He hadn't thought much about not having a close-knit family since he'd left home, but Nadia made him consider what he'd been missing.

A teenager in a uniform approached their table with a serving tray.

"Hey, Lyla, thanks for bringing that out here." Nadia helped her unload two glasses and a silver pitcher of milk.

Lyla looked a little confused by the odd request until she spotted the bag of cookies. Then she smiled and nodded knowingly. "You have to dunk."

"My kind of girl." Nadia handed Lyla one of the cookies. "That's for you but you have to get your own milk."

"Thank you, Ms. Hamlin. Have a good night." She nodded at Penn and left.

"Good way to get out of eating half a dozen cookies," Penn said once they were alone again.

"Oh, I gave her one of yours."

He grinned in spite of himself. "You know all your employees' names?"

"Not the newest ones, usually. Lyla has been with us for two years. Her very first job."

"Lucky her."

"Maybe. We've had to reduce a lot of the service staff's hours in the past few months. We've been able to avoid layoffs so far but the loss of hours has hit people in some departments hard."

Penn filled both short, fat glasses with milk. "Apparently we're supposed to dunk." He picked up another cookie and broke it in half so it would fit into the glass.

"Wait," Nadia said. "You have to do it the right way."

"The right way. Educate me, please, Ms. Chocolate Chip Expert."

She took on an exaggerated, official air. "You

dip the cookie in about an inch and then you hold to the count of three."

"Not four."

"Three. To get the proper dunkage effect without turning it into sog."

He raised his eyebrows at her.

"Technical terms. Trust me."

"Oh, I do, at least in the art of cookie dunking."

"Ready?"

He sat up straighter, taking on a formal cookie-dunking stance. They dipped their cookies in at the same time and Nadia counted aloud. Then they both took a bite.

She was right. It was even better dunked. "Tastes like chocolate chip ice cream," he said.

Nadia's eyes were closed, and the look on her face as she savored her cookie… He had to glance away to stop the dirty thoughts from circulating through his head.

"Where can I buy some of these?" he asked, dipping another bite.

"Just text your friendly hotel rep and she can set you up." She held the sack out to him. "You can have the rest of these."

"Lucky for me, Zoe left a jug of milk."

"It has to be whole milk. None of that watered-down skim stuff or you won't get the ice cream sensation."

"Whole milk and cookies for dinner and yet

you don't weigh much more than a bird. How is that possible?"

Nadia laughed and popped the last bite in her mouth. "It'd have to be a very large bird. Ostrich, maybe?"

"You've got better legs," he said matter-of-factly.

"Aww, thanks. You're too kind. I already confessed I don't exercise enough. I'm a sloth."

"Most sloths aren't still at work at—" he checked his watch "—8:45 p.m."

"The night is young."

"For those of us still in recovery, it's time to call it a night," Penn said. "I need to go home so you can get back to business."

Penn stood, maybe too quickly, with not enough regard to his tired muscles, and a pain shot through his lower back. He squeezed his eyes closed against it, then exhaled slowly, quietly, trying not to alert Nadia when his every instinct was to yell an obscenity or twelve.

"What's wrong?" she said, taking a step forward.

He clenched his fist and it was all he could do to keep from banging it on the table. Damn worthless body. He'd give anything to have the old one back.

"Are you okay?"

"No, I'm not okay," he bit out. He reined in the

urge to tell her exactly what he thought of his injury and what had caused it.

He straightened the rest of the way slowly, waiting for another stabbing pain. He searched the patio for the best escape route. "How do I get out of here?"

"I'll show you."

"Just tell me."

She looked at him searchingly. Again. "Are you sure you're okay?"

He gritted his teeth. "Dandy. That door over there?"

"That takes you to the lobby and you can go out the front from there. But I can give you a ride."

"No." His answer was curt.

"You look like you might collapse," she said.

Blow out a couple of disks and that was one of the results.

"Really, Penn. This isn't the time to let your pride get in the way."

He turned to face her, his jaw stiff. She was less friendly and more quietly determined. But her determination was no match for his rage.

Penn managed to speak in a low, even voice when he finally answered. "Hate to break it to you, Nadia, but pride is one of the few things I have left."

With that, he turned and made his painfully slow way to the door.

CHAPTER FOURTEEN

NADIA FELT AS THOUGH Penn had slapped her.

She glared at his back as he crossed the patio, refusing to allow any sympathy to seep in. If he wanted to walk home in pain, who was she to argue?

Taking a different route from him, she went through the staff door Lyla had used and marched to the front desk to greet the night staff on her way to her office. Lucas, one of her favorite employees who'd worked there for eighteen years, had several funny lines for her and managed to make her laugh. Then she spotted Penn.

He was still walking toward the main door. Slowly. Not quite limping, but his gait definitely had a catch in it. She could tell from here that he was in pain and she growled in frustration.

"Everything okay there, Miss Nadia?" Lucas asked.

"Just fine," she said, watching Penn for as far as she could see him once he exited the building.

"'Fine' doesn't normally elicit angry animal noises."

Penn slipped out of view and she met Lucas's questioning gaze. "Stupid, stubborn man. Men can be such idiots. No offense."

He chuckled. "None taken. I'm sure you can change his mind, whoever he is."

Nadia shook her head and drummed her fingers on the marble counter. "I already tried. You have a good evening, Lucas."

"You do the same," he said as she strode toward the executive offices.

She'd no sooner entered her office than she muttered a curse, put on her shoes, grabbed her purse and took off toward the side exit to where her car was parked.

She was just reassuring herself. That was all.

There were only two routes Penn could take to get home, so she shouldn't have to search too long. He'd never even know she was checking up on him, and once she saw with her own eyes that he was making progress—from a distance, of course—she'd turn around and go back to work.

She turned onto the main street from the parking lot and scanned both sidewalks. The streetlights were lit, but a lot of the businesses were dark since it was late and off-season. Moving at a crawl, she hunted the shadows.

She spotted someone a block away, but as she got closer, it became obvious that it wasn't Penn. The person was jogging. And female.

At Pebble Street, she turned right. It was darker off the main boulevard, so she slowed down even more, afraid she would whip right past him and not only risk missing him altogether but get busted checking up on him in the process.

Penn lived one block south of Pebble, and when Nadia reached his street, she still hadn't seen a hint of him. There was no way he'd already made it home—not at the rate he was walking. She quelled her growing alarm by reassuring herself that if he'd been hit by a bus or fallen over on the sidewalk, she would have seen him. He must have taken the other route.

Looping around to the second option, she again watched for someone walking. This street was more deserted. She was almost back to the hotel when she hit her brakes hard. Luckily she'd been going so slowly they didn't squeal.

Nadia stared in her rearview mirror but couldn't see clearly enough. Putting the car in Park, she twisted and craned her neck to look out the back window. There, under the streetlight, was a figure on the bus stop bench, lying down, knees pointed to the sky. Bare knees. Tennis shoes. Dark hair.

Penn. She was almost sure of it.

She was going to kill him for refusing a ride.

He didn't even look her way when the car door slammed shut. She crossed to his side of the street, and narrowed her eyes as she approached. Yep, that was Penn all right.

When she stood at the side of the bench peering down at him, he opened his eyes.

"What are you doing?" she demanded, unable to keep her anger in check.

"Resting," he said with a decidedly blow-it-out-your-ear tone.

Nadia clenched her jaw so hard her head throbbed. She was trying to control her temper, to be calm and reasonable. Unaffected by his blockheadedness. She'd have to work on mastering that later.

"Get in the car, Penn."

He stared at her without changing his expression. "I said I'm resting my back."

"Let's get you home to your bed and you can rest it all night, for all I care."

"*Let's* nothing. This is my problem. Stay out of it."

He had to be hurting something awful to have stopped like this, but her sympathy was currently buried by frustration to the nth degree. "Penn, come *on*." She shifted to the end where he rested his head. "I can't believe you were too stubborn to accept a ride in the first place. See where that got you?"

"Halfway home so far."

"In between grimaces of pain."

Her blood pounded as he ignored her.

Sucking in air to try to calm herself, she unclenched her fists and looked up and down the street. They were alone, not that that mattered. An audience wouldn't stop her from...what? What was she going to do? She couldn't move him. Even if he wasn't a hundred pounds heavier than her, she didn't dare touch him, for fear of hurting him more.

He watched her with a mix of wariness and defiance. His body took up the entire bench, so Nadia lowered herself to the pavement in front of it.

"What the hell are you doing?" he asked.

"Waiting."

"Bus just came through about five minutes before you got here." His forced nonchalance was almost as annoying as his hatefulness.

"Maybe you'll get tired of the game before the next one comes along."

"Why are you doing this?" Penn shifted his arms from behind his head to cross them over his chest stubbornly.

"That's a good freaking question," Nadia muttered, hugging her legs in an attempt to find a semi-comfortable position.

"Guilt can be a bitch."

She glared at him.

Another five minutes passed with neither of

them speaking. Nadia, who'd shed her jacket in her office hours ago, shivered as a light breeze picked up. A little wind wasn't going to scare her off. This battle had become personal and she wasn't leaving Penn until he was in his condo. She glanced over and caught him watching her.

Penn eased himself up and swung his legs to the ground, and she could tell he was fighting hard not to show how much the motion hurt.

"Let's go," he said. "You're too stubborn to admit you're cold."

Nadia hopped up and, once he was standing, firmly grabbed his hand. She wasn't going to let him walk off now. "The car's right there."

He removed his hand from hers and she tried—unsuccessfully—not to take it personally.

They walked to her BMW. She got in the driver's side and prayed he wouldn't decide to walk off now. The passenger door opened and he sat with his back to her, then slowly turned toward the front.

"Son of a bitch," he said.

It was all she could do to not remind him he would have been home and more comfortable ages ago if he'd listened to her in the first place.

"If I'd known your seats had such top-notch lumbar support, I would've accepted long ago."

Nadia was too irritated to respond to his sarcasm. They didn't speak again until she pulled the car into his lot, not bothering to find a parking space, just stopping as close as she could get to his walkway.

He stared straight ahead for a moment. "Well. This night didn't go well."

She didn't know what she'd expected him to say, but it wasn't that.

"Understatement."

He met her gaze and held it for a few seconds, as if he was going to say more. Instead, he turned away and opened the door. "Good night, Nadia."

He'd shut the door before she could wish him the same.

Inexplicably, tears gathered in her eyes as she watched him walk away. Just minutes before, she'd been so mad she'd wanted to punch something—and she'd never been a particularly violent person. Now... *God.*

He moved stiffly, ramrod straight, so that someone who didn't know him couldn't tell what he'd been through in the past month. But his pace and that subtle catch with every step gave it away. He went at the speed of someone forty years older. The contradiction between the way he looked—young, strong and, okay, admittedly hot—and the way his body obviously felt...

She couldn't have stayed mad if she'd wanted to. Her throat tightened with sympathy, sadness.

And as he'd suggested, guilt. If she hadn't been out in that storm…

With blurred vision, she stared after him until he turned the corner out of her sight.

His life had been rocked irrevocably, and she ached to be able to wrap her arms around him and make it better.

CHAPTER FIFTEEN

THERE WAS NO POINT in going back to work tonight.
Nadia was done emotionally.

Ten minutes after Penn left, she dried her eyes
and pointed her car toward Faith's, hoping like
crazy it wasn't too late to drop in. In the pre-Joe
days, she wouldn't have hesitated. She, Faith and
Mercedes had always had that kind of friendship,
where the hour didn't matter. If something was
wrong, they sought each other out.

Tonight qualified.

As she drove, she didn't try to pinpoint what
was wrong. Didn't want to think about it too
hard. She just proceeded on instinct, knowing
she didn't want to be alone, didn't really want to
hang out with her mom, definitely didn't feel capable of being productive.

After parking in the street, Nadia climbed one
level to Faith's front door, relieved to see lights
shining out from inside. She knocked softly.

The outdoor light went on and Nadia blinked
in the brightness. She felt herself being looked at
through the peephole, and then the door opened.

"Hey, you," Faith said with a smile. She wore yoga pants and a sports tank, and Nadia's gaze automatically went to Faith's middle. Faith's followed. "Can't see the baby yet. Everything looks the same but…" Her laugh was a touch bittersweet. "Everything's different. Come on in."

"Am I interrupting anything?" Nadia asked, glancing around for Joe. Their two cats were curled up together on the easy chair but they seemed to be the only other living creatures present.

"Not at all. I was just working on some wedding details and was about to go for the Ben and Jerry's. Joe's on duty so there's no one to stop me."

"Don't look at me to hold you back. Pregnant women are supposed to exist on ice cream. You have to get your calcium."

"See, that's exactly what I needed. Logic." Faith led her to the kitchen and went directly for the freezer. "Want some?"

Nadia shook her head. "I'm not hungry."

Faith studied her more closely as she took a pint container out. "Ice cream doesn't require you to be hungry. It slides in the cracks. What's going on?" When she set the container on the counter, she narrowed her eyes. "Have you been crying?"

Nadia lifted her chin and stared up at the ceiling, willing herself not to start again.

"You have. What's wrong, Nadia?"

Nadia exhaled in a cross between a laugh and a sigh. "Good question. Penn came to the hotel tonight."

"To see you?"

"He said he was on a walk to get out of his condo."

Faith turned her back on the ice cream and gave Nadia her full attention. "And he just happened by the Silver Sands. Oh, and you just happened to be there, of course." She grinned knowingly. "I'd say between that and your supersecret visit to his place the other night, something's going on between you two."

"It's not like that." Nadia leaned against the dishwasher, unable to even fake any lightness or nonchalance.

"You're not attracted to him?"

She briefly thought about their awkward but memorable kiss. "That's not the point."

"Okaaay." Faith crossed her arms, still staring at Nadia. "Talk to me. Tell me the point. And everything else."

The breath Nadia took in was shaky. "I feel terrible about his injury. It's my fault he lost his career. My fault he's walking around in pain."

"Oh, no, Nadia." Faith left the ice cream sitting on the counter and locked her arm with

Nadia's, dragging her out to the living room. "Let's sit down."

They curled up on a love seat in the corner, facing each other. Nadia picked up a throw pillow and hugged it to her chest. She briefly told Faith how Penn had strained his back getting up, how he'd been so physically fatigued he could barely walk. "He wouldn't let me give him a ride home."

"Doesn't surprise me," Faith said. "Firefighters are a proud, stubborn breed. Especially the male ones."

"He's not a firefighter anymore. His career is ove—" Nadia darted a look at her friend, realizing Penn might not be the only one in those circumstances. "Crap. I'm sorry, Faith."

Faith shook her head. "Don't worry about me. I'm thinking seriously about going back to work once the baby is born."

"Good for you," Nadia said. "If anyone can balance it, it's you two."

Faith shrugged, not looking entirely sure of herself. "Back to you and Penn. Sometimes all you can do is try. You gave him the option of not walking home. He chose not to take it. What are you supposed to do, force him into your car?"

"Well…" Nadia's lips quivered upward at the corners. "Yeah. Pretty much." She recounted the rest of the story. "He definitely didn't thank me when he got out of the car."

"Y chromosome."

"He was moving so slowly, Faith. Not quite walking right. This big, beautiful, burly man can barely move and it's killing me."

"You have to let go of that guilt, hon. As a firefighter, he had a dangerous job. We all know that going into it and, believe me, we're reminded of it every time we go out on a run."

"I can't let it go. He won't let me."

"What?" Faith sounded scandalized.

"He blames me. He already resented my dedication to my job because of when I had to cancel our dates."

"How do you know he blames you?"

"He's said things. He blows up at me."

"And you've bought into the idea that it's your fault."

"If I hadn't decided to go back to the office for files at the last minute, I wouldn't have needed to be rescued. He wouldn't have been injured."

"You don't have anything to feel guilty about. A piece of debris disabled your car, Nadia. You didn't push him to the ground yourself."

Nadia eyed her, annoyed with the drama. "Gray area. Nothing was intentional, but that doesn't mean I'm not responsible. If a driver runs someone over without meaning to and kills the person, he's still guilty."

"In this case, then, the debris is guilty."

"You're warped," she told Faith.

"But I'm right." Faith leaned forward to emphasize her point. "If our roles were reversed, you'd tell me the same thing."

"Maybe," Nadia conceded, "but being able to see that logically doesn't take away the regret."

"Fair enough. It doesn't help if he's quick to remind you."

"Right. I want to help but I think I only make things worse when I'm with him."

"Maybe stepping away and giving him space would be best."

Nadia pursed her lips as if that could hold in all the emotions storming through her. Closing her eyes, she whispered, "I can't."

"You care about him," Faith said, her voice gentle. "You liked him a lot before you ever went out."

"I thought he was good-looking," Nadia clarified. "I didn't know him enough to 'like him a lot.' Even after our disastrous half date, I didn't know him." It'd been obvious from the first time they'd met—or even before they'd officially been introduced, really—that he was easygoing and well liked. Whenever she'd seen him at bars and firefighter gatherings, he'd been surrounded by people, frequently laughing. She'd been drawn to that, just like everyone else.

"You do now."

"I know him better. Weren't you in desperate need of ice cream?" Nadia hopped up and hurried to the kitchen to get both of them some.

"Nice," Faith said, following her. "At least try to be less obvious about your avoidance."

Nadia took a large spoon out of the silverware drawer and jabbed it into the softened ice cream. Drops of it splattered out. She licked her fingers and grabbed two bowls from the cabinet. "What all is in this stuff?" she asked as she scooped out the vanilla with...lots of somethings.

"Cake, chocolate, sugar, calcium, as you mentioned."

"As long as it's health food. I had cookies for dinner."

"You need to stop living like a single man." Faith took one of the bowls and got spoons out for both of them.

"I live like a single woman who works long hours."

They wandered back out to the living room and retook their seats.

"You were about to admit your feelings for Penn," Faith said with her mouth half-full and a wicked grin.

Trying to convince Faith she wasn't attracted to Penn was futile, and besides, that attraction wasn't the issue here. Not exactly.

Nadia scooped a spoonful of ice cream in her

mouth, closed her eyes and let the first bite sit on her tongue. "Pure heaven. Why do we bother with such things as meat and veggies?" She took another bite.

"Stalling," Faith said, drawing out the word.

She stared at her bowl, stirred the melting ice cream in it. "He's not handling anything very well. He's just wasting away, and if I let him, that's just going to add to my guilt. And yeah, I do care about him."

Faith nodded once, as if gratified Nadia had finally fessed up.

Nadia filled her spoon but set it down without eating. "I shouldn't even tell you this because you'll never let it go." She bit her lip and met Faith's gaze. "The night Mercedes and I had dinner here? When I went to Penn's beforehand?"

"Yeah?"

"I kissed him."

Faith leaned forward, one hand braced on her thigh, the other gripping her bowl. "I *knew* there was more to the story. *You* kissed *him?*"

"Yes. So I guess I'm busted. I care about him. I'm attracted to him. But there's no way anything could develop because of all the bad mojo between us."

"Mojo in this case being his anger toward you and your feeling guilty."

"Bingo."

"So the first step is for you to work through your guilt."

Nadia scoffed. "Yeah, right. How?"

"Be there for him. And if he throws the blame at you again, remind yourself he's mad at his situation and that what happened was an accident."

It made perfect sense to the logical part of Nadia's brain. "I'll work on it. I can be there for him. It's harder to let his anger roll off my back."

"If it gets too hard, you always have the option of walking away."

Nadia nodded slowly. She wasn't ready to desert Penn, even when he acted the way he did tonight.

"Until you reach that point, Great-grandma Hamlin's cookies never hurt."

Nadia breathed a little easier. "Chocolate chip cookies can sometimes work wonders."

"I can't believe you didn't tell Mercedes and me about the kiss before now."

"I had this suspicion you might make a big deal of it," Nadia said dryly.

Faith reached out for Nadia's empty bowl, stacked it with hers and set them on the end table behind her.

"We've accomplished ice-cream-ness. Now what wedding stuff are you working on?" Nadia asked. "What can I help with?"

"Thought you'd never ask. Will you help me

decide on a centerpiece style for the reception? I found several online that I think we could make."

Nadia followed her to the computer on the built-in desk in the kitchen. After her own dilemma, centerpieces were a welcome walk in the park.

CHAPTER SIXTEEN

VODKA MADE JUST ABOUT everything better.

It was true of cooking, as far as Penn was concerned. He hoped it was true of food, as well, as he consulted his laptop and reread the online recipe for penne alla vodka for the third time.

Far be it from his sister to stock his kitchen with things like frozen pizzas and Hamburger Helper. Evil wench that she was, Zoe had bought ingredients for a handful of fancy dishes before she'd left. He either had to drag his butt to the store for something else or break down and figure out how to cook them. He wasn't a complete novice in the kitchen but anything with more than about five ingredients was a stretch.

He pulled out his phone to text his sure-to-be-smug sister.

What the hell is molto al dente and what's so bad about boxed mac and cheese?

Her response was almost immediate. Basically it's when the pasta is almost done. Anything that orange besides carrots and yams surely causes some kind of terminal disease.

Penn shook his head and peered at the pot of boiling pasta. There was a reason he wasn't the cook in the family.

Don't suppose you want to define "almost done," he typed.

Taste it. Mostly tender but just a little hard when you chew it.

Just perfect. He eyed the open vodka bottle, then reached to the back of one of the cabinets and dragged out a shot glass. Filled it with Absolut and downed it.

Aah, yeah. The burn could only help his cooking adventure.

He took the spoon he'd used to stir the penne and fished out a couple of pieces to taste. He stuck them in his mouth, forgetting to blow on them, and howled and sucked in cool air to soothe the burn on his tongue. Swallowing the scalding pasta whole, he let out a creative stream of swearwords.

The cream sauce in the other pan gurgled, reminding him to stir it. Then he captured another piece of pasta, blew on it and sampled it.

Perfectly almost done, as far as he could tell.

He drained the penne and stirred the sauce again, starting to feel like he was on the verge of conquering Rome.

"What's cooking, honey?" Cooper asked in a falsetto voice as he walked into the kitchen. His hair was wet from the shower and his face was sunburned. He came up to the stove to peer into the pots.

"Penne alla vodka," Penn said grumpily. "If you get the hell away from me, I might share."

"Smells good. Where's the box it came from?" Coop opened the lid of the wastebasket as if searching for evidence that Penn had cheated.

"Going out tonight?" Penn asked, ignoring the accusation. He added the pasta to the oversize pot with the sauce.

"Nah. Got my fill of beer and socialization at the beach today. Felt like June out there, not late October. You missed it."

Just as he'd missed everything else for the past month. Penn bit back the words and reminded himself that his roommate wasn't trying to rub it in.

"Shit, I'm sorry, man," Coop said, making Penn suspect he hadn't hidden his reaction as well as he'd thought. "You need to come out with me next time."

"We'll see. Beach volleyball is the least of my worries." Penn flipped off the burner and poured the pasta and sauce into a large bowl that had previously only ever been used for microwave popcorn.

Coop took a couple of beers out of the fridge, opened them and slid one to Penn. In return, Penn handed him a plate.

"Help yourself."

After they'd filled their plates, Coop sat at the bar and Penn stood at the counter to eat.

"Damn," Coop said with his mouth stuffed full. "You can cook for me anytime, sweetheart."

Penn replied with some choice descriptive words.

"Seriously, this is really decent."

The thing was, Penn agreed. He sort of impressed himself, not that he'd admit it out loud. "Call me Betty and I'll kill you in your sleep."

The sound of their forks scraping the plates filled the room.

"So. Any luck deciding what the heck you're going to do?" Cooper asked after a while, still shoveling the food in.

"Do?"

"In general. Got any ideas yet?"

"For a job?"

"Yeah. Gotta earn beer money somehow."

"I don't have a clue."

"Have you checked job sites?"

Penn frowned as his gut tightened. "Hell, no. I wouldn't know where to start."

Cooper slid Penn's laptop over and starting typing.

"What are you doing?" Penn asked, not masking his annoyance.

Without answering, Coop typed some more. Waited, clicked. "Let's see… 'Number one furniture company is seeking professional sales associates. Previous experience preferred but not required. Weekends mandatory.'"

Penn shot his roommate a killer look.

"Okay, true, can't see you in a tie," Coop said. "How about this? 'Swing bridge operator, midnight shift. English required.' You speak excellent English. Or you could be a rent-a-cop. That'd be an easy one."

"As long as they assigned me to the old folks' home," Penn said.

Cooper finished a bite and took a swig of beer while he perused in blessed silence. "No way. These aren't your answer." He shut the laptop and pushed it aside.

"Could have told you that before you started."

"What about something in the department? Dispatch or training or something?"

Penn didn't want to think about any of it. He hadn't yet fully accepted that he wouldn't be fighting fires. He supposed the idea of still being involved in the fire department was decent but… dispatch? Seemed like second prize—or third or fourth—in a beauty contest. Miss Congeniality, even. "I don't know. I could make more money as a bartender."

"There you go. Have Derek set you up at the Shack pouring drinks."

Nothing against Derek or his wife, Macey, but just the thought of it made his stomach turn.

They wolfed down pasta in silence for several minutes.

"What would you do?" Penn eventually asked.

"If I couldn't be a firefighter?" Coop looked thoughtful for a moment. "Marry some rich chick."

"Classy."

"You keep cooking like this, you could make yourself one hell of a wife for Nadia."

"Hate to blow your fantasy there but I don't think Nadia's a rich chick, in spite of the Bimmer."

"Is that what's holding you back from her?" Cooper came around the bar and heaped some more food on his plate. "Money?"

"We're going down this dead end again?" Penn asked, pushing his empty plate away.

"I'm stumped, dude. Beautiful woman who seems to want to spend time with you, and you're dragging your feet." He returned to his place. "I'm not trying to be insensitive, but you have spare time out the wazoo right now. Why not get to know her better?"

"Think about it, Coop. Where can it go?"

"I'd say that's up to the two of you."

"Exactly. It's going nowhere."

"Why is that, if you don't mind me asking?" Cooper took his seat at the bar and started shoveling pasta into his mouth again.

"I do mind you asking."

"So answer, anyway. Hot woman who keeps turning up here. Guy with little to do besides rehab. What gives?"

"Really? You have to ask?" Penn wished he could avoid this conversation, but Coop didn't seem likely to let it drop.

"Apparently I do."

"She's the reason I'm sitting here with little to do besides rehab. I can't seem to get past it."

"It was an accident. A freak accident. Depending on how you look at it, you could even argue that she was being responsible by trying to keep up on her workload in the middle of a hurricane."

"I tell myself that. Well, not the responsible part because her love affair with her job is over the top, but the accident part. I know she didn't do anything on purpose, man. You think I've got rocks for brains?"

"Yeah, actually."

Penn chugged the remaining third of his beer and set the bottle down with a clank. "I tried to apologize to her the other night. For the way I keep treating her. I know it's not fair. I couldn't make myself do it. If I were her, I would've told me where to go and been done with it long ago."

Coop raised a brow at him. "That's messed up, dude."

"Yeah, well, that's pretty much where I live these days."

"I kind of get it," Coop said sympathetically. "You'll get there. Doesn't seem like it right now, but everything will fall into place for you, Griff."

"Yeah." Glancing at the mess he'd made on the stove and the counter, he said, "I cooked. You're up for KP."

Once the possibility of resuming the career he loved, the only thing he knew, was taken away, Penn had no damn clue what "everything" his roommate thought would fall into place. Penn didn't believe that any more than he believed selling furniture was his destiny.

CHAPTER SEVENTEEN

"THANK GOD YOU'RE HERE." Paul Leder, the night manager, stood in Nadia's office doorway, concern evident on his face.

Nadia smiled in spite of the foreboding that raised the hairs on the back of her neck. "Hey, Paul, I'm pretty much always here, aren't I?"

"Well, so is your mother, but I can't find her anywhere and she won't answer her cell phone." He entered the room and helped himself to a chair opposite Nadia.

"What's going on?"

"I've got the guy from the roofing company out at the desk looking for her. They've run into some kind of a snag and need to talk to her."

"What kind of a snag?" Nadia asked warily. She was in on a lot of aspects of the hotel, more than were relevant to the events and marketing departments, but maintenance wasn't one of them.

"Something about one of the air-conditioning units being potentially unsafe."

"Where's Lois?" Her mom's assistant would likely know where she was.

"Apparently she left this morning for the West Coast. Her grandmother had a stroke."

Nadia wondered how she'd missed that news, but then she had been in back-to-back meetings for hours. She stood as she pulled out her cell phone and hit the button for her mom. "You've looked everywhere?" she asked Paul.

"Two or three times. The guy's been waiting out there for a good twenty minutes. They're trying to go home for the night."

Her mom's voice mail kicked in.

"Mom, call me ASAP. You're needed at the hotel. Bye." Nadia picked up the landline and dialed the number that connected her to the hostess in the restaurant. "Hi, Mandy, it's Nadia. Have you seen my mom lately?"

"I've only been here since four, but I haven't seen her once."

"If you do, please tell her I'm looking for her?"

"You've got it."

Nadia hung up and tried three more departments with the same results.

"I can't remember the last time your mom was gone before 6:00 p.m. on a weekday," Paul said, also standing.

Neither could Nadia. On those very few occasions, her mom had told her where she'd be and had usually planned to return later in the evening.

"Where is this roofing guy? I'll see if I can take care of it."

"Thanks. I left him in the lobby."

Nadia followed Paul down the hall toward the front desk area, trying her mom's phone again. She ended the connection as soon as the recording started, wavering between concern and annoyance. Paul led her to a fifty-ish man wearing old, dirty jeans and a navy Island Roofing T-shirt.

"This is Nadia Hamlin," Paul told him. "She's one of our directors and happens to be Joyce Hamlin's daughter."

"Hi," Nadia said, shaking the guy's calloused hand. "I understand there's a problem?"

"There might be or there might not be," the roofer said. "How familiar are you with our project?"

"Not very," Nadia said regretfully. She'd had no reason to be. "I know the damage was all on the north end."

The guy didn't bother to hide his annoyance. "Your mother gave us a strict deadline to get it finished. The presidential suite can't be rented out while we work."

"And we need it by the weekend," Nadia said, having heard her mother mention repeatedly the bind they would be in if the roof wasn't done in time for some politician's stay.

"Right. We're on schedule but we just discovered one of the A/C units is loose, probably from the storm. It's not something my company can fix."

"Okay," Nadia said slowly, completely out of her element. "So we need to get someone up there who can."

"Right away. It might be easily fixed, but I'm worried about that unit. It's not at all secure. Might be a pressing safety issue."

He had Nadia's full attention with that, and her adrenaline started pumping.

"It needs to be checked out immediately. You get a little wind and that unit could cause all kinds of damage."

"Got it."

"My crew needs to get started no later than eight tomorrow morning or the deadline might not be possible," he said with a scowl.

"I hear you. Thank you."

The roofer headed for the door without another word, but Nadia had no time to worry about his irritation. She had no idea what company her mother preferred to work with, whether the unit was under warranty, whether it was old or new or how much effect it would have on the guest rooms if it had to be replaced. She didn't even know exactly what kind of company she needed to contact.

She made a beeline for her mother's office,

trying her cell again to no avail, her frustration mounting with every step. Her mom better have a damn good reason for being incommunicado.

"How NICE OF YOU to drop in." Nadia didn't bother to look up from her laptop when her mother wandered in.

"Hello to you, too," Joyce said. "What are you doing in my office?"

Nadia finished typing the last sentence of an email and hit Send. She closed her laptop and met her mother's questioning gaze. "Did you not get my message?"

"I was just about to sit down and check my phone. What's going on?"

Nadia's rage had been put on hold for the past few hours as she'd shifted into problem-solving, fix-it-even-though-you-don't-have-a-clue-how mode. Suddenly she was shaking with anger as she stood. "Let's see. The roofers notified me that one of the A/C units was loose and needed to be fixed ASAP so that their tarring schedule wouldn't be interrupted. It took me a while to track down a company that could send someone out this week, let alone tonight. They got here about seven and confirmed that, yes, there was more damage from the storm than we knew about and that, oh, yes, we damn well better get this taken care of right this stinking minute before the unit causes more damage. Of course, they don't have the type of unit we need just sitting around, so they had to order one. In the meantime, they're removing the immediate danger and we're moving guests to the south wing of the building because the cooling system on the north side is down until they can get the new unit installed."

Her mom had dropped into one of the chairs across the desk from Nadia, the color drained from her face. "Oh, my Lord." She ran her hand through her hair, which Nadia now noticed looked windblown. "Do we have enough rooms available to keep.everyone comfortable?"

"Guests were given the choice to stay where they were, but given that it hit almost eighty degrees today, no one's interested in being without air-conditioning. It's crowded but we can get by tonight. Tomorrow...I haven't even looked at the reservations yet."

Her mom stood and came around the desk, having apparently recovered from her initial shock. "What company did you end up getting out here?"

Nadia handed her the business card with the information on it and answered her mother's other questions, assuring her that, for now, all they could do was wait as the workers removed the danger from the situation.

Joyce frowned at the card. "Not my first choice but it sounds like you didn't have a lot of options."

"No." Nadia spoke through clenched teeth, her arms crossed tightly over her chest. "Not a lot." As in, zero.

Her mom shrugged and Nadia's pulse hammered through her head. "We'll hope for the best."

That did it. "Where in the hell have you been all evening?"

Joyce sat in her own chair now and, unbelievably, smiled. "Gene called me this afternoon and invited me to go out on his boat for a picnic dinner."

"You were on a *date?*" Nadia threw her arms up in frustration.

"Yes," her mom said firmly. "I was. It was after five o'clock and I didn't intend to be gone so long."

"And you didn't tell me—or anyone—where you were going? I called you a dozen times!"

"I didn't realize we'd be out of range for my phone."

"You might want to check into that before you go off for a little champagne and fried chicken. You know you can't be out of touch like that, Mom!" She turned her back and took several steps away.

"Keep your voice down, Nadia."

"What?" She spun around in disbelief.

"There's no need to let the entire hotel know of our disagreement. That's never been our way."

"It's never been our way to take time out of a workday to go frolicking around with a man before, either."

The grin that once again spread across her mother's face made Nadia want to scream. "I can assure you I'm too old to 'frolick.'"

"Mom! Do you not understand what I've been going through for the past few hours? While you were having the time of your life? *Because* you were having the time of your life?"

"This is the whole dating issue again, isn't it?"

"No. This is a you-were-irresponsible and I've-been-at-my-wit's-end issue."

"Would you be this upset if I'd been at a doctor's appointment?"

"Yes," Nadia said without thought. She was too pissed off to try to think straight. "Unless you want to teach me every aspect of your job, then you need to be reachable."

Nadia had aged five years in the past two hours. She could handle events crises with barely a blink of the eye, but operations and maintenance…that had always been something her parents had handled.

"Maybe it's time for you to learn more," her mom said, surprising her. In the past, she'd been more apt to try to ease Nadia's workload than to suggest adding to it.

"Let me get the events manager hired and brought up to speed and I'll consider it," she snapped.

"That's fair. Now…when is the new air-conditioning unit supposed to be here?" her mom asked.

"They can install it Friday, assuming the roofers will be out of their way."

"It has to be done for Saturday night. All of it." Joyce jotted something on a sticky note and stuck it on the bottom of her computer monitor.

Nadia reached across the desk and grabbed her laptop from her mom's workspace. "I assume you can take it from here? I was supposed to get back to Tessa on the marketing campaign several hours ago. I haven't even started looking at the final materials and I'm sure she's gone home by now."

"You'll be around if I have any more questions?"

Pausing in the doorway, Nadia said, "Of course. Staying in communication has always been our way."

Until recently. Until her mom had decided a man was more important than the family business.

CHAPTER EIGHTEEN

THE NEXT DAY AT 9:47 A.M., Nadia had yet to leave the hotel. She'd stolen an hour-long nap in her hotel room around four in the morning, but unfortunately her room was on the north end and the temperature was starting to climb to uncomfortable levels. She'd woken up in a sweat, taken a quick shower and returned to her office.

She and Tessa, the marketing manager, had been locked away hammering out changes to the marketing materials for almost an hour. Tessa had just left, and in thirteen minutes, Nadia was expected to be at the weekly executive meeting with her mom and the other directors and managers.

Her eyes burned and her body tensed at the thought of sitting at a table with her mother and pretending nothing was wrong.

Screw it. She couldn't do it. Not this time.

For the first time ever in the four years she'd been on the management team, Nadia was going to deliberately, emphatically skip a meeting. And maybe she was being immature, but she wasn't going to tell her mother in advance, either.

Without giving it more thought, she shut down her laptop and closed it, grabbed her purse and left everything else behind.

She was grateful no one saw her sneak from her office to the parking lot. She had no interest in explaining herself, not to mention no real excuse other than exhaustion, which wasn't an abnormal state for her. Exhaustion and, okay, she could admit it, irritation.

Just as she was about to open the door to the outside, doubt hit her. What if she missed something important? What if Tessa needed her to help her explain their last-minute changes? Shaking her head, she shut the questions down and went outside. She was too tired to say anything coherent, anyway, she told the nagging voice of guilt that persisted in trying to make her turn around.

The sky was overcast, which added to her uncharacteristic need for refuge. She ducked her head and jogged to her car.

A gust of wind pushed her door shut before she was ready, nearly catching her purse. It was nothing compared to the storm winds of a few weeks ago, but thank God they'd taken care of the loose roof unit last night.

Along with the wind came a sudden downpour, and she leaned back against the headrest, telling herself the sound of the rain hitting the roof and the isolation were exactly what she needed.

Maybe it was the fatigue and the remnants of last night's stress, but instead of peace, she felt... alone.

Since she'd been out of college and working with her mom, they'd rarely had disagreements. In general, the hotel had been the priority for both of them, and they worked well together. She couldn't say why she resented her mom's recent decisions to take time away, but she did.

Nadia jammed her keys into the ignition, started the car and sat there leaning her head against the side window, wondering where the hell to go. She sucked at playing hooky.

Penn would be home.

The thought came out of nowhere, but once she had it, she couldn't deny she wanted to see him. Maybe there was a subconscious—or not so subconscious—idea, too, that if her mom could skip out to spend time with a man, then so could she.

She turned on the BMW's windshield wipers and pulled out of the parking lot, heading toward Penn's building.

The lot was half-empty, probably due to the midmorning hour and people being at work, so she was able to park close. She glanced at her reflection in the mirror on the visor and questioned what she was doing here. She looked like, well, like she hadn't slept for a couple of days. The shower and minimal makeup this morning hadn't done much to disguise that. But she'd seen Penn during some low times, when he hadn't looked his best.

She forced herself out of the car and walked down the sidewalk toward his building, thankful the rain had stopped. When she turned the last corner, she recognized Cooper heading in her direction and her step faltered.

"Hey, Nadia." He gave her a knowing grin.

"Hi, Cooper. Is Penn home?"

"Sure is. Go on in. The door's unlocked. He's in his room."

Cooper walked on by, seeming in a hurry, and she tried to calm her nerves. Penn might not want to see her. He might still be upset from the other evening. She should have thought to pick up some cookies, but she was tired of coming up with excuses—to herself as well as to Penn—for why she kept stopping by.

She was here because she wanted to see Penn. Maybe he needed some company as much as she did.

When she got to the condo, she hesitated before twisting the knob and opening the door as Cooper had suggested.

"Hello?" she said into the silence.

She could see from here that the door to his room was mostly closed. With her heart hammering, she made her way down the hall and stood outside his room, listening. "Penn?"

When he still didn't respond, she pushed his door open, suspecting he was asleep. Should she have walked away at that point and let him sleep? Probably. But if she was going to start second-guessing her decisions, she had a handful to get through just from the past half hour. It was a little late for that.

It took several seconds for her eyes to adjust to the relative darkness, but she could see enough to set her heart pumping double-time. Penn was stretched out on his back, one arm propped behind his head, one resting on his bare abdomen. Gray cutoff sweatpants sat low on his hips and covered his legs to the knee. His upper body was beautifully naked. She allowed her gaze to linger there, admiring the solidness of his pecs, the ridges of his abs.

She moved closer and watched his face for a sign that he was faking sleep. It looked like he hadn't shaved yesterday, and she wanted to touch the stubble on his chin. She sat on the edge of the bed, expecting him to awaken. His steady breathing continued. The sound was lulling, peaceful. Especially alluring to a girl who was seriously sleep-deprived.

Nadia slipped her shoes off and leaned forward, bracing her weight on the mattress. He still didn't stir. She stretched her body out against him, slid her arm across his middle and rested her head next to his shoulder.

After the way they'd left things the last time they'd seen each other—with him walking off mad—there was a better than average chance he wouldn't be happy to find her here. She'd deal with that when it happened. Right now she was too drowsy and too comfortable to work up much concern.

PENN TRIED TO LOWER HIS ARM from above his head and ran into…something. *Someone.* What the…?

"Nadia?"

With his other hand, he rubbed his blurry eyes and confirmed that Nadia was indeed draped across him.

He'd finally broken down at close to three in the morning and taken one of the sleeping pills his doctor had given him. He wasn't sure he'd so much as stirred after that. It was the hardest he'd slept since his back had given out. Now he was having the damnedest time waking up. An even harder time figuring out the day and time.

Judging by the light coming through his window, it was daytime. He raised his arm again, the one on Nadia's side, and squinted at his watch—10:22 a.m. Wednesday.

Where was Coop and what the hell was Nadia doing here?

Not that he was complaining.

She'd been on his mind ever since she'd dropped him off the other night. On his mind and in his dreams. In spite of the unsettled, unhappy note they'd parted on.

He breathed in deeply, relishing the hint of vanilla and shampoo from her hair, just inches from his nose. Shifting enough to lower his arm, he wrapped it around her, resting his hand at her waist. Her blouse had come untucked from her skirt, and he couldn't get enough of the silky feel of her skin. He couldn't have stopped his body from responding if he'd wanted to.

"Nadia, what are you doing here?" he whispered.

She mumbled and moved slightly, curling more closely against him.

That was a good enough answer for him. He gave in to the grogginess again and drifted back to sleep.

The next thing Penn was aware of, God only knew how much later, was Nadia's leg sliding over his. And then immediately after, his blood pounding southward. Her chin nuzzled his chest and he touched her golden hair. She made a sleepy, sexy sound, her eyes still shut. He'd have to be dead not to want to kiss her.

Penn cleared his throat. "Aren't you supposed to be at work?" he asked, his voice rough.

She lifted her head and blinked her eyes slowly open. Mesmerizing sky-blue eyes with long sleepy lashes. He swallowed hard and fought the need to lift her more fully on top of him. Even though he felt no pain as he lay flat on his back, his body would protest any effort of the sort.

"I wanted to see you, make sure you recovered from Monday night," she said.

"See me? Or sleep on top of me?"

"Both, apparently." The shy grin she gave him didn't help his fight to ignore the heat that was building. "Sorry. I didn't sleep much last night."

It was on the tip of his tongue to tell her she could sleep on him anytime.

"Your back is better than the other night?"

"It's fine. I pushed too hard then."

Nadia shifted, bringing her lips an inch from him and, *damn,* she had a way of setting him on fire. Her lashes lowered as she glanced down at his lips. Every muscle in his body tensed as he anticipated contact.

"I'm *not* going to kiss you," she whispered. "This time you have to kiss me."

CHAPTER NINETEEN

PENN DIDN'T NEED ANY encouragement to silence the arguments in his head and take what Nadia offered.

He drew her mouth to his, his hand at her nape. When their lips touched, everything else faded away. He became lost in the taste of her, the softness of her mouth, the heat of her tongue as it twisted with his. He touched her greedily. Her silken hair, her slender torso just beneath her ribs, her delicate jawline.

Her knee slid to the other side of him, centering her body on his. She pulled away just enough to look him in the eyes as if having second thoughts.

He drew her back to his mouth, hungrily, aching for more of her. All of her.

He ran his hands down her sides, inward at the waist, flaring out over her hips. If anyone had told him three weeks ago, when he'd been in the worst pain of his life, that he'd have this sexy hourglass-shaped woman climbing on top of him, he wouldn't have believed it for a second.

Now it seemed natural to have Nadia in his bed. Natural and as necessary as air.

He palmed her ass and drew her lower body into his, which elicited an arousing moan from her. His hands continued their journey downward, until they found the bare flesh of her thighs where her short skirt had ridden up. Her legs were firm, muscular. The hem of her skirt teased his knuckles and he trailed his hands up under it. Farther, still, beneath her satiny panties.

Nadia's breath caught. She fit their bodies together, making him crazy with need. He wanted her naked, every last inch.

Trying to slow down and regain an ounce of control, he moved his hands back to her waist. She was so small, so feminine in his hands, and that unleashed an odd, primal possessiveness he didn't know he had in him.

She raised her upper body, strands of her hair draping over him, and pressed her hips into him. An appreciative growl came from deep in his throat. His hands roved upward and he explored the lace-covered curves of her breasts, inching his way beneath the material. With one hand, he reached behind her and released the snap. He couldn't get enough of her.

Nadia leaned down and they kissed again, a light, erotic teasing that left him breathless. She lifted her head and peered down at him, her lids heavy with lust. Penn ran his fingers over her jaw, pushed her hair back. Her lips curved into a lazy, sensual smile. "You're okay, right?" she asked.

He leaned up to reassure her with a kiss and swore under his breath as pain jabbed at him. That motion was apparently a no-go. The pull in his lower back wasn't as bad as two nights ago but it was enough to make him stop in his tracks, so to speak.

"You're not okay." Nadia seemed to snap out of lust mode and sat up quickly. "Why didn't you say something?"

He collapsed on the pillow and threw his head back. Closed his eyes. Wanted to hit something.

"Because I *was* okay." *Damn traitorous body.* "I'm fine now."

He nudged her gently, wanting, *needing* to kiss her again, feel her body on his, needing more, but Nadia's veil of desire seemed to dissipate into thin air. She leaned in to kiss him chastely on the lips.

In that moment, Penn knew frustration like he'd never known it before, and he figured he'd become something of an expert on it in the past few weeks. He wished for nothing more than to show this woman how much he wanted her, to lure her back to the place they'd been just moments ago, but he couldn't even lean up enough to kiss her. He was at her mercy.

"Come back," he whispered to her, gently using

his hand on her neck to urge her closer. She pressed her lips to his for a few gratifying seconds and he attempted to convey his need for her with that kiss.

At first, Nadia responded. As soon as he deepened the kiss, though, she pulled away, opened her eyes, shook her head. "No. You're not up for this yet."

"On the contrary, I'm very up for it, Nadia."

She laughed huskily at his deliberate double entendre, a sexy sound that didn't do a thing to cool his jets.

Her look of sympathy, however, did.

Sympathy.

Just what every guy wanted to see from the woman sprawled across him like a golden-haired goddess.

"Let me up." He couldn't keep the frustration out of his voice and frankly he didn't give a rat's left nut.

Nadia moved to the side of him and sat up, looking startled. He rolled the other way and sprang out of the bed on the opposite side. "Dammit!" He'd moved too fast, neglecting to use the care necessary to avoid more pain.

"Penn." The tone she used for just that single word was soothing and he could tell she was about to go into calm reasoning mode. None of which improved his temper.

His back to her, he breathed in, eyes closed, waiting for her to say what he was sure he didn't want to hear.

"It's okay. We don't need to rush anything," she said.

"It's not okay, Nadia." His volume climbed. "*Nothing* is okay."

He went over to his closet and took a random tee down from the shelf. Pulled it over his head, ignoring the relatively minor twinge in his lower back when he stretched.

He felt her approach him from behind. Ignored her closeness.

She touched his shoulder lightly. "Don't beat yourself up. I can be as patient as I need to be."

He jerked away from her touch and increased the space between them, searching for his sport sandals.

Patient. Shit. When it came to sex, what guy wanted to force patience on a woman? Wouldn't that just make for a winning personal ad: unemployed, physically challenged man seeking a woman who is beautiful, funny, intelligent and *patient.*

"Patience isn't going to do jack," he said, managing to keep his voice under control, "when this worthless body of mine won't do what I want it to. Now if you'll excuse me, I have a lot of nothing to do today." He stormed out into the hallway.

As he rounded into the kitchen, a knock sounded at the door. He turned toward it ominously, in no mood for a visit from anyone and more than ready for Nadia to hit the road, as well. She appeared at the end of the hall, having hastily straightened her clothing but still looking tousled and aroused. She looked from the door to him. Swearing under his breath, he went to answer it.

"Mom?" He didn't bother to hide his shock at the sight of her.

"Your sister didn't lie," his mother said, looking him over. "You're upright. Mobile. This is good."

"Uh, yeah." He looked past his mom for Zoe, but she was alone. "What are you doing here?"

Nadia stood off to one side, watching with interest.

"How about 'Welcome to my home, Mom, come on in'?" Her short red hair, slightly spiky on top, hadn't changed for as long as he could remember. She smiled broadly and he noticed the fine lines at the corners of her eyes and around her mouth. He didn't remember seeing those before. Of course, it'd been two and a half years since he'd been to Colorado to see her, give or take. That was the norm.

Her showing up at his door was not.

"Come in, Mom." He stood back to let her enter, a black suitcase rolling behind her. He'd have to come up with a polite way to ensure she didn't think she was staying with him—soon. "And then back to what are you doing here?"

"Visiting." She stood on her toes to kiss his cheek. "Taking a vacation. And yes, checking up on you."

"You sent Zo for that. I'm still fine. This is my friend Nadia Hamlin. Nadia, my mother, Nell Griffin."

The two women shook hands and sized each other up.

"It's nice to meet you," Nadia said. "Welcome to San Amaro."

"Thank you. I've never been here before. I have to admit, just judging from the cab ride in, it's gorgeous. I'm overdue for a nice, relaxing trip."

Penn was going to need a nice, relaxing trip as soon as his mother's was over. "Smells like Coop left a pot of coffee. Want some, Mom?"

"No, thank you, I'm wired enough as it is. Been up since 4:00 a.m., drinking caffeine since 4:05." She adjusted her suitcase—large enough to stow away a Great Dane—up against the front wall.

"Love your bag," Nadia said, pointing at the expensive-looking monstrosity. "It's a Louis, isn't it?"

"It is," his mom said, obviously warming up to Nadia. "A bit of a luxury but I travel so much for work, I decided it was worth it."

"The texture is gorgeous." Nadia ran her fingers across the leather suitcase, then straightened. "I need to get back to work and let you two catch up."

"It's been a while for us," his mom said, patting his upper arm. "Where's work?"

"My family owns a hotel on the beach. The Silver Sands. I'm the director of events and marketing."

Nell raised her brows, impressed, and looked at Penn.

"You would love the Silver Sands, Mom." Perfect solution.

"You said on the beach? I'm sold. Is it possible for you to save me a room and Penn can take me there later?"

"Absolutely. When you go to the front desk, have them page me," Nadia said, edging toward the door. "It was nice to meet you, Mrs. Griffin."

His mom reached for Nadia's hand as if they'd been friends forever. "Please, call me Nell. I'll see you and your beach hotel later."

Penn moved to the door to see Nadia out, hoping to give his mother the appearance that there was no tension—of any kind—between them. He was already going to get the third degree.

"I'll talk to you later, Penn," Nadia said on her way past. She managed to pull off a hint of warmth, although he could tell it was fake because of the set of her jaw.

If his mom had to show up at his place, there couldn't have been a better time for her to do it. Her presence allowed no room for further conversation between Nadia and him. Thanks to her, he could avoid any situation that forced him to make false pleasantries or promises. Because those were two things he just couldn't muster right now. Possibly ever.

CHAPTER TWENTY

PENN STARED AFTER NADIA even once she'd disappeared around the corner, stalling as best he could before turning around to deal with his mother.

"She seems like a nice girl," Nell said, her smile evident in her voice.

"Yes. She is." Penn shut the door and faced his mother. "So what are you really doing here, Mom?"

"Isn't it obvious?" She glanced around the living room. "Let's sit down. Catch up."

"Obvious," Penn repeated, frowning. He gestured to the couch and dragged his handy-dandy straight-back chair away from the window to join her. "There's nothing obvious when it comes to my mother showing up on San Amaro for the first time in the twelve years I've lived here."

"Has it been twelve years? My word…" She sat on the couch and smoothed out her navy slacks, as if they needed it.

Most people got off an airplane looking at least a little wrinkled and fatigued. Not Nell Griffin. Her clothing was impeccable, her face looked fresh, as if she'd gotten up an hour ago and taken a rejuvenating dip in natural spring water.

"I can't get over the fact that you didn't even call me after your injury, Penn."

"I already went over this with Zoe. Didn't she fill you in?"

"She said you're holding your own. Starting to recover."

"Going to be a long process, but there's nothing you or anyone else can do."

"A mother never accepts those words where her children are concerned. I love you, Penn. It pains me that you're struggling." She moved to the edge of the cushion and leaned forward as she spoke.

"I'm fine, Mom."

"You're going to be fine. Absolutely. You have so many opportunities ahead of you, so much promise."

Shit, not this. He stood. "So, no coffee. What about water? Orange juice? Soda? Scotch?"

"I'll help myself, Penn. You need to sit down and rest your back."

"Dammit! I don't need to sit down. I can get my mother a goddamn glass of water when she finally shows up at my place after twelve years."

"That's bothered you," she said, casually rising from the couch.

"I haven't lost sleep over it." He headed to the kitchen to get her a drink and prove a point. She was going to have water whether she wanted it or not.

His mom followed him in, her shoes clicking authoritatively on the tile floor. "You know my job is—"

"Demanding and time-consuming." Penn said the last part at the same time she did.

"I should have made a point of coming before now," Nell said, sounding regretful.

"Ice?" Penn asked before filling the glass.

"Please."

He took some cubes from the freezer, dropped them in and filled it with water from the tap. As he handed her the glass, the front door opened and closed.

"Hey," Coop said as he strode into the kitchen. He did a double take when he spotted Penn's mom. "Hello."

"This is my mom," Penn said tiredly. "Nell Griffin. Mom, this is my roommate, Cooper Flannagan."

His mom was stepping toward Cooper, her hand extended, when understanding dawned on her face. "Oooh. So you're Cooper."

"That's me."

"I've heard all about you."

"Penn lies," Coop said.

"I've heard more from Zoe in the past week

than Penn has told me in all the time you two
have lived together."

Penn narrowed his eyes at his mom, then
looked at Coop to gauge his reaction. His roommate wouldn't have been able to wipe the grin
off his face to save his life.

"What did Zoe say?" Penn asked, curious as
hell.

"That I eat like a four-year-old with no parents,
I'm sure." Coop opened one of the cabinets and
took down a bag of sour-cream-and-onion chips,
holding it up proudly as if to prove his point.

"She did mention you have a penchant for less
than nutritious foods," his mom said. "Among
other things."

Penn continued to stare at his friend, wondering again if Coop was screwing around with his
little sister. He wasn't sure he wanted to find out
until he was physically able to kick Coop's ass.

"Zoe was nice enough to leave us a boatload
of groceries when she left, and fortunately, Penn
here has been bored enough to figure out how to
cook them."

"Zoe's a good girl," Penn's mom said, and
just like that, he was right back where he'd been
twelve years ago. Zoe and their mother—and
really, their father, too—were cut from the same
cloth. The intellectual, overachieving cloth. Penn
had tried that path, had forced it on himself for

the first eighteen years of his life. His mom's innocent statement had him feeling like a failure all over again.

As if he needed more of *that* right now.

"Where have you been?" Penn asked his roommate, determined to ignore the crap feeling trying to overcome him.

"Red Cross. I went with Cale to help with the preschoolers."

The preschoolers. Penn hadn't even thought about missing them. Each month, a few of the firefighters volunteered to help the three-year-olds with craft time, and he'd tried to be in on it whenever he wasn't on duty.

"Was Alberto there? Tiny little guy with the grin as big as his face?"

Coop laughed. "Yep. Alberto was there. That dude is loud for his size. Cuter than hell."

"Alberto is loud for any size. Man, I miss going."

"You could still do it. Don't have to lift anything but some glue and crayons."

"Maybe," Penn said noncommittally. The visit was a big deal to the kids each month because they were *firefighters*. Firefighters were like superheroes in their eyes. He wasn't sure he was up for being the guy who *used* to be a firefighter.

Coop took a can of soda out of the fridge. "I've got some errands to run. See you later. Mrs. Griff, it was good to finally meet you."

"Likewise."

"Later," Penn said, realizing it was lunchtime, and that he hadn't even had breakfast yet. Not that his schedule mattered much.

The front door again shut and the quiet between him and his mom seemed to suck all the oxygen out of the air.

"He's a friendly young man," his mom said, clinking her ice against the side of her glass.

"Is there something going on between him and Zoe?"

"You'd have to ask your sister that. But she talked an awful lot about him when she got home. So." Nell leaned her elbows on the bar, grasping her glass in both hands. "I was trying to apologize for not making time to visit you earlier."

"No big thing." He searched the refrigerator for something suitable to offer his mom or any guest for lunch.

"I'm sorry I couldn't come right away when you were hurt," she continued. "We were in the middle of negotiations on a major deal and I thought if I sent Zoe down, she could help you until I got here. It's taken some doing but I finally managed to hand everything off or postpone it so I could get away for a week."

"A week?" He wasn't aware that his mother had ever taken an entire week off from work. He could count on one hand the times she took a full day off when he was growing up.

"Seven days. You look like I just announced a torture regimen."

"I just don't know how to take a visit from you, I guess," Penn said, closing the fridge empty-handed and at a loss for what to feed her.

Seven days? What would he do with her for seven days? Zoe had had studying to do, and who knew, maybe Coop had helped in the entertainment department, but his mom was different and this was longer.

She was staring at him, her head tilted.

"What?" he asked in dread.

She pursed her lips and continued to watch him. "Why don't you and I get along better, Penn?"

The question caught him off guard. She seemed genuinely confused and, for once, not judgmental.

Penn leaned against the counter and crossed his arms over his chest. "You don't understand me, Mom. You don't know me. You never have."

Her brows furrowed as she considered. "Why is that?"

"Why don't you understand me?" he asked in disbelief.

She nodded. "You lived at home for eighteen years. And you're right. I feel like I don't know you."

"You've always been..." He searched for words

that wouldn't get her hackles up. "You've been too preoccupied by your job to realize that I'm different from you."

"How are you different?"

Was she for real? The shorter answer would be how he was similar to her.

"I'm a college dropout, for starters." He straightened to his full height when he said it.

She nodded slowly, still staring at him as if he was a specimen under a microscope. "I'm betting the reasons behind that would be an excellent start in discovering how we're different."

"Might be but I haven't eaten yet today, and I can promise you, that's not something I'll get into willingly. Especially without food. I could make grilled cheese sandwiches pretty fast."

His mom waved off the idea. "I'll take you to lunch, Penn." She took a drink of water and set the glass in the sink. "Maybe we can change some things while I'm here this week."

"Such as?"

She faced him. "I'd like to spend some time together. It doesn't have to be anything special—I know you're recovering. But maybe we can get to know each other a little better. What do you say?"

Penn shrugged. "Worth a try, I guess." He attempted a grin to hide his lack of optimism. "I sure don't have anything else going on."

"Well, then, we've got the conditions for a perfect storm," his mom said. "You're bored out of your mind and I'm stuck on an island. I think we can work with that."

Penn's smile became less forced. "You ready for lunch? Or have you been up long enough to go for dinner?"

"If I skipped to dinner, I'd miss out on one of my meals. Can't have that," she joked. "Where would you like to go?"

"Ruiz's has decent Mexican food."

"That sounds lovely. I take it you're ready to leave now?"

"I was ready a half an hour ago. Let's go." He grabbed his keys from the hook Coop had put on the kitchen wall. He stopped in his tracks midway through the living room. Muttered a curse under his breath. "You'll have to drive my Jeep. I can't drive yet. Doctor's orders."

"As long as you can direct me, that won't be a problem. I'll take my suitcase and we can head to the hotel after we eat."

Penn took over rolling her luggage as soon as she had the handle extended. As they walked toward the parking lot, his mom squeezed his upper arm.

"I'm glad we talked, Penn. It's going to be a good week."

He nodded halfheartedly. Family harmony, getting along with his self-absorbed mother, those

weren't his strong points. They were a better fit
for Zoe's cerebral, empathetic abilities. Penn was
always more comfortable and a lot more confident with physical endeavors—if you needed a
sink fixed or a fire put out, he was your guy. Or
he *had* been. Now that he wasn't even able to lift
a suitcase or drive his Jeep, he had no idea what
the hell he *was* good for.

CHAPTER TWENTY-ONE

NADIA WENT PAST THE executive office hallway, through the lobby and directly into the women's locker room in the hotel's first-floor fitness wing. She walked without seeing anything as she tried to stop her head from spinning.

She hadn't had much of a plan at all when she'd headed to Penn's, but one thing was certain— she absolutely hadn't expected any of what had happened. Even when she'd lain down beside him, she'd been tempted simply by the promise of comfort and rest. Nothing like the chemistry that had exploded between them. Her breath became shaky just thinking about it.

The guilt that had engulfed her when he'd hurt himself again had gradually morphed into guilt over missing work as she'd driven back to the hotel. Her mom was no doubt livid and concerned. And still, there was no way Nadia could just walk into her office, sit down and get back on task.

She'd probably pay for taking several hours off, but at this point, what was one more hour? Her head wasn't going to be in the game if she went back now, anyway.

The locker room was deserted, which was typical for early afternoon, after the lunch rush and before new guests checked in. Not that she was a frequent user or anything—she was normally too caught up in work to exercise—but she'd heard rumors.

In spite of her sporadic fitness habits, she had her own permanent locker where she stored some workout clothes and a couple of swimsuits. She opened it now with her key and took out one of the suits. At first she was thinking about the hot tub, but then she changed her mind. She needed to sweat out some of the crazy stuff going on inside her today. Once she shed her rumpled clothes and pulled on a no-frills one-piece suit, she headed for the sauna.

As she expected, it was empty, as well. She set the timer and stretched out on one of the wide wooden benches.

Heaven.

She really needed to do this more often.

She really needed to do a lot of things more often.

Her muscles slowly began to loosen, and as she relaxed, the knot of rejection that had lodged in her gut at Penn's lessened. It didn't go away entirely, but space and two-hundred-degree heat helped her see beyond the surface.

On the bright side, though he'd been angry as a bull, he hadn't taken it out directly on her. Hadn't thrown around blame or reminded her of her role in his injury.

That was progress.

And still, it was always there, between them, like an invisible trip wire.

His anger... It took so little to set him off. The first sign of pain, among other things, made him explode. His resentment was never far away and today his self-disgust was undeniable, as evidenced by his "worthless body" comment and the remark about getting busy doing nothing.

That was his problem, she realized suddenly. He had nothing to do except think. No goals, beyond getting to PT every couple of days. Nothing to challenge him mentally or give him hope that he'd ever have a normal life again.

He needed purpose. Needed to move forward, to find something to occupy him, whether it was a hobby or a career path to start pursuing or training for...something to take his mind off what he'd lost.

Maybe she could help him with that. Heck, maybe there was an opportunity for him to work at the hotel. They had so many departments and different possibilities, perhaps there was something there that Penn could be interested in. If not there, she could encourage him to start looking other places.

And though she had every intention of backing off physically until he had a chance to heal more, in due time, she could help him focus on the things his body could do, instead of the things it couldn't. Martyr that she was.

Penn had lost perspective, or rather, had been overwhelmed by the negative. She'd give him a couple of days to cool down, but if she could bring him around to a different, more productive point of view, maybe in some small way that would counteract the damage she had indirectly caused.

"I WOULD HAVE THOUGHT you'd find a better way to show you were mad at me."

Nadia tensed at the sound of her mother's voice behind her in her office doorway. It'd been quite the day so far and she wasn't ready for another confrontation. Without looking at her mother, Nadia continued to her desk. She'd just put out a fire, figuratively speaking, with one of the convention groups and wanted to wilt into her chair for a precious five minutes. Alone.

"We discussed some pretty significant budget issues at the executive meeting," Joyce continued.

Even though Nadia still didn't look up, she

could see out of the corner of her eye that her mom stood in the doorway, arms crossed, leaning casually against the doorjamb.

"Sounds like nothing blew up in my absence."

"That's not really the point, Nadia." Her mom came in and sat across from her and Nadia could no longer avoid eye contact.

"I was tired, Mom. Up most of the night. I didn't have anything to contribute."

"If that's the real reason, it's perfectly understandable, but you should have let me know."

Fatigue mixed with lingering anger and Nadia couldn't make herself act contrite.

"Where were you? I called around to just about every department and no one had seen you. It's not like you to miss a meeting."

"I was off premises," Nadia said stubbornly.

"Doing what?"

"Taking a nap, if you must know."

There might have been a few minutes this morning when Nadia had entertained the idea of throwing it in her mom's face that she, too, was spending time—*work* time—with a guy. Kind of an eye-for-an-eye thing. But whether that had been her motivation for going to Penn's at first or not, it hadn't ended up that way. It didn't feel right to even mention it now. She didn't want to cheapen her time with Penn by turning it into revenge or *I'll show you*. Even if he had rushed her out in the end.

Joyce narrowed her eyes. "What's going on, Nadia? Between us?"

"I missed a meeting, Mom. It had nothing to do with you." A little lie, but she could see now that skipping the meeting because she'd been pissed off was immature.

Nadia's in-house phone rang. "This is Nadia."

"Hi, Nadia, this is Lucas at the front desk. I have a Nell Griffin here who says you asked her to page you when she arrived."

"I'll be right there, Lucas. Thank you." She hung up and glanced at her mother. "Duty calls," she said, and headed out the door by herself.

CHAPTER TWENTY-TWO

SO FAR, PENN HAD SURVIVED three days of his mom's visit.

There'd been some ups and downs, but neither of them had killed the other yet—or even threatened it—so he considered that a raging success. It turned out, though, that entertaining her was exhausting.

To recuperate, and avoid the overquiet condo, he'd been soaking in the building's community hot tub since she'd left for her hotel. He'd had it to himself for the past twenty-five minutes, probably because it was late on a weeknight and most normal people had to get up for a job in the morning. Wasn't he a lucky bastard to have nothing? Yeah, not so much.

The chilly night air caused steam to rise from the water. His muscles were beginning to loosen at long last, the discomfort of sitting less of an issue in here.

"I thought that was you." Nadia's voice came from behind him, startling the ever-loving life out of him. He hadn't heard her approach over the sound of the jets and bubbles.

"You quit early tonight, huh?" He couldn't prevent the slight edge from slipping into his voice. Didn't want to. The way she'd invaded his dreams the past few nights, he needed to put on a suit of armor, show her he wasn't sorry about how they'd last parted ways.

She moved more fully into his line of sight and he noted she'd at least changed out of her usual business clothes. Dressed in yoga pants and a Silver Sands sweatshirt, hair pulled back in a ponytail, she obviously wasn't trying to impress him. And yet, he couldn't deny that his pulse reacted to the way she looked faintly illuminated by a distant streetlight.

That truth was irritating as hell.

"I saw your mom heading up to her room for the night," she said. "She said Cooper was working and she felt bad for leaving you alone."

"So you thought you'd swoop in and rescue me."

Nadia lowered herself to the pavement a couple of feet away from him, set her purse aside and hugged her knees to her chest. "Nah. I'm not big into the superhero scene."

Neither was he, these days.

"And you didn't bring any cookies." He said it as a joke, but he wouldn't have argued if she had.

Though his mom had taken him out for dinner again and ensured that he ate enough for a full fire crew, he could always find room for those cookies.

"I don't want you to get spoiled."

"Gotta watch out for that. Living the high life these days." He kept his eyes on the bubbles right in front of him as they reflected the light, all too aware of every move she made. "You going to join me in here?" he said in an effort to turn the tables and throw her off-kilter, knowing full well she wouldn't.

"I didn't bring a suit."

"We've got the place to ourselves. Suits not required."

"You're naked?"

He chuckled roughly. "Careful. You sounded a little too eager there."

Nadia reached into the hot tub and splashed some water in his face, surprising him, striking a playful chord in him that hadn't surfaced for weeks. He stood, his instinct to drag her into the water, but just as quickly, he remembered that lifting her, even though she couldn't weigh much more than a hundred pounds, would wreck his back. The thought was an instant buzz kill.

"What exactly are you doing here, Nadia? You're a busy woman. I've got to think you have better things to do than watch me sit here."

"I figured you missed me by now," she said, smirking.

He didn't respond. He didn't like the truth, and she wouldn't like a lie.

"I've been wanting to talk to you about something."

Dread knotted his gut. Talking had never been his favorite thing. Not with a woman he'd rolled around in the sack with. *Rolled* being a nonliteral term, of course, as that was something he was still trying to master again.

"Have you had any ideas about what you might want to do for a job once your rehab is over?"

Hell. He'd rather discuss his sad performance in bed than that. Almost. It was a toss-up. Why in the name of God did everyone feel it was necessary to ask him that question?

"Let's see," he said with a cavalier tone. "I considered a paratrooper with the air force but I really don't care much for heights. Then I thought about crab fishing. Those guys on TV make it look fun and all, but I've never managed to develop my sea legs—"

"Seriously, Penn."

"Why would that be any of your business?" he snapped.

There was no denying he was trying to goad her into an argument. That would be a better way to spend his evening than discussing his future.

Because he was looking right at her, he was able to see the effect of his words on her, just for a fleeting moment before she neutralized her expression. They'd hit their mark.

The knowledge wasn't as satisfying as he'd hoped.

"No, Nadia, I haven't had any job ideas. Haven't given it much thought."

"I had some thoughts about it," she said, less confidently.

"So did Coop. His suggestions didn't pan out."

"I was thinking that we have a broad range of types of jobs at the hotel—"

"No."

She paused. Stared at him. "No? Really?"

"Do you like 'hell, no' better?"

"Not especially."

The timer on the hot tub ran out and the noisy jets turned off. The sudden silence was disconcerting and peaceful at once. He made no move to get up and reset the timer.

"What's wrong with working at the hotel?" she said, able to speak more quietly now. "You could do so many things there—customer relations, concierge—"

"Please don't say bellhop."

"Group sales, operations—"

"No."

His refusal was at first answered only by a frog croaking at regular intervals in the distance.

"Why not?" she finally said, scowling.

"Let me count the reasons. One, I don't have any interest in working in a hotel. Two, I don't want a job given to me out of sympathy—"

"It wouldn't be."

"You'd hire me based on my vast hotel industry experience?"

"*I* wouldn't be doing the hiring, lucky for you," she said sharply.

"Good, because three, I wouldn't want you for a boss."

"I'm going to give you the benefit of the doubt and ignore three. Are you going to get out?" She indicated the tub with a wave of her hand.

"Hadn't planned on it. It's cold out there, and warm in here. Sure you don't want to join me?"

He said it again to get under her skin. When she straightened and scooted closer to the edge, he thought for a minute she was going to call his bluff.

If she did join him, particularly if unclothed, he *would* pay dearly. Because he wasn't sure he'd be able to keep his hands to himself. Though she was physically tempting, there were a hundred reasons touching her again would be a mistake.

"Okay, you don't want to work at the hotel, but maybe it's time for you to start thinking seriously about possibilities. If you decide to do something that requires training or extra schooling, you could start that now while you're still rehabbing."

Just the thought of school brought back bad memories. Particularly classes in a subject area he had no interest in, which, coincidentally, would be just about everything right now.

He swished a hand back and forth, just under the surface of the water, making his own mini-currents. "Why are you harping on this?"

"Harping?"

"Asking," he amended.

"You need…a kick in the rear."

"I need a lot of things but that isn't one of them."

"What's wrong with you tonight?" she asked in a quieter, sadder voice.

"Same thing that's wrong with me every other night, I guess. I was doing fine until you came around trying to pin me down on the future."

"I had this crazy idea of trying to help."

"Why?"

"Because I care about you."

Her words struck him more deeply than he wanted to acknowledge, even to himself. His only defense, being the son of a bitch that he was that evening, was a good offense.

"Do you care or do you want to assuage your guilt? How can I tell the difference?"

She looked as if he'd hit her physically. For a moment. Then she narrowed her eyes and he subconsciously braced himself for her temper. Which he deserved, no doubt about it, but acknowledging that to himself wasn't enough to make him back down.

"Keep being a bastard all you want, Penn," she said, her spine stiff. "I don't scare off so easily."

"You didn't answer the question."

"You're right and I'm not going to. One of these days you'll have to find the courage to face your future. I'm not saying it'll be easy but it is necessary. If you ever want someone to bounce ideas off, I'm willing. If you want help researching possible careers or courses or trade schools, I'm all over it. But you have to decide to start, and until you do, you're just going to sit around and mourn what you've lost. While that is necessary to an extent, how long are you going to do that?"

"Until I feel like doing otherwise. Which, I can promise you, is no time soon." He sounded a little like a pouting child even to his own ears. He didn't like that but he didn't know how to stop it. Friendliness and repentance didn't seem to be in his arsenal tonight.

Beyond the hated topic of conversation, what it came down to was that he was afraid to let his guard down with Nadia. Afraid to slip up and let her in, as he'd done the other day.

He stood and climbed out of the hot tub in a slow, deliberate way, catering to his stubborn left leg that still rebelled against doing what his brain wanted and possibly always would. He'd left his towel on one of the patio tables so he wouldn't have to bend down to retrieve it. As he dried his upper body, Nadia came up next to him.

"You've made up your mind to lock me out tonight," she said. "I may be stubborn but I'm not an idiot. I'll talk to you soon." Without waiting for a reply, she strode off.

Penn busied himself drying his body, having to sit in one of the chairs to do so. He didn't allow himself to look after her. Tried to pretend the past half hour hadn't happened. But try as he might, he couldn't forget that he'd just once again been a royal jackass to a woman who, logically, he knew didn't deserve it. Maybe one of these days he'd learn—but he didn't hold out a lot of hope.

CHAPTER TWENTY-THREE

FOR AN HOUR OR SO, Penn felt like his old self.

Sitting on the patio of the Shell Shack, eating a double burger and cheese fries, trading insults with the guys.

When Coop had asked Penn and his mom to join him and a couple of other people from the station for dinner, he'd hesitated. The guys could be crude. While Nell Griffin was no prude, there was typical male bullshitting and then there was that of firefighters. She'd wanted to get to know him better, though. One way to do that was to meet some of the guys he'd spent day in and day out with.

Luckily, his friends were on their best behavior, so his mom was holding up pretty well. She even seemed to be enjoying herself, now that she'd relaxed a bit. A couple of times, she'd laughed until her eyes filled with tears. He couldn't remember ever seeing his mom this laid-back and social.

"Did Penn ever tell you about the time he had his very own stalker?" Dylan, one of the newest guys at the station, asked her.

Penn cringed. "First off, of course I didn't tell her. That's not the kind of story you tell your mom, especially when she's a lawyer. Second off, how the hell would you know? It was before your time."

"Legendary, man," Dylan said. "That story will be passed down for another fifty years at least."

"I have to hear the story now," Penn's mom said, squeezing a lemon slice into her water.

Dylan looked to Cooper, who was renowned for his storytelling abilities. Coop took a drink of his lemonade, grinning the whole time. He set down his cup. "It was a couple years ago, late one night, and we got a call to the retirement village over on Sunrise. The call was for the truck, which we thought was kind of odd because normally the assisted-living calls are for EMS. All we knew before we got there was that a sixty-nine-year-old woman was stuck."

"Stuck?" Penn's mom repeated, as the guys all tried to hold in their laughter for the rest of the story.

"Yeah, stuck," Penn said, grinning.

"So long story short, this woman, Ursula, had dropped her wedding ring into the toilet."

"Oh, nooo," Nell said, completely into the story.

"And when we get there, she's at this odd angle, and her arm is stuck in the toilet."

Dylan could no longer contain a chortle, and Cale Jackson, one of the lieutenants, was laughing so hard his shoulders shook.

"That poor woman," Penn's mom said, grinning.

"She was understandably in a panic," Coop continued. "And while the rest of us were trying not to laugh, Penn here kept it together and talked her through her fear while we tried everything to free her. We were afraid of breaking a bone, quite frankly. Delicate operation, that."

"How'd you get her out?"

"We had to break the toilet in the end."

By this time, everyone was cracking up, Penn included. It took several minutes for them all to calm down and stop making bad jokes.

"That's not the best part of the story," Coop said. "Ursula apparently developed a raging crush on our boy Penn, here."

Penn shook his head, eyes closed.

"*She* was his stalker?"

"She used to send him handwritten letters that reeked of perfume."

"She looked so meek and harmless with her arm in the toilet," Penn said.

"Oh, that poor woman." Nell wiped her eyes carefully so that her makeup didn't run.

"Kind of what we thought until she started

showing up at the station at 7:00 a.m. after every one of Penn's shifts."

His mom's eyes widened and she looked to Penn to confirm.

He nodded. "And here at the Shack a few times. At all the fire department charity events. It went on for months. I finally had a cop buddy talk to her."

"Did you get a restraining order?" his mom asked.

"Nothing formal like that. He just explained that what she was doing was considered stalking. It seemed to do the trick."

"Unbelievable story," she said. "You guys must deal with some real kooks."

"You wouldn't believe the half of it," Cale said. "We could write a book. But then so could every fire department in the country, I imagine."

"Every now and then, Penn still gets called Mr. Ursula," Dylan said, laughing again.

"I never knew my son was such a ladies' man." His mom winked at him.

"Like I told you, there's lots you don't know."

Derek Severson, a firefighter and the owner of the Shell Shack, hurried over to their table then. "Just got paged. Anyone else?" he asked. Penn automatically reached for the front pocket of his shorts, where his pager would be, then clenched his empty fist. The other four pulled theirs out and checked them.

"Yep," Cale said, standing as his pager buzzed in his hands.

"Me, too." Coop shoved the last quarter of his double burger in his mouth.

"Ditto," Rafe Sandoval, one of the paramedics, said.

"Looks like they hit all six of us," Dylan said.

Penn's heart rate had kicked up immediately, as he was sure everyone else's did, at the first mention of a page, the department's means of calling off-duty guys into work. It meant something big was happening. But glancing around the table now, doing a headcount, he felt nauseous. "Make that five," he said. Derek, Coop, Dylan, Cale and Rafe.

Dylan swore. "Sorry, man. I can't get used to it. You're still one of us."

Penn tried to smile but had nothing to say to that. He stole a fry from his mom's basket and pretended he didn't feel like the odd man out times twenty.

"You got this place covered?" Cale asked Derek, referring to the bar.

"Macey's handling it fine for now and she's going to call someone else in."

Dylan, Rafe and Cale finished their sodas and

simultaneously set their empty cups down on the table.

They all knew roughly how much they owed for their dinners—that was what happened when you ate at the same place multiple times each week—and they tossed some bills toward Derek.

"I'll run this in to Mace before I go," he said. "Meet you guys there." As an afterthought, he turned to Penn and his mother. "Nice to meet you, Mrs. Griff. We'll fill you in on all the details later." He directed the last at Penn before he jogged off with the other guys' money.

"I'll be sure to have a beer for each of you," Penn said, and received a concerned look from his mom. "Not really."

Epic fail on the self-consolation effort.

Within thirty seconds, Penn and his mom were left in the relative calm of having five big, loud guys take off.

"Wow," Nell said, watching them in the parking lot. "They're…quite a group. Are they always like that?"

That made Penn grin. "They're usually twice as loud and ten times as vulgar. They were on their best behavior for you."

"I haven't laughed so hard in ages," she said. "I like them."

He tried not to show his surprise. For the first ten minutes, she'd been uptight, though she'd done her best to hide it. "They're good guys, every last one of them."

"Did you want to order a beer? I could sit out here and listen to the surf all night."

"Nah. But I'm happy to stay for a while if you're not in a hurry." The chairs here weren't the best but then no chair was particularly comfortable.

"Where would I have to go? This is paradise. Front row seat, right here."

She stared out at the darkening waves and the contrast of the light sand. The sun was slowly sinking in the sky behind them and the patio lights were coming on.

"You picked one heck of a place to settle down, son of mine."

Macey Severson, Derek's wife, walked up to the table. "Hey, Penn, how are you doing?" She began clearing the baskets and trash the guys had left.

There was a hint of general sympathy in her voice. He was starting to get that a lot and it made him want to lash out. Fortunately, he liked Macey and knew her enough to recognize she meant well. He'd have to learn how to blow off that tone or he was going to develop high blood pressure— or a violent streak—in no time.

"Doing pretty well," he said, stacking his and his mom's now-empty baskets to hand to her.

"I've been showing my mom here around San Amaro this week." He briefly introduced the two.

"You guys need anything else?" Macey asked.

He and his mom looked at each other and shook their heads. "We're okay."

The cell phone in Macey's pocket rang and she excused herself, setting the trash on the empty table next to theirs and taking the call a few feet away. As she did, Penn told his mom about her and Derek and how the Shell Shack had become the unofficial bar of the San Amaro Fire Department.

"That was Derek," Macey said, less than two minutes later. "He heard on the radio on the way in that there's a strip mall on the southern end of Coral Road on fire. They said they have two full blocks closed and are diverting traffic."

"It's a big one, then," Penn said, immediately scanning the sky to the south. It'd become too dark and they were too far away to detect smoke.

"It sounds bad." Macey pressed some buttons on her phone. "I'm calling Andie to see what she's heard. I think Clay's on duty." She cradled the phone between her shoulder and ear, picked up the baskets and trash and headed back inside.

"Let me know if you learn anything," he said as she went back into the open-air shack.

Penn didn't realize he'd exhaled loudly until his mom turned to him.

"You miss your job, don't you?" she said.

If anyone else had referred to his firefighting career as his "job," Penn wouldn't have thought twice about it. But with his mom, it was different. What he did wasn't a career to her. Not the way law was a carccr.

"Like you wouldn't believe." It took some effort to shake off the annoyance, but he was admittedly sidetracked by the thought of what his colleagues—*former* colleagues—were up against and what they were doing at that very minute. "I'll get over it." In a decade or two, hopefully.

He breathed in deeply, trying to smell the smoke in the air, but the wind wasn't cooperating. He thought he knew the strip mall Macey had described, and if so, there would be multiple challenges, depending on what parts of the building were engaged.

"Anything I can do to help, Penn?" his mom asked after a minute of distracted silence.

He sized her up. "Ever been to a fire?"

"You mean besides a bonfire? When I was a junior in college, one of the old buildings on campus was struck by lightning and caught on fire. My roommates and I went and paid homage for a few minutes, but by then things were mostly under control."

He drummed his fingers on the tabletop, suddenly infused with a surge of energy as he considered. "You said you want to get to know me better. What do you say you drive me to the fire and I'll show you what I've spent twelve years of my life doing."

She frowned and his spirits sank. He shouldn't have asked.

"Isn't it dangerous?"

"We'd stay well out of the way. You're tired, though."

"It's seven in the evening, Penn. I'm fifty-two, not a hundred and two. Let's go check out the excitement."

He was out of his chair, faulty back and all, before she could reach for her purse.

CHAPTER TWENTY-FOUR

PENN COULD SMELL the fire before he could see it. And that was saying something because as soon as they turned onto Coral Road, about two miles north of where he suspected the engaged building was, they could see the sky glowing as if a bank of stadium lights had been turned on.

There was extra traffic, most likely gawkers curious about the blaze. Just like him, he realized. He was on the outside, with the rest of the world. The realization left a bad taste in his mouth that had nothing to do with the tainted air as they drove closer.

"Wow," his mom said, gazing ahead of them as she drove. "It looks bad. You're sure we'll be okay?"

"I know a thing or two about fires. I'll keep you out of harm's way."

An ambulance turned onto the street up ahead of them, lights flashing, heading for the scene and kicking up Penn's adrenaline an extra notch.

"There's going to be a grocery store up here on your left. We'll park there and walk," Penn said, checking to make sure his mom wasn't wearing some impossible high-heeled shoes. They could undoubtedly drive a little closer but walking would be quickest, judging by the congestion up ahead.

As soon as his mom stopped the car, Penn was out, back injury be damned. His heart was racing in his chest and it was all he could do to wait for his mother to emerge from the Jeep.

"Let's go," he said when she joined him on the sidewalk.

"You're like a kid on the way to an amusement park," Nell said, grinning but managing to match his pace.

The foreboding in his gut was incomparable to the happy anticipation she described. "My friends are inside that," he said, pointing as the actual structure came into view. He shook his head, unable to say more.

Heavy smoke filled the air. The structure was more than 50 percent involved and it appeared to have spread from the north end, which had been a diner.

"Looks like they're doing an interior attack," he said to his mom. When she looked confused, he explained, "They've got the hoses inside the building at this point."

All three of the department's rigs and the chief's truck were on the scene, but he didn't see any other departments. Yet. From the looks of it, it wouldn't be long.

A crowd had gathered and Penn slowly made his way to the front, his mom sticking close behind him. He took in what probably looked like chaos to the casual observer. Though it was impossible to see faces or read names from this far back, he could pick out some of his former coworkers by their stance and size. He recognized Joe Mendoza's animated wide frame and Dylan, who was the shortest in the department. The chief was giving orders nearby, as well.

More sirens approached the site, growing louder. Within seconds, an engine and a truck from a neighboring fire department on the mainland arrived, just as he'd expected.

"This is terrifying," his mom said into his ear to be heard over all the noise.

Penn had forgotten she was there. He looked down at her. Her eyes were wide and glued to the scene. She lifted the collar of her shirt over her face to filter the air. Without thought, Penn put an arm around her and squeezed her reassuringly.

"Are you going to be okay?" he asked, unable to imagine leaving so soon after arriving. But he didn't want his mom to be upset.

She nodded without moving her gaze from the fire.

A fire scene was always scary, he supposed.

He was just programmed to act on that fear or ignore it. Maybe if she understood more of what was going on, saw the rhyme and reason of fighting the fire, she'd be less fearful.

"See those guys over there?" he said, pointing to a pair of firefighters who'd just arrived. "They're prepping a line and will probably take it in over there."

"It doesn't look safe."

Penn stifled a grin. "No. *Safe* is probably not a word I'd use to describe the job. But they're smart guys with years of training to handle all kinds of variables once they get in there."

They watched without further discussion for a few minutes. The battle raged on, with the men and the fire seeming to trade the advantage back and forth. This one was going to take a while.

"What are they doing?" His mom pointed to a ladder and a firefighter barely visible through the smoke.

"They're going up to the roof to ventilate."

"What if the roof is weakened? Can't they fall through?"

"They'll watch out for that."

"Crazy," she said. "Which job did you do?" his mom asked after some time.

"Which job?"

"Did you go on the roof or run in with the hose

or stand around outside like that guy over there and watch everything?"

Penn chuckled at the thought of what the chief would say to the accusation of standing around and watching. "He's the one in charge. Giving all the orders. That's the chief, and no, that wasn't my job."

"What was?"

"All the rest of them. Depended on the day and what I was told to do."

"What was your favorite?" she asked.

"Easy. Nozzle."

"Nozzle?"

"Manning the hose. Being the guy who gets to shoot the water on the fire." He smiled just thinking about it.

She dragged her eyes from the blaze and studied him silently. The attention made him fidget.

A substantial crowd had gathered behind them and seemed to be closing in. "Let's go over that way," he suggested, spotting a less populated area to the side by two ambulances that would be upwind from the smoke.

It took several minutes to get to their destination because they had to work their way back through the crowd and skirt around the gas station in the parking lot near the street. Once they did, the air was somewhat clearer. There were only a few observers scattered here and there on this side.

"Better," his mom said, finally releasing her shirt.

"Little bit," he agreed.

They were closer now to the diner, and he could see that there had been a collapse at this end of the structure. Two firefighters were manning the hose from outside. He could imagine what was going on inside.

"Isn't that Nadia?" his mom said.

Dragging his attention from the action, he followed her line of sight to a group of three women to their left, close to one of the ambulances. Sure enough, the one on this end looked like Nadia, though he couldn't be certain because the back of her blond head was to them.

"Might be."

The woman next to the blonde had dark hair pulled up on the back of her head. As she turned to say something to her friend, he realized it was Faith Peligni. Which made it highly likely that the blonde was indeed Nadia. The third woman paced nervously away from the other two, then returned, and he recognized her as Andie Marlow, the wife of firefighter Clay Marlow.

"Why would she be here?" Nell asked.

"She's with Faith." He pointed her out. "Faith's a firefighter and her fiancé, Joe, is a captain. I saw him earlier. Looked like he was safety sector command."

"Safety what?"

"He's keeping track of which firefighters enter and come out of the structure."

"At least he's not one of the ones going in."

"He's got the responsibility for the others," Penn said. "Sounds easy but in this chaos…"

His mom frowned. "Are you going to talk to her?" She nodded in Nadia's direction.

He shook his head, fighting the urge to watch Nadia.

"No? Aren't you two an item?"

An item? He didn't know what an item was, exactly, but he did know he and Nadia were not one. "She's…just a friend."

Or something. He wasn't sure he'd consider her a friend because most of his friends didn't make his body react the way she did. He looked at her again. She'd turned her head so she was in profile now, her dainty nose and tempting lips outlined against the brightness of the fire. And yep, his body reacted, his blood heating up as if a fire just a few feet away wasn't enough excitement.

"Just a friend," his mom said smugly, "who happened to be there in the middle of a workday—looking flushed—when I arrived the other day."

He had nothing to say to that. They both turned

their attention back to the action, with her asking periodic questions about what was happening.

A few minutes later, it appeared there might have been an injury somewhere inside. Casual bystanders wouldn't notice anything, but he sensed that the tension had ratcheted up. Two paramedics hurried with a cot toward the building. Sure enough, a firefighter came out carrying the victim. It was tough to see from where Penn stood, and then there were lots of people in the way, including Rafe and Paige, the paramedics who carried the cot toward the ambulances. From what he could tell, it wasn't a firefighter.

In front of him, Andie grabbed Faith's arm and held on, obviously scared for her husband, wherever he was. Nadia had taken several steps away and was squatting down for a better vantage point. She was in profile to Penn and the look on her face told him the scene was really getting to her.

He and his mother angled to try to see and found themselves closer to the three women. Penn's attention was again diverted to Nadia as she straightened and turned away from the medical scene, her hands covering the lower part of her face as if she was deeply disturbed.

Without bothering to consider his actions— or the tense way they had parted last night—he came up behind her, wanting to offer comfort.

"Hey, Nadia."

She turned to him and he didn't wait for her to speak—he could see her dismay in her eyes. Instinctively, he pulled her to him and wrapped his arms around her, wishing he could make that fear and sadness disappear. He felt her arms wrap around his waist and hold on.

"That girl…" she finally said, and shook her head.

"They're doing everything they can for her."

He felt her nod against his chest, beneath his chin. Several seconds later, she inhaled and straightened.

"You must have heard about this on your scanner."

"I was at the Shack with Cooper and some others when they got called in. You were with Faith?"

"Working on wedding stuff." She shot a glance toward the huddle of paramedics and closed her eyes. "Intense."

"I wish I could say you get used to it." At least when he was on the job, he'd had so much on his mind in the midst of an emergency that he'd been able to compartmentalize and block things like casualties out until afterward. The view was different from this side.

"Hey, Penn," Faith said when she looked away from the medical scene and noticed him. "It's tough being out here, huh?"

"Like sitting on the bench with an injury during the championship ball game. Hi, Andie. Clay working?"

"Somewhere. I haven't seen him yet but I'm sure he's here."

His mom introduced herself to Faith and Andie and they all turned their attention back to the scene. After a while, he felt Nadia watching him. When she wrapped her arm around his, he looked down at her. She rested her head against his arm and tensed as the paramedics got the patient into the back of the ambulance and prepared to hightail it out of there.

"Are you sure you want to stay?" he asked in her ear. "There could be more of that before it's over."

"I don't want to leave Faith."

"I'm guessing my mom's ready to go. I bet she'd give you a ride. I can stay with Faith."

"Isn't this…really hard for you?"

"No harder than sitting at home wondering what's happening," Penn said. "I need to be here."

She gazed up at him, her eyes narrowed as if making sure he was okay. Finally, she nodded, as if granting her approval. An unspoken connection arced between them for a moment and the answer to last night's question became clear to him. She did care about him. Whatever role guilt played in her ongoing attention to him, there was genuine affection there, too.

When he asked, his mom admitted she'd seen enough and was ready to get off her feet, so she took Nadia and Andie, whose stepdaughter was due to be dropped off by Clay's parents, with her. Penn explained to Nadia where they'd parked, just in case his mom got turned around, and then watched them walk away.

"So the rumors are true," Faith said with a knowing smile.

"What rumors?"

"You've got the hots for my friend."

He started to deny it but there was no point. "No comment. You think they're making any headway with this fire?"

The two of them discussed what was going on and analyzed what needed to be done to put it out, talking details as they hadn't been able to with the others. Penn felt more mentally alive than he had for weeks. Physically, well, he put that out of his mind for as long as he could. He wasn't leaving because of a little fatigue, not when his friends were working to exhaustion. Not until he knew all of them were safe.

IT WAS AFTER 1:00 A.M. when the firefighters began salvage and overhaul. There had been two more serious injuries, both of them to firefighters from the mainland department. Several others had suffered minor injuries that had been treated at the scene. Faith was able to talk to Joe for a couple of minutes and then she turned to Penn, relief in her eyes.

"You ready to get out of here? You must be wiped."

"Doubt I'll be able to sleep," he said.

"I know the feeling. I'm parked about two blocks that way."

They walked in silence for a ways before Faith spoke again. "Are you keeping up on department gossip?"

"I'm going to go out on a limb here and guess you're talking about your pregnancy? I heard it from Nadia, actually. Not from anyone in the department."

Faith smiled, maybe a little thinly, and nodded. "Yep. Got myself knocked up."

He knew Faith well enough to suspect that joyful congratulations wasn't the best response. Knew how dedicated she was to her career. They'd actually discussed, late one night at the station after a run when they'd both been too hyped up to sleep, her plans to work until she was closer to forty and then make a decision about starting a family.

"I don't really want to say I'm sorry to that

news," he said as they began walking again, "but my first thought when I heard it was…shit, Faith."

She laughed. "Extra points for an original response. I've had mostly 'congrats,' a couple of 'oh, no's,' but you're the first 'shit.'"

"You're not still working, are you?"

"It's been sixteen days since my last shift. I was out a week on sick leave because I honest to God was sicker than a poisoned dog every morning and didn't know what it was right away. We told the chief last week and word's pretty much gotten around. Plus my favorite blonde and yours…"

"She and I really aren't…" Hell. No use trying to convince her of anything. She probably knew more about what had happened between him and Nadia than he did himself, the way women shared stuff. "We're talking about you. What are you going to do? You going to go back after the baby's born?"

"I was. I'm parked over here," Faith said, pointing toward her Subaru. "We'd decided, or really I had decided, I'd go back after maternity leave. Joe and I talked about it a lot but he said it was ultimately my decision. He'd support me either way."

They got into car and Penn could swear he'd never been so glad to get off his feet. He leaned back against the headrest and just breathed for several seconds.

"You're going to pay tomorrow for standing so long tonight, aren't you?" Faith asked.

He chuckled. "Tomorrow and right now. You said 'had decided.' You changed your mind?"

Faith put the keys in the ignition but she didn't start the engine. "I've thought about nothing else for two weeks. Once the enormous shock wore off and we faced up to reality..." She shook her head. "It wouldn't be fair to our child to have both parents work crazy schedules and have dangerous jobs."

"So tell Joe to become a house husband," Penn said, mostly kidding. "He's had more years on the job than you. Plus you have to take nine months off, anyway."

Faith laughed. "He'll love your idea and your rationale, I'm sure."

"That sucks, Faith. Not the baby part but—"

"I know what you mean. Once the baby's born, I'm sure I'll fall in love with him or her and won't even want to work but right now..."

"It sucks," Penn said again, this time with more emphasis than he'd intended.

"Especially watching a fire like that and knowing I won't be fighting those anymore. You and I are kind of in similar situations."

"And you seem to be handling it a lot better than I have," Penn said.

"I don't know about that."

"I've punched things. Blown up at people."
Like Nadia.

"I cried for twenty-four hours straight."

They looked at each other, on the verge of
laughing.

"You're such a girl," he said, and then they did
laugh.

Faith started the car and backed out of the parking spot. "I might have it a little easier than you,"
she confessed as she drove. "For one thing, my
decision, in the end, was just that—mine. Not out
of my control. Plus, I get a baby out of the deal.
A son or a daughter."

"That's pretty amazing."

"It helps. I've been clinging to that positive
thought like crazy. Trying not to focus on what
I'm losing. Making a point of appreciating the
good stuff and looking to the future. The baby.
Joe. Having a family."

"And I've just been being bitter and hateful,"
he said, grinning with self-deprecation.

She pulled into the lot of his condo. "Wish I
had better advice for you. Short of having a baby,
I've got nothing."

"I'm not sure my back could take the pregnancy," he said.

She swatted him lightly and stopped the car
where he directed her to. "Ha, ha. If you need to

rant or rave, I'm here. And I'll probably join in and rant with you."

He nodded, turning somber. "It may not seem like it all the time, but you've got a good future ahead of you, Faith."

"Yeah." She looked over at him, but he continued to stare out the front window. "You can, too, Penn. I honestly believe that."

He left her comment unanswered, climbed out of the car and headed home, too exhausted to argue.

CHAPTER TWENTY-FIVE

NADIA HAD BEEN TO FIRES before.

She vaguely remembered watching one of the hotels on the island burn when she was a kid. She'd gone to a couple of smaller blazes with Faith over the years. But for some reason, the one last night had really gotten to her, more than the others ever had.

Honestly, she knew the reason she couldn't get it out of her head, even though she was extraordinarily busy showing Jamie Castigliego, the newly hired events manager, the ropes. No matter what she did, she couldn't erase the image of the blonde woman who'd been carried from the building from her mind.

Though it'd been difficult to see, because of the darkness and the throng of people, Nadia would bet that woman was young, in her twenties maybe. Her age. And though Penn had said she was still alive when the ambulance had sped off with her in the back, Nadia couldn't find any solace in that. Not until she could know for sure the woman was okay.

She caught herself staring at the wall of her office. Again. A glance at her watch told her it'd been exactly four and a half minutes since the last time she'd been distracted from the report she was trying to write.

Obviously this wasn't working.

She picked up her desk phone and dialed Jamie's extension. When he answered, she explained that she had to go out and that their final meeting would have to wait until tomorrow. After hanging up, she stood and did something she hadn't done for ages, if ever. She acknowledged she was done for the day—at 4:27 p.m. Pushed a button on her phone to forward calls to her voice mail. Left everything but her purse and headed to the hotel room that was starting to become more like her home.

She'd been to her actual home twice in the week since she and her mom had argued, both times to get specific clothes, both times when her mom was nowhere to be found. Nadia had planned it that way. They were civil to each other at work, and the roof and air-conditioner project had been completed in time for the politician last weekend. Nadia wouldn't exactly say she was upset with her mom—she just wasn't in the mood to be friendly. Either Joyce felt the same way or she sensed Nadia's lack of warmth and had left her alone, as well. That and her mom was apparently busy. She'd seen her with Dr. Morris a couple of times and heard others mention him, too.

Nadia kicked off her shoes as soon as she was inside her private room. She was overdue for maid service, she realized. Before she could have anyone clean, though, she needed to tidy up—bigtime. She picked up the shoes she'd just taken off, along with three other pairs, and put them in the small closet. Next she attacked the various articles of clothing, either hanging them or tossing them on the bed to take to the hotel's dry cleaner. As she systematically hung one item after another, her mind wandered back to the blond hair draped over the stretcher last night.

"Forget it," Nadia muttered, dropping the rest of the pile of clothes. "The mess will wait."

She shed the business suit and blouse she was wearing and left those on the floor with everything else. Pulling on a pair of wrinkled denim shorts and a Bahamas tee someone had given her, she didn't even bother to check her appearance in the mirror. She slid her feet into blessedly comfortable flip-flops, picked up her purse, ensured that her keys were in it and made her way to the parking lot.

She *had* to find out how that girl was doing.

She needed to see Penn. He'd calmed her last night. Centered her. She craved that feeling again.

She drove straight to his condo, briefly wondering if his mom would be there. Fortunately, she and Nell Griffin got along well. Last night, when they'd returned to the hotel after leaving the fire, they'd stopped by the Hour Glass for an order of fried mozzarella and a drink to relax them, let themselves come down from the adrenaline.

No one immediately answered the door when she knocked, but she could hear the television on inside and guessed that Penn would get there eventually. And he did. As he stared down at her, she had the fleeting thought of how unreasonably good it felt to lay her eyes on him. And it wasn't because he was shirtless, though that certainly added to the allure.

"Hi," she said. "I should have called first."

"You're fine. What's up, Nadia?" Instead of inviting her in, he stood in the doorway.

"That girl from last night," Nadia said. "Do you know how she's doing?"

His gaze dropped and he grasped one of her hands, wove their fingers together. She instantly sensed the news wasn't good, and then he shook his head.

"She didn't make it."

Nadia squeezed her eyes shut. Penn increased the pressure on her hand reassuringly. She was glad he was there and didn't really understand why she was so upset by the death of someone she'd never even met, but she was.

Penn looked back into the living room behind him. "Coop fell asleep watching TV. I need to walk, anyway. Want to go with me?"

Nadia nodded.

"You can come to my room while I get ready." He pulled her inside and shut the door without a sound.

She sat on his bed while he put on a shirt and some sport sandals, neither of them speaking. They didn't say anything until they'd left the condo, walked across the expansive parking lot and reached the street.

"Why is this bothering me so much?" she said as they headed toward Coral Street. "I didn't know her. Don't know a thing about her."

"Doesn't matter," Penn said. "Still gets to me every time. I think it gets to all of us in the department even though we see it more than most people."

"Do you know how old she was?"

"Twenty-two. She worked at the clothing store next to the diner, where they think the fire started. They believe she'd fallen asleep on a couch in the back room after the store closed. That building was old enough that it didn't have appropriate firewalls to slow down the spread."

"Do they know what started it?"

He shook his head. "They won't start investigating until they've got all the hot spots taken care of. Might be today. Might be a few days."

They turned left on Coral, the noise of the traffic increasing.

"Where's your mom today?" she asked.

"She took Coop and me to brunch, then was going to go shopping. I told her she was on her own for that."

"So you do have some 'typical male' in you, huh?" she joked.

"If that means I can skip out of shopping, yes, I do."

"I like your mom."

"A lot of people like my mom," he said noncommittally.

The generic statement made Nadia smile. "But…you don't?"

"We have a history." He shrugged. "She's okay, I guess. She's been decent for this visit."

"I'm blown away by your overwhelming enthusiasm," she said dryly. "What kind of history?"

"Stereotypical overdemanding mother. Growing up, I tried too hard to please her."

"What about your dad?" Nadia asked with trepidation. She didn't even know if Penn's dad was living.

"They divorced when I was six. He lives in Ireland."

"Wow. Why Ireland?"

"He met an Irish woman. Married her and moved there."

"Do you see him very often?"

"I've gone over a few times. We're not very close but I don't hate him or anything. I can kind of understand why he couldn't live with my mother."

"She seems like a sweet enough woman," Nadia said, frowning.

"She has her good points. We just have a lot of differences."

"You hide it pretty well when you're around her," Nadia said. She had a hundred questions, was itching to know more about Penn, his family, his past, but knew she'd only get so far with that, as he wasn't the type to talk her ear off about himself.

"We've gotten along better this visit," he admitted. "Probably because I don't worry so much what she thinks of my life and my choices anymore."

"Choices like…your career?" she guessed. Nadia had the ultimate respect for firefighters, especially knowing Faith as well as she did, but she could see how a powerful corporate attorney might have a different view.

"You're good."

They stopped at a busy intersection and waited for the light to change.

"What did she think you should do instead of firefighting?" Nadia asked.

Penn chuckled. "Anything. Part of the problem was my fault. I can admit it now."

"Yeah? Why's that?"

Penn looked up at the sky and inhaled, as if he didn't like the topic. "As a kid, I busted my ass to get good grades. Because that's what my mom expected."

"Okay."

"I went to University of Colorado for the same reasons."

"I didn't know you went there." She'd assumed he'd gone to a community college and studied fire sciences, as Faith had.

"I didn't last long," he said. "It took me about five days to decide I hated it."

"You dropped out after five days?" Nadia said incredulously.

"Nah. Maybe that would have gotten my mom some of the tuition money back, but no. I spent a semester screwing around. Failed every class I'd enrolled for. Apparently that happens if you don't go to class or do the work." A hint of a smile tugged at his lips. "My mom still hasn't forgiven me."

"I guess I can see why she was pissed."

"It was immature," Penn said. "I can admit that now. I should have owned up to it as soon as

I knew it wasn't for me. Instead, I used my book money on beer."

"So…you skipped everything for a semester, flunked out and became a firefighter?"

"That's the short version. My mom has always hated that I 'ended up' in a blue-collar career. She doesn't understand that I didn't go into it as a last resort. That I loved what I did."

"Have you ever told her that?"

"No. She's never asked. She's just…judged." He crossed his arms. "I don't want to talk about that anymore."

Nadia didn't push it. "That's fine. Penn?"

He looked at her sideways.

"We're almost to the fire scene. Is that where you meant to go?" Now that she'd realized they were so close, she wondered how she hadn't noticed the smell lingering in the air.

"Not consciously, no. I wouldn't mind checking it out in the daylight, though. See if it's still smoldering."

He stared toward the site, which they could see from where they stood, and a change came over him as Nadia watched him. It was subtle, something she wouldn't have noticed if she hadn't been looking directly at him. He stood straighter, and his face came alive, his eyes more animated.

"What?" he asked, looking down at her.

"You're sexy when you think about fire." She tried to keep a straight face.

Their eyes locked for a moment and she was taken by how green his eyes were in the sunlight. He broke eye contact, shook his head minutely then started across the street.

She entwined her arm with his, trying to stretch out the light moment. "You don't like being called sexy."

"A guy who can barely tie his own shoes is not sexy."

"You don't get a vote."

There were two police cars and several fire vehicles, including the chief's truck, at the burned-out strip mall. The south end, which housed a music store and an ice cream store, was still intact, though the windows were missing and the formerly light-colored exterior walls were scorched with black. The other end where the diner had been…it looked like a bomb had gone off. Crime scene tape outlined the entire area.

"Crime scene?" Nadia asked as they got closer.

"There was a fatality. That guy over there is an arson investigator."

"Makes sense." She frowned, for the first time considering that the blaze could have been started deliberately.

As they approached the scene, they stopped.

The chief called out a greeting to Penn, and then two others did the same.

"Do you want to go talk to them?" Nadia asked.

"They're picky about who they let in since it's a crime scene."

"You're still technically a firefighter, though."

"It's not me they'd have a problem with."

"I'm not allowed," she said unnecessarily. She looked around and spotted a coffee shop about a block to the north. "I'll wait for you there," she said, pointing. "You go talk fire stuff."

"You sure?"

She could tell he was dying to get in there and discuss what had happened. "Absolutely."

He looked doubtful and she prodded him in that direction.

"I'll come find you in the coffee shop in a few minutes."

"You can buy me dinner when you're done," she said.

"You drive a hard bargain for a short thing."

"Don't forget it." She walked away, happy to see Penn come alive. And happier still about the prospect of having dinner with him.

CHAPTER TWENTY-SIX

NADIA HAD DOWNED two large mochas with whipped cream, trying all the while not to watch the clock on the wall of the coffee shop.

How freaking long was she supposed to wait when he'd said "a few minutes"? She had above-average math skills and she'd go out on a limb and say that an hour and a half was more than a few.

She pushed her chair back, causing the metal legs to screech loudly on the floor, picked up her empties and threw them in the trash on the way out. Maybe she'd misunderstood where they were supposed to meet, except it was hard to misinterpret "in the coffee shop."

Fresh air helped marginally. Sitting there watching people come and go while she waited and tried to concentrate on the newspaper someone had left… Her agitation had grown with every new customer's coffee order.

It was almost completely dark. Surely Penn and the others couldn't see enough to still be working. They must be talking.

Nadia tried sending him a text message and

then walked toward the strip mall tamping down her annoyance. Penn had been more excited than he'd admit to go discuss the intricacies of the fire with his friends and colleagues. She shouldn't begrudge him that. *Didn't.*

As she got closer to the fire scene, she could see that bright lights had been set up toward the rear of the north end. Without crossing the street—the yellow tape was as far out as the sidewalk in places, anyway—she veered to the right so she could see if they were behind the former diner.

She had a clearer view of the lights, which were shining from the back of a truck, but the area was deserted. Several vehicles were still parked on this side of the tape, so they had to be there somewhere.

Unfortunately, she couldn't exactly stroll over and look for them.

Her stomach rumbled and her irritation soared again. It'd been an hour and forty minutes now. She truly hadn't minded Penn going in there, but now she felt like a desperate loser to wait so long for him. There was a fine line between being understanding and being an idiot and she suspected she was well over that line.

She crossed the street and followed the yellow tape around to the front. A policeman sat in his cruiser and watched her but didn't get out or ask her if she needed help. She didn't, anyway. She wasn't about to have the guy run inside the building, where Penn and the others had to be, to remind him he'd forgotten all about her.

Humiliating much?

To give him the benefit of the doubt, she texted one more time and then kept walking until she'd done a complete circle of the building. Nothing. No one.

Forget it.

She strode back to the front and kept on retracing her steps to the coffee shop. As she went, she pulled her phone out and called Faith to ask for a ride.

The unrest and distress about the fire victim that had plagued her all day had been blown away by anger. On the bright side, the best thing for her to do when she was angry had always been work. So much for quitting early—she couldn't wait to get back to the peace and predictability of her office.

WHEN PENN, DAVE APPLBAUM, who was the arson investigator, his assistant, Robert Benitez, and the chief emerged from the fire-ravaged building, they were deeply engrossed in their discussion. Penn hadn't expected to get so caught up in the investigation when he'd shown up. He'd been around during investigations before, been questioned numerous times about how a fire had advanced and behaved, but he'd never gotten involved beyond that. Following Dave around today, listening to him explain what he'd learned after several hours on the site, had been intriguing. Penn had gotten more than a little caught up in the process and had lost track of…

Oh, shit.

He'd left Nadia waiting for him.

It hit him that it was now fully dark. The portable lights were shining down like noon, even inside what used to be the diner, so he hadn't noticed the sun had set.

It was going on seven o'clock. More than an hour and a half since Nadia had gone to the café. She had to be pissed.

"Is my watch right?" he asked. "Six forty-nine?"

Dave looked at his and nodded. "I've got 6:50."

"I'm in trouble. Thanks for letting me barge in and for explaining everything. Good luck finishing up."

Dave chuckled. "Thank *you*. Who knows how much time you saved with your find. We call that beginner's luck."

The group of them, including Penn, laughed. He waved and hightailed it out of there—as quickly as he could with a leg that didn't like taking directions from his brain.

As he walked toward the coffee shop, he dug

his phone out to text Nadia and found her messages waiting for him. He called himself some choice names and typed in an overdue reply.

On my way. IOU big-time.

By the time he got to the shop, he hadn't received a reply. When he saw she was gone, he didn't figure he'd hear from her tonight.

His stomach was growling and his body ached now that he'd pulled himself away from the fire investigation, but he ignored both and took off toward the most likely place Nadia would be—the hotel. He had a good half-hour walk to figure out how to make it up to her.

If his first day on the job was any indication, Jamie Castigliego was going to work out just fine as the events manager.

When Nadia returned after hours away, she found him still in his office, familiarizing himself with some of the upcoming conventions. When she'd suggested they have their canceled meeting, after all, he'd been all for it even though it was long after 5:00 p.m. Of course, for a manager at the hotel, five o'clock quitting time was a myth, anyway. They'd decided to grab dinner in the restaurant while she brought him up to date on the upcoming podiatrist conference details since they had a meeting with Stacy Keller, the planner, in a few days.

The catering chef had been on his way home for the day and had made the mistake of exiting through the restaurant just as Nadia and Jamie were discussing menu possibilities. Now they were three.

"According to Stacy," Nadia said, "they want to go all out for their Saturday night dinner on the patio. She wants us to show her a couple of custom menu options that will impress."

"What kind of parameters?" Lyle, the chef, asked.

Nadia snuck in a bite of her turkey club and finished chewing. She smiled, knowing Lyle would like her answer. "No parameters except classy. Of course, I'm sure budget will play into it at some point."

"What about some kind of seafood buffet?" Jamie asked. "You could have an oyster station. Maybe do a medley of shrimp dishes…"

"And a fish entrée, depending on what I can get fresh at that time. And I would suggest a veal or sirloin option for those who don't care for fish, as well as some other nonseafood side dishes."

Lyle carried on, throwing out more ideas than they could use, and Jamie was jotting them down religiously.

Nadia's phone buzzed and she glanced at the screen. She'd been ignoring texts all evening, especially those from Penn, but this was a call from the front desk.

"This is Nadia," she said, stepping away from the table so as not to disrupt the men's conversation.

"Hello, Ms. Hamlin. This is Elena from the front desk. I have a man here asking for you by name."

Nadia could guess just who that man was. "Wearing black shorts and a gray T-shirt? Short brown hair, really nice green eyes?"

"Yes, ma'am." Elena's voice held amusement.

"Tell him I'm in a meeting and will call him tomorrow, please."

"Oh. Yes, ma'am."

"Thank you, Elena." Nadia ended the call and attempted to focus on the menu conversation, which had turned to Asian cuisine options.

"Everything okay?" Jamie asked her.

Taking a drink of her ice water, she nodded, but her attention veered back to Penn.

He must have walked all the way here when he realized he'd screwed up. If he thought she was going to honor their last-minute dinner plans, he was sadly mistaken. And now he could turn around and walk back home, since his mom wasn't expected to return to the hotel until later.

Realizing she held her glass with a vise grip, she pushed Penn out of her mind completely and got back to business.

CHAPTER TWENTY-SEVEN

NADIA BROKE OFF midsentence as she, Jamie and Lyle walked out of the restaurant. She promptly lost all sense of what she'd been saying.

"I see someone I need to talk to," she finally said. "Jamie, we can finalize this before we meet with the planner next week. Thanks for joining us, Lyle. Go home to your gorgeous wife."

The two men said goodbye and headed toward the employee lot. Nadia took a deep breath before turning around.

"Penn?" she said, walking across the wide hall-way to where he stood. "You're still here? Standing instead of sitting?" It'd been well over an hour since Elena had called to tell her he was at the front desk.

"Looks like it. No place close by that I could sit and I didn't want to miss you." He held out a white paper bag. "Last in the house."

She took the bag from him and peeked in, even though she knew what it was without looking. "Cookies."

"Repentance cookies. I'm sorry, Nadia." His

determined stare said more than his words. "I screwed up."

There were people all around them, half of whom she knew. She wasn't in the mood to invite Penn to get comfortable and stay awhile, though his apology—and the cookies—were starting to wear down her anger. "Let's move," she said, pointing toward the front doors of the lobby.

He didn't argue, though he did look worn-out, making Nadia question her decision. They could sit on one of the benches out front.

"Is your mom back yet?" she asked. They neared the doors and she nodded at Henry, a bellman who'd been with them for a dozen or so years.

"I don't know. I came here to see you."

"Elena was supposed to tell you I'd call you tomorrow."

"She did. I stayed to safeguard your health. Didn't want you to fume at me all night and mess up your beauty sleep."

"God forbid."

"Not that you need any," he said, backtracking. "Beauty sleep."

A half grin tugged at her lips, darn it. She breathed in the chilly November night, waiting until they'd distanced themselves from the doors and all the people going in and out of them.

"You said a few minutes, Penn. It was an hour and a half."

"I know. I'd be pissed, too."

"I even went over to look for you." She sat on a bench at the end of the hotel's curved driveway. "I walked all the way around the tape trying to see you."

"We were inside. I lost track of time."

"You committed the worst of all sins possible," she said. "You got carried away with your job. Or rather, *a* job."

The look he gave her told her he understood. He'd done the same thing she had, which he was still punishing her for.

"On top of that, I'm a dumb male."

"You make it really hard to stay mad at you," Nadia said, studying him.

"Charming dumb male. Are you going to share your cookies?"

"Did you walk all the way here?" She opened the sack and took out two cookies, then gave him one.

"It's not that far."

"You must be tired."

"It's getting easier. Walking is good, according to my therapist. And since you weren't answering my texts, if I wanted to apologize to you it had to be in person."

"There's that. I was in a meeting."

"Didn't intend to interrupt. Thought you'd left work for the day."

"I had. Opportunity arose and here I am." She bit into her cookie and closed her eyes to savor it. "Did you find out anything more about the fire?"

"We think we pinpointed the origin."

"'We'?"

Penn made a sound of disbelief. "Dave, the arson inspector, took me through everything he'd figured out so far today. I learned so much my head is swollen."

"I thought it looked big."

"He was showing me the area where the fire appeared to have started. It was in the diner, back in the kitchen. He was bending down, pointing out some stuff, looking for evidence. I, of course, couldn't really bend like I wanted to, so I had a different angle or something. Anyway, I was shining the flashlight he loaned me around the area and spotted what appears to be the very end of a fire-starter stick."

Nadia tilted her head as she tried to follow.

"An unoriginal method of arsonists," he said.

"So someone started it on purpose?"

"Dave and his people have some more work to do but it appears so."

"And you found the clue?"

"One of the clues. A small but important piece

of the puzzle. It was luck, really. And looking from a different perspective, since I couldn't move normally."

"Penn, that's amazing!"

"I hope it leads to them finding the sick bastard who did it."

She nodded, her thoughts drifting to the twenty-two-year-old woman again. The cookie had lost its appeal and she put the uneaten half back in the sack. They sat in silence for a few minutes, watching the cars pass on the street, some of them turning into the drive.

"I never really thought about the existence of arson investigators before," she said, an idea sparking. "Tell me about what they do."

"They're a combination of a firefighter and a detective, basically. They need to have the fire background to some extent, but they also have to know investigation techniques."

"But they don't have to fight fires, right?"

"Right. They come in once the fire is out."

"So no extreme physical superpowers necessary," she said.

He looked at her warily.

"You should look into it."

Penn didn't answer.

"The more I think about it, the more perfect it seems," Nadia said, pulling her legs up to sit cross-legged on the bench. "You've got the background for it. You've been trying to figure out what you could possibly do for a career."

"Have not."

"You're supposed to be. What would you have to do to get into the field?"

"Take a bunch of classes. Get certified. Be able to move right and bend down, among other things."

"It's perfect, Penn."

"Because I'm so good at moving."

"You're one month off back surgery. Getting better every week. I assume the classes would take a while."

"I assume." He kept his voice noncommittal, and though she tried to read some hope into his features, it wasn't there.

"What's holding you back?" Nadia did her best to curb her impatience. "From where I'm sitting, this job has Penn Griffin written all over it."

Penn blew out a loud breath, his shoulders sagging. "It's hard to swallow having to start over from scratch."

Her irritation dwindled. "There's not a doubt in my mind you can handle it."

He scoffed. "How do you know what I can handle? Practically all I've done since I've known you is lie around uselessly."

"Are you kidding me?" Nadia stared at him, stunned. "I've watched you fight every single day since your surgery to get your mobility back. Remember that first day home, when you wanted to rip off my head for suggesting a three-minute walk? And today you went miles. If you make up your mind, you can do it."

"That was a sweet little rah-rah speech but I never said I *couldn't* do it."

"Then get off your butt and do it."

"Swing bridge operator sounds a hell of a lot easier."

"Right. Except you don't seem like the kind of guy to take the easy route on anything."

"I'm sitting here with you, aren't I? Definitely not easy."

With an almost-smile, he touched her thigh and made her long for more contact.

She wasn't going to initiate anything physical, she reminded herself. He had to do it when he was confident enough, assuming he wanted to.

"I should get back inside," she said, even though she hadn't yet decided if she would go to her office or revisit her earlier plan to take the night off. All he had to do was suggest it and she'd gladly spend the evening with him.

Penn stood. "I'll walk you in."

She didn't allow herself to be disappointed,

fully aware it was going to take him time to come around. "I'd ask if you wanted a ride home," she said, "but I have a sneaking suspicion you'd turn me down flat."

"Your suspicion would be right. Besides, I should see if my mom is in her room yet."

They went back in the hotel. At the hallway to the executive offices, they paused. She took out her half-eaten cookie from the sack and offered the remaining cookies to him.

"You don't like my gift?" he asked.

"It's the best. But I sense that you need them more."

He took the bag from her. "Sacrifices." He looked toward the elevators, then back at her. "I owe you dinner."

"Good point. Unfortunately, I've already eaten."

"I didn't mean tonight," Penn said. "Tomorrow. It's my mom's last night. I'll put something together for both of you."

"Are you sure you don't want to have her to yourself?"

"She likes you better than she likes me. Why don't you come over around six-thirty. If I haven't burned the condo down, we can plan to eat around seven."

"I'll bring dessert."

For a second, the way he looked at her, she imagined an unspoken comment about another kind of dessert, just hanging there between them. Inwardly shaking herself from the idea, she smiled and walked away.

CHAPTER TWENTY-EIGHT

NADIA'S SHIRT—BLOUSE, T-shirt, whatever you wanted to call it—was going to be the death of Penn.

From the front, it looked classy and modest, a light blue, short-sleeved, loose-fitting shirt that matched her eyes. No low-cut neckline, no cropped waistline. The back, though... It showed a lot of skin. Smooth, soft-looking skin. With just a strap of fabric at the top, the cutout swooped almost down to her waist and, most intriguing, made it obvious there was no way to wear a bra with it.

He'd been fine during dinner because her back had been out of his sight. He could pretend it was just a T-shirt. Nadia and his mom occupied stools at the bar and Penn had been more comfortable standing at the end. Now, though, the women had insisted on doing the cleanup and forced him to get out of the way. Though he wouldn't admit it out loud, he was glad to sit. He was starting to get into this cooking thing, but all that standing was tough on his back.

He'd argued halfheartedly for a couple of minutes, then parked his straight-back chair near the wall where he could still talk to them—and watch. He pulled one of the stools closer so he could prop his feet on the foot supports. The pose he struck—arms crossed, legs extended, posture not as straight as it should be—made him look cool and collected, he hoped.

Inside, he was anything but.

His fingers tingled with the urge to wrap his hands around Nadia's tiny middle and feel the soft warmth of her flesh. And then he wanted to inch his hands upward and palm her bare breasts.

"Are you sure you've never cooked Thai food before?" his mom asked as she rinsed the plates. "Your red curry with beef ranks right up there with my favorite Thai restaurant in Boulder."

"I've never cooked much of anything before the past month or so. Unless you count grilling."

"Grilling doesn't count," Nadia said. "Guys are born with the grill gene."

"That's so true, isn't it?" Nell handed the plates to Nadia to load in the dishwasher. "Men and fire."

"Some men more than others." Nadia spun around to smile at him and caught him staring at her.

"I have to tell you, Penn, I've had a fabulous trip but probably the best part of it was going to that fire with you. Hearing you talk about it, the ins and outs of how the firefighters were attacking it, what they were watching for, how they knew when to change tactics…" Nell stopped and looked at him. Shook her head slowly. "My mind is blown. As ridiculous as it sounds, I had no idea how much science was involved in putting out a fire."

"I took classes for two years before I could even get hired," Penn said, thinking back to the days when he'd done construction work by day and studied at night. "And that was just the beginning."

"I can see that now." His mom dried her hands on a towel as she came over to the other stool and sat on it. "I said I wanted to get to know you better while I was here. I didn't know how I was going to do that when I said it, and it turns out that with all the sightseeing we did and all the talking… Watching and listening to you at that fire taught me so much more about you than anything else did."

Her frankness made him uneasy, especially with Nadia on the other side of the bar, her sexy back to them as she continued to clean up but her ears perfectly capable of hearing everything. "Glad you enjoyed it," he said simply.

His mom nodded and looked to the side, as if deep in thought. "I…" She cleared her throat.

"Forgive me for getting into some family stuff here, Nadia."

Nadia turned around. "If you want privacy, I can go in the other room."

"No, not at all." Nell smiled. "I'm not going to say anything bad except maybe about myself. Penn…"

He lowered his feet and sat up a little straighter, curious.

"It's such a long time ago, but I think I owe you an apology."

"For?" He'd never seen this side of Nell Griffin before.

"When you dropped out of college—"

"Flunked," he corrected. If they were going to be honest with each other, he could own that.

"Whichever. I was so upset I wanted to strangle you. You were such a smart kid and to me it seemed like you'd thrown every opportunity I'd ever worked to give you right out the window."

In a sense, that had been his intention, though he might not have fully realized it at the time.

"I knew you were smarter than that and I couldn't fathom how you could ever make something of your life if you didn't get a four-year degree. I see now how wrong I was."

Penn's eyes widened at her admission.

"Don't give me that look." She snapped the towel lightly at his legs. "I'll admit I was being exactly what you accused me of back then—an intellectual snob."

He couldn't help grinning a little, but as he looked at her, it was with a new appreciation. Eating crow didn't come easy for anybody, but his mom was a harder case than most.

"Some of the things you taught me the other night make my head spin, they're so technical," she continued. "And that doesn't even begin to take into consideration the sheer bravery..." She broke off, emotion flooding onto her face and into her voice.

"Okay, stop it, Mom," he said, laughing. "No more mushy stuff when I have a girl over."

"Don't mind me," Nadia said with an amused look. "It's fun to watch a firefighter-type squirm."

Penn studied his hands, ready to get this uncomfortable moment over with but needing to say one thing. "If we're doing true confessions, I'm sorry I wasted your money at CU."

His mom shooed that off. "It wasn't the money. You never did like school, did you?"

"Wasn't my favorite thing."

"And yet you worked your tail off to get good grades throughout high school."

Penn grinned again. "You didn't give me much choice."

"I don't regret pushing you, but we should have

had a serious conversation before you went off to college."

It was his turn to shrug. "It is what it is. That's all long over."

Nadia finished wiping the counter and placed the sponge near the faucet, then turned around to face Penn and his mom again.

"I should really get going," she said. "Dinner was amazing, Penn. Thank you."

"Don't let Ms. Serious here scare you off," he said, making a joke of it when he didn't want her to leave. Though he really didn't want to want her to stay.

His mom raised her hands in surrender. "I'm done, I'm done. Please, don't go because of me."

Nadia located her purse on the counter. "It's your last night together. Now that you have all the serious stuff out of the way, you two need to enjoy it."

She came around the bar. "It was so good to get to know you this week, Nell. Have a safe trip home."

Nell stood and pulled Nadia into a hug. "I'll do that. Thank you for your fantabulous hotel. It's been perfect." She drew back to look Nadia in the face as Penn sat there feeling like the odd man out. "Keep an eye on this guy, will you?"

"I intend to."

The women shared a wily female grin and then Nadia threw a quick glance his way.

"Thanks again, Penn. I have to admit you surprised me with your mad cooking skills."

He stood and followed her to the front door. With a perfect view of her back.

"Thanks for coming over. Sorry you had to sit through that uncomfortable bit."

She turned to him and lowered her voice. "It was good for you two to talk about that. With or without me here." Rising on her toes, she kissed him full on the mouth, teasing him with her taste, ending the contact almost before it'd started. "Now go have fun with her."

Mom fun wasn't what he wanted right now, but he didn't have much choice.

When Nadia was inches from him, it was easy to bury his doubts. He made a promise to himself: *soon*.

CHAPTER TWENTY-NINE

THOUGH SHE WAS DREADING it, Nadia closed the file on her computer at 4:55 p.m. the next day and headed to her mom's office.

They always met on Wednesdays at five o'clock to indulge in Chinese food while they discussed hotel business. Sometimes it was Nadia's events and marketing stuff, sometimes her mom talked through general hotel issues, but it was always a set-in-stone date. Canceling would send the message that she was ticked—and she wasn't. Not really. Mildly annoyed, maybe.

"There you are," her mom said as Nadia entered her spacious, gulf-view office. "I wondered if you'd show up."

So they were going to act as if nothing was stilted or tense, then. Okay.

"And miss out on cashew chicken and pepper beef?" Nadia said, forcing nonchalance into her voice. "Don't count on it."

The food was already on her mom's desk, along with their usual soft drinks. Nadia took her seat across the desk from her mom, setting her notebook aside. Since these were informal meetings, she rarely took notes, but she came prepared, anyway.

Joyce handed her a paper plate and they served up their food family-style, as usual. Nadia checked the delivery bag and reached in for the chopsticks. She unwrapped one set and dug into the chicken.

"Starving," she said, which was true, but stuffing food in her mouth also conveniently filled the unusual silence between them.

"How are things?" Her mom's question wouldn't sound all that unusual to an outsider, but the fact was, they were normally in contact so often that they didn't have to ask. They knew.

"Good. Jamie Castigliego is my new hero." She launched into a praise fest of her new events manager between bites.

Next, she updated her mom on the impending conferences and the newest prospects for events and conferences.

"I'm so glad you found Jamie," Joyce said. "You've been doing too much for too long."

"He's going to be worth every penny." Nadia washed down her food with a long drink of soda. "So what's new with you?"

Her mom ran through the laundry list of issues she had to deal with on a regular basis. It'd always been their family's way to discuss business at dinner, even when Nadia was a kid. Her mom and dad had made a point of the three of them sitting down to eat together as often as possible, and the hotel inevitably came up. They'd never tried to hide concerns or problems from Nadia, believing that one day she would have to face the same things if she took over.

As they finished the last of the food, her mom leaned back in her chair and became strangely quiet. Disconcertingly so. Nadia frowned and asked, "What's going on, Mom?"

Joyce exhaled and tapped her fingernails on her desk. "I met with Ross Hennington this week. Of Hennington Lodges."

"Why?" Nadia sat up straight, concern taking hold in her gut.

That her mother didn't meet her gaze was telling. "It was just a discussion," she said. "We talked about some possibilities if Hennington purchased Silver Sands."

"You *what?*" Nadia wished she hadn't just wolfed down so much food. It was threatening to resurface.

Her mom crossed her arms and looked to the side. "We're barely keeping our heads above water, no matter how hard we work. It's a different world than when your father and I got into the business and...I don't know. Sometimes I wonder if it's time to take a step back. I was just exploring options. Options are good."

"Not if they include selling *this!*" Nadia spread her arms. "This is our lifeblood. Our family's past and its future. Yeah, it's hard, but really? You want to give up?"

"I didn't say that, Nadia—"

"It sure as hell sounded like it to me." She was on her feet now, her chair shoved backward. "What are you thinking, Mom?"

Her mother finally looked her in the eye and Nadia saw doubt there. Fatigue.

Yes, it was tiring to fight through this recession, the downturn in travel, the upswing in competition. But that was what they did. That's what they lived to do.

"Is this because of Dr. Morris?" Nadia asked.

She expected her mom to deny it, regardless of whether it was true or not, but Joyce hesitated.

"In part," she said noncommittally. "You and I both seem to have other things on our minds lately. I care a lot about Gene. Sometimes I just want to be with him without feeling guilty about working a measly twelve-hour day."

Still stunned, Nadia fell back into her chair and stared at her mom.

Who was this woman? What had happened to the heart and soul behind the hotel?

"Think about it, Nadia. All the things we miss out on because we're buried in here working our butts off and getting virtually nowhere. You're young. You're supposed to be thinking about starting a family."

"I'm twenty-seven, Mom. I have time."

"What about whomever you've been spending time with lately?"

Nadia clamped her mouth closed, taken aback that her mom had even noticed. It wasn't as if Nadia had been home enough that her mother could monitor her comings and goings. And she wasn't spending a *lot* of time with Penn. She had nothing on Joyce and Gene.

"Is that why you're doing this?" Nadia asked. "Because I've taken a few hours off here and there?"

"I'm not 'doing this.' I'm merely thinking about it. But yes, you're part of the equation. I worry about you. Maybe it's time we both learned to live more."

"I *am* living more. And I can still handle the job. Is my performance lacking? Have I dropped any balls?"

"There was the executive meeting…"

"That was because I'd been up all night. And it's the only meeting I've missed. If you want to punish me for it, dock my pay or something."

"You're being ridiculous."

"*You're* being ridiculous." Nadia stood again, rage boiling inside of her. "Does my opinion not matter in any of this? I was always under the impression it was a family business. I would have thought getting rid of it would be more of a democratic process."

"Nadia." Her mom used her stern voice—Nadia hadn't heard that tone for years. "I haven't signed any agreements yet. Hennington knows I'm exploring options, plural. You need to think about this rationally. You need to calm down, honey." She'd transitioned to her lecturing-a-child voice.

Nadia was shaking, inside and out. She stared at her mother, confused. Astounded. In a matter of weeks, Joyce Hamlin had become someone Nadia didn't even recognize.

"I need to go." Nadia didn't bother to grab the blank pad of paper she'd brought in with her. She marched out of her mom's office and straight to the nearest restroom, barely making it into a stall before her dinner came up.

FINANCIALLY SPEAKING, a vacant presidential suite was bad news for the hotel. For Nadia personally, though, it was relief.

Ever since she was about twelve, the presidential suite had been her haven. Back then, she'd had help on the inside in the form of Lucas at the front desk. If the suite was unbooked when she asked, he'd slip her a key card and turn his back. The agreement was that she had to stay back from the edge of the balcony—the only way someone could have seen her—and return the suite to its original state. As she'd gone through the hotel's housekeeping training and was careful not to mess the suite up, it was a small price to pay. Though her parents had never mentioned it to her, she suspected they'd known her secret.

As a member of the executive team and the general manager's daughter, she didn't need to explain herself to use it. She could check its vacancy and let herself in without anyone knowing.

That's exactly what she'd done this evening after the bomb her mom had dropped.

The gulf-facing side of the suite had floor-to-ceiling windows from one end to the other. The first thing Nadia did after letting herself in was to push the sheer curtains all the way to one end and open the sliding doors. The fresh sea air filtered in, and Nadia inhaled deeply, letting the salty, humid aroma fill her lungs and begin to calm her.

Without turning on the lights, she sank into one of the lush white sofas, letting the darkness, the air and the sounds envelop her. She tried to blank her mind. The idea of selling the hotel to, well, anyone… It didn't bear thinking about. Her mother insisted it was only a possibility, and Nadia was nowhere near done trying to talk sense into her if she continued to pursue it.

So much was storming through her she couldn't begin to sort it out. Nor did she have the energy to try. She just wanted to disappear for a while, to ignore reality. She kicked off her shoes and stretched out on her back, relishing the peace. Her eyes drifted shut and she didn't fight it.

She'd been blissfully floating on the edge of sleep for several minutes when her phone buzzed, rousing her. She attempted to ignore it but the thought struck her that it could be her mom. If it was, she swore she'd turn her phone off completely.

Growling in frustration, she removed her phone from her pocket to find a text message from Penn.

Are you working?

The discord from the past hour slid away with those three words and she smiled as she typed her reply.

Not. Even. Close. Where are you?

Out walking. Call me Forrest Gump.

Didn't he run? she typed.

Call me FG Wannabe.

Are you close to hotel, FGWB?

Might be. Who wants to know?

Was he flirting with her?

Her heart picked up as she responded. Just making conversation. ;)

Happen to be walking on beach outside SS now.

SS as in Silver Sands?

Nadia jumped up and went out on the balcony.

There weren't many people on the beach, as the temperature was down in the sixties tonight. She strained her eyes in the darkness trying to find Penn.

It wasn't difficult. He was strolling about half-way between the hotel property line and the waterline.

She texted him again. I see you. Dark shirt?

She watched him move closer to the hotel and could tell he was scanning the main level for her. She grinned as she typed.

Look up.

When he got closer, his gaze rose to maybe the second story.

Way up.

She leaned over the balcony and waved her arms. She could tell when he finally spotted her. He raised both arms in question as if to ask what the heck she was doing.

Nadia laughed again, tired of communicating with a tiny keypad. She patted her rear pocket for the key card that allowed access to the suite. Slipping back inside, she looked around the room for a light object and settled for taking a box of facial tissues from the bathroom. She hurried back out on the balcony, stuffing the key card into the box as she made sure Penn was still there.

Tossing a present. Watch for it.

His only response was ???

She threw the box out as far as possible so it would clear the palms bordering the patio below. It plummeted and she kept her eyes glued to it for as long as she could. She didn't see it hit the ground, but she could estimate where it must have landed. Nowhere close to Penn.

He again threw out his arms in question and she tried to point at the box.

Look twenty feet to the northeast.

When he read her message, he did as she said. She watched in amusement as he spun around and canvassed the general area.

What am I looking for?

White box.

About five minutes later, he found it. Again, the questioning arms came up followed by another text.

You threw me tissues???

Without hesitation, she instructed him. Card inside. Use it in east elevators to sixth floor.

CHAPTER THIRTY

PENN HAD THE EAST ELEVATOR to himself. Which was handy since it took him a while to figure out the key card was the only way to get the "six" button to light up.

He had no idea what Nadia was up to and he didn't care. He just wanted to see her. Hell, he wanted to do more than see her.

Cooper had taken Penn's mom to the airport that morning, then driven on to Austin to visit a friend. The condo was so damn quiet Penn thought his head was going to explode. Way too much time to think.

He'd tried to read a book but all he could think about was Nadia. Nadia being kind to his mother. Bringing him cookies. Wearing the backless shirt. Climbing into his bed…

He'd done nothing but push her away. Denied himself. Nursed his damn wounds.

He shook his head as the elevator slowly climbed. His wounds weren't going away any-time soon. He didn't know what would happen in the future, and he didn't care. All he was concerned about was the present.

Something Faith had said had been nagging at him all day. The bit about focusing on the good elements in her life. For her, the baby on the way and Joe.

For Penn? Well, it might be Nadia. If she could get past the way he'd treated her too many times…and forget about the future for a while.

He didn't know exactly what she was to him, didn't want to think about it too hard. All he knew for sure was that he liked her. Wanted her.

The elevator stopped and the doors opened. He stepped out and looked to the left and then to the right. There were four doors in the small landing, two on the wall opposite him. The other two were on either side of the elevator. He checked the key card for a clue as to which door it would open.

Lucky for him, the hottest woman in the world opened one of the doors opposite him and smiled coyly. Without a word, she eased the door open the rest of the way to let him in.

Sticking the key card in his back pocket, Penn did a quick scan of the moonlit suite and found that they were alone. He shut the door, closed the gap between them and kissed her.

She sucked in a gasp of surprise, then promptly clutched a handful of his T-shirt and pulled him closer. One of the things he loved about her—

her ability to just go with things, even when they weren't expected.

He let the tissue box fall to the floor and wrapped both his arms around her waist. As he deepened the kiss, one hand slid up to cradle the back of her neck to hold her in place.

Not that she was trying to get away.

His senses swam in all that was Nadia... The warm, delicate skin at her waist. The taste of minty toothpaste and berry lip gloss. The vanilla and shampoo scent of her silken hair draping over his hand.

When the kiss ended, Nadia opened her eyes and made a sound of regret. "Wow. Hello to you, too."

Penn pressed a kiss to the tip of her nose. "Hi, honey, I'm home. Great place to play house."

Nadia laughed, her voice husky. "Welcome to my humble abode for the time being."

"Beautiful." He didn't take his eyes off of her.

"You can't even see."

"I don't even care."

Nadia walked away from him and switched on a dim lamp on an end table. She turned around and looked at Penn. "Just wanted to make sure it was really Penn Griffin coming on to me."

"Do you let a lot of men into your darkened lair?"

"Only the ones I recruit off the beach."

He looked around him at the luxurious room. Pristine white couches, muted blue ceramic tile on the floor, a full kitchen with granite counter-tops and a chandelier above the dining table.

"What are you doing up here?" he asked.

"Hiding." She ran her slender hand over the back of the couch as she walked toward the balcony door. "You should see the view."

He was watching the view right now and definitely liked what he saw.

"The waves in the moonlight," Nadia clarified.

With a smirk, Penn joined her outside. They stood at the railing staring out at the water.

"Who are you hiding from?" he asked.

"Everyone but you, apparently." She brushed her hair out of her face as she stared at the gulf. Penn took in her profile, the swell of her lips, the long lashes…the shadows under her eyes.

"I started coming up here years ago," she said. "If I was upset or lonely or whatever, I'd find out if the presidential suite was vacant and pretend I lived here."

"So what is it tonight? Upset, lonely or whatever?"

She frowned as she considered. "A and C. The company so far is pretty decent." She flashed a smile at him, then sobered. "My mom told me she might sell this place."

"Silver Sands?" He couldn't hide his surprise.

"The one and only."

She was gripping the railing. Penn caressed the back of her hand as he let that announcement sink in.

"The hotel has been struggling, money-wise," she said without looking at him. "All kinds of reasons. Economy, newer competitors…" She broke off. "Too many factors to list."

"And your mom wants to get out while the getting's good'?"

"I don't know what she wants. I have no idea what she's thinking. This is our world. It has been since I was seven." Her voice was filled with emotion. "And while there may come a day when selling it is the thing to do, that's not now." She swallowed hard before continuing. "She didn't even ask my opinion."

Without thought, Penn moved behind her and rubbed both of her shoulders. They were hard with tension and he tried to massage the knots out of them. At first, she resisted, seeming to fight to keep her shoulders stiff, but within thirty seconds, she eased her head back and moaned in appreciation. He managed to ignore how erotic the sound was. Mostly.

"You love this place, don't you?" he said.

"It's all I know. I barely remember life before we moved here. It's always been a part of my future. I've never once questioned that, and now…" Her voice cracked.

As the tightness in her shoulders eased bit by bit, his touch lightened, and he traced circles with his fingertips.

"When I first met you, I thought your work addiction was about money," he confessed. "The BMW didn't do anything to persuade me otherwise."

"I bought it used five years ago," she said, straightening.

"Shh. It doesn't matter. As I was about to say, now I can see that what drives you is a passion for what you do. A belief in it. Total dedication to making this hotel the best it can be." He stopped rubbing and wound his arms around her, resting them on top of her upper arms, which she'd placed on the railing.

"I admire that," he said into her ear.

She leaned into him and held on to one of his arms. "Thanks," she whispered, and he barely heard it over the waves and the wind.

They stood like that for some time, without talking, just holding on to each other, his body pressing gently against her back. For the first time in ages, he didn't feel useless. She gave him the sense that she needed him, that he was maybe helping her in some miniscule way.

Eventually he felt her shiver.

"Cold?"

"A little." She turned around to face him. "I should stop whining to someone whose career has already been taken away. It's only a possibility for me right now."

"Seems more like you're taking up arms and prepping for battle than whining." He brushed her hair behind her ear. "Believe me, if I had the option, I'd fight to the death for the career I loved, too."

"I'd fight for yours if I could, as well." She looked earnestly up at him before her eyes dropped to his lips and lingered. "The other times we've kissed haven't turned out too well," she whispered.

They were so close, he could feel her breath on his skin when she spoke. "I'm thinking the third time's going to be a charm."

Her lids lowered again, and when her eyes met his, there was no mistaking the heat in her gaze.

"Hypothetically speaking, if I were to kiss you, would you freak out again afterward?"

"Don't plan to."

"Because if this continues, there's a good chance I will get really hacked off if you change your mind again."

He could only take so much anticipation, and he'd been craving her touch since last night. Even before then. He brushed his lips over hers. Lightly at first. Their breaths mingled and he kissed her harder, unable and unwilling to take it slow or gentle.

She wasted no time in responding, sliding her arms up around his neck and holding on. He pressed his body into hers, needing to let her know how she affected him, needing to feel her heat and show her that his body did work, that he wasn't broken, at least not when it came to this.

Minutes slipped away—he had no concept of how many. All he knew was that he could spend days here with Nadia and never tire of kissing her.

"You mentioned you were cold," he said eventually. "We could go inside if you want to."

She ran her fingers over his jaw and met his eyes. "I'm not cold anymore. At all. But we can go inside if *you* want to."

Going inside would lead to more than just staying warm, and they both knew it. It hung between them, disguised in her suggestion.

What if his body once again didn't work properly? What if he let both of them down…again?

The lower half of him knew exactly what it wanted to do, but the part above his neck was getting in the way. To buy himself some time, he leaned forward and ran his tongue over her lip. Nipped it lightly. They fell into another long, exploring kiss.

The first time after his accident was going to be

worrisome whether it was now or in two months. The one thing he was sure of was that he wanted it to be with Nadia.

He felt her hands inch up under his tee at the waist. They roved upward slowly, lovingly, to his chest. The simple touch made his blood pound harder. The kiss turned urgent, deeper, both of them more demanding.

Penn eventually managed to pull away and tried to catch his breath. And his thoughts. He leaned his forehead into hers.

"Nadia."

She breathed out with a nervous laugh. "Yeah."

He swallowed, tried to figure out what he needed to say to not sound like a complete moron. "I want you. So much."

She nodded and inhaled. "Me, too." She looked at him with a question in her eyes.

"I haven't…" Welcome to life's most awkward conversation ever. "Since my injury…"

She nodded again, her lips curving upward. "I get it. Are you allowed…?"

"When I'm comfortable with it," he said. His doctor had brought the subject up and, at the time, Penn had scowled and figured it was a pointless discussion. He exhaled nervously, wanting this conversation over with. "Let's just say I'm comfortable if you are."

Nadia answered by kissing him, her tongue

and lips tracing a slow, seductive path around his mouth. "More than. If you're sure it will be okay."

"I'd say the time you attacked me in my bed taught me my limits."

"Attacked?" Her eyes sparkled as they caught the moonlight. "Up until you moved wrong, I'd say you liked being attacked."

"Definitely a tolerable offensive. But I think the whole hypothesis should be tested further...."

"Yeah?" She dipped her hands into the back of his shorts. Her fingers on his ass kicked up the need to get this discussion the hell out of the way. "Science was never my strong point but I'm willing to do my best."

"I have a feeling you'll ace this experiment," he said.

The question was, would he?

CHAPTER THIRTY-ONE

NADIA'S HANDS MOVED around to the front, and before Penn knew what she was doing, she'd unsnapped his shorts. She kissed him as she worked one hand beneath his briefs and grasped him, making him suck in a breath.

"I can pretty much promise you one thing that won't work and that's standing out here on the balcony," he said in a strained voice.

"Then we should definitely go inside."

He reluctantly pulled her hand from his shorts and entwined their fingers. Led her back through the open doors. "Do we need to shut these?"

She shook her head and pulled him to the room to their right. The bedroom was bathed in dim light coming in from the living room, not that he took the time to check out the accommodations in detail. Nadia's hands were under his shirt again, lifting it to his shoulders. He pulled it over his head and threw it aside. The hunger in her eyes as her gaze lingered over his bare upper body made him vow to thank his physical therapist for pushing him to continue to work out regularly.

Penn drew her close and kissed her. He sought her skin, lifting her shirt enough to slick his hands against her. He felt her taut belly and her ribs, then the bottom edge of her bra.

Before he could explore further, her hands were at his shorts again, and shc shoved them easily to the floor.

"No fair," he said into her ear. "You're getting ahead of me."

She laughed wickedly. "Poor thing." She slid his underwear off and ran her hands over his bare ass as he pulled her lower body into his.

"Not thinking it's the worst deal ever."

He felt the back of his good leg hit the mattress. He lowered himself to it, then lay down carefully, silently begging his body to cooperate. There was only the slightest twinge in his lower back, so minor he wouldn't have thought twice about it if he hadn't been waiting for it. Even if it had been a ten on the pain scale, he would have quickly forgotten about it because at that moment Nadia stood at the edge of the bed easing her shirt upward, exposing her body inch by beautiful inch. She lifted it over her head and threw it behind her, revealing a silver leopard-print bra edged in lace.

She unfastened her pants and worked them over her hips as Penn enjoyed the show. When she straightened, he was treated to a tantalizing view of her silver string bikini panties. Holy hell, she was moving too slow for him. Unfortunately, sitting up and dragging her onto the bed would probably wrench his back and put an early end to the night.

"You're a tease," he said, propping his hands behind his neck, as if he was lying there leisurely and relaxed. His body blatantly said otherwise, and he caught her checking that out firsthand.

"A tease would be someone who doesn't follow through. You're just impatient."

"I'm at your mercy." His anticipation ramped up along with the pounding of his blood when she reached behind and unfastened her bra. She dropped the lingerie to the floor.

Penn growled at the sight of her nearly naked body. Couldn't wait to taste her, tease her nipples with his tongue. "Get over here."

She stopped, tilted her head and raised her brows at him.

"Please?" he said with a grin.

"Love a boy with manners." Nadia crawled onto the bed, leaning over until she could kiss him.

Penn's hands were on her the instant she was in his reach. They roved over her everywhere and within seconds he'd discovered the silver panties were a thong. Their lips still locked, he filled his hands with her ass and pulled her more firmly against him.

He palmed her breasts, loving the heaviness of them in his hands. She raised her body enough to give him better access. He toyed with her pebbled nipples, captured the tips between his fingers and thumbs, eliciting a moan from her.

"Your body is beautiful," he whispered.

"So is yours." There was so much desire in her eyes as she looked down at him. After all the crap in the past few weeks, he would swear at this moment he was the luckiest man in the universe.

Hands around her slender torso, he guided her upward so he could taste one of her breasts, suckle it until she was begging him for more.

"Grab my wallet. Back pocket of my shorts. *Please*," he added, but she didn't seem too concerned about manners anymore.

The view as she made her way back down the bed was erotic as hell. He didn't take his eyes off her as she located his pants and took his wallet out. She tossed the whole thing to him and peeled her panties down her legs.

Penn took out one of the condoms—yes, he was either optimistic or well prepared, maybe both—and unwrapped it. As Nadia moved up next to him, he sheathed himself, then started to turn his body toward her. His back had other plans and let him know it quickly. Frustration was only momentary, though, because Nadia slid her leg across him and straddled his thighs. Bending down, she kissed around his belly button, swirled her tongue over him, then slowly trailed her mouth toward his chest. Two could play the torture game. He kneaded her breasts, ran the tip of his finger around one nipple. She continued her way to his neck, jaw, ear. He nearly bit his tongue when she whispered in his ear exactly what he made her want to do.

When he could manage to speak, he said, "You forgot your manners."

"Time and place for everything." With a mischievous grin, she rotated her hips against him, teasing him with her heat.

"Some day," he murmured, "I'll be on top and the one in control. Just remember payback can be hell."

"Promise?"

He never got to answer because she lowered her head and kissed him like she meant business. He grabbed her ass and guided her where he wanted her.

At last, she lowered herself onto him, taking him inside her so achingly slowly Penn thought he might lose it. She leaned her face closer and their eyes locked.

"Everything okay?" she asked.

"Very okay, unless you plan to take a nap like that, in which case I'll be forced to summon my bionic powers and flip you over."

She raised her brows as if challenged. Began to move her hips, slowly, torturously. Determined to make her as wild as she was making him, Penn played with her nipples. He moved one hand lower, and when he touched her where their bodies met, she threw back her head and sucked in a breath.

"You don't play fair," she said, her voice lower than normal, sexy as sin.

"Time and place for everything." He purposely mimicked her earlier words.

The games and teasing were forgotten as she moved faster, took him deeper. He started to respond with his lower body and realized instantly that wasn't going to work. Though it took some effort not to move the way he wanted to, he'd gladly deal with that hardship every day till he died if it meant having her naked and on top of him.

Their rhythm became fervent, their bodies slickened with sweat. He held on to her hips and knew she was close by the sounds she made and the things she said. She was even more beautiful as she came unglued.

He watched her climax, the look on her face shattering his own control. He came seconds after her, arching into her, ignoring the twinge in his back. At that moment he didn't care if he pulled it badly enough to need another surgery. The only thing that mattered was Nadia and the way she made him feel.

He became aware that she was kissing him along the jawline, working toward his lips. With an unhurried kiss, she nuzzled her head in next to his chin and relaxed on top of him.

Penn ran his fingers through her hair, waiting for his equilibrium to return. "That wasn't so bad," he said once his breathing leveled out.

Nadia's head popped up and she narrowed her eyes at him. Penn chuckled, realizing his error.

"What I meant to say was that was toe-crackingly amazing."

"That's a little better…." She propped her chin on top of her hands on his chest.

He hesitated. "Have to admit I was a little… concerned."

"About your back?"

He nodded.

"And it was okay?"

"Okay enough."

"You think you can walk?" she asked, grinning smugly.

"Don't know why I'd ever want to move from this spot, but yeah. Think I'll make it." He closed his eyes, trying to ignore the doubt nagging at him.

Hell. The best way to deal with that was to ask.

"Was…that okay for you?"

Nadia's drowsy eyes opened all the way. She laughed, a quiet, sexy sound. "Do you have to ask, Penn?"

He shrugged, relief starting to seep in. "That wasn't my usual M.O. Just want to make sure…"

She eased up even with his face again. "You—" she pressed a kiss to his lips "—are the sexiest man on the entire island." Another kiss. "You could be sitting in the hardest, straightest-back chair in the world, and sex with you would still rock my world."

Her words struck a chord in him, more so than he would admit. He attempted to lighten the moment, distract himself from thinking too hard about it. "We'll have to try that sometime. The chair thing."

"Does that mean you're not going to walk out of here and avoid me, then?

"The only place I'm walking to right now is the bathroom, if that's okay."

"I guess this once I'll allow it."

When he returned, Nadia had switched off the light in the other room, and climbed in beneath the covers on the king-size bed. If he'd had any hesitation about staying, the sight of her lying there in the moonlight erased it.

He stretched out next to her and was able to roll to his side to put his arms around her. Two weeks ago, he wouldn't have been able to handle that small move and he thanked God for the progress he'd made.

A comfortable silence fell between them for several minutes. If not for the light movements of her fingers on his side, he might have believed her asleep.

"Got something on your mind?" he asked.

"I'm thinking we've spent a record amount of time together tonight without arguing once."

"Wonders never cease," he said, caressing the curve of her hip. As long as they avoided certain topics, he felt certain they could continue to get along. In fact, the less talking, the better. He kissed her lightly.

"Faith and Joe's wedding is next weekend. Are you going?" she asked.

"Yep. Haven't had any better offers yet," he joked.

"Want to be my date for it?"

"I think that qualifies as a better offer."

"You think?" She traced a finger over his lips. "I'm a bridesmaid so you'll be on your own for part of it, but once the official stuff is over, I'm yours for the night."

"I like the sound of that," he said, not planning to wait until then to have Nadia like this again.

She propped herself up on one elbow. "Would it be pushing my luck too much to ask you to the rehearsal party on Friday?"

"Isn't it a little late to be inviting an extra person?"

"Well, you see, I have some connections."

"It's at the hotel?"

"Kind of. It's on the beach but the hotel is putting it on. It's casual. Not your typical rehearsal dinner, just a buffet, an open bar and a party."

"I wouldn't want a pretty girl like you to be dateless for any of that," Penn said.

"Is that a yes?"

"Definitely a yes."

Though a party on the beach sounded like it could present multiple problems for him with his limited abilities, he pushed his worries aside and rolled to his back, pulling Nadia with him.

NADIA ROLLED OVER, needing a moment to figure out where she was. As soon as she felt Penn sleeping inches away from her, she relaxed, intending to drift right back to sleep.

Her brain had other plans.

Instead of allowing her to bask in the contentment of being with Penn, her mind fixated on her mom's admission about the hotel. It ticked her off that such a stressful thought could infringe on her time with this man. She fought it with all kinds of rationalizations and reassurances to herself that she could worry about it later, but nothing helped. Nothing could erase the panicked feeling that pumped through her veins.

Her mom had said she was only exploring the possibility of selling the hotel, but no matter how Nadia reasoned with herself, she couldn't stop the questions.

What if she could no longer work at Silver Sands? What would she do? What if she was able to keep her job but hated the new management? How could she fill the hours of her life that were now taken up by her career?

The thought struck her with the force of a wrecking crane: without her job, she would have nothing.

Just like Penn.

She'd spent so much of her adult life making sure she didn't prioritize anything above the hotel. It was suddenly crystal clear how that just might bite her in the butt.

It felt like an invisible fist had closed around her chest, forcing her heart to beat twice as hard and sucking all the air from her lungs. The darkness seemed to swallow her up.

Penn stirred, and before she could gather her wits, he wrapped an arm around her middle. Grateful for the interruption in her freak-out, Nadia snuggled into him, breathed in his masculine scent. Her heart slowed to a more normal pace.

She allowed herself to revisit her potential crisis but the panic was gone. She was more centered now. Calmer. Able to think rationally.

She had her job for now, and maybe for as long as she wanted it. But maybe it was time to make some changes.

Nadia wanted Penn in her life. Not for just random run-ins or chance cookie dates. She longed to know him better, to understand him intimately. To be comfortable enough with him that they could do anything together—talk, watch mindless TV, cook, whatever. For the first time, she could imagine herself walking away from work before her usual ungodly quitting hour—to be with Penn. Starting right now, Nadia was going to work on balance. Less work, more Penn. After years of such single-mindedness, it wouldn't be easy, but she finally understood how such a change could be exactly what she needed.

CHAPTER THIRTY-TWO

HINDSIGHT WAS twenty-twenty, Penn thought as he vacated the chair Nadia had insisted one of the hotel's events staff track down for him. His *special* chair. The one that set him apart as being less than normal. As if he or anyone needed a chair to remind them of that.

He never should have agreed to come to Faith and Joe's rehearsal party.

The sun had set a couple of hours ago and the party was in full swing. Tiki torches were wedged into the sand next to the Silver Sands, and long buffet tables filled with appetizers and finger foods lined the patio. The volleyball net had finally been deserted due to darkness, and now a group had gathered near the speakers that were pumping out bass-heavy dance music.

"Hey, you." His sister, Zoe, sidled up to him and made him smile in spite of himself. "Where's your woman?"

"Nadia's in the middle of that." He indicated the large group of people dancing.

"I *knew* there was something between you two when I was here before. Knew it!"

"At that point, there wasn't."

"It was there," Zoe said. "The guy is just usually the last one to know."

"Speaking of last one to know, why didn't you fess up about you and Coop?" He was still trying to wrap his head around the fact that his roommate and his sister, opposites in so many ways, had started a long-distance thing after she'd left San Amaro. Serious enough that she'd flown back to town to be his wedding date. "I suspected you guys had a thing for each other when you were in town before, but I nearly fell over when you showed up on his arm. Couldn't even warn your brother you were coming back to the island, huh?"

They stood along the edge of the party, watching several crazy-ass firefighters who were in the wedding party—Cooper included—as well as the groom's rowdy stepbrothers and an assortment of beautiful women form a conga line on the sand.

"That's kind of the point of a surprise," Zoe said. "The look on your face was priceless."

"All you two did while you were in town last time was bicker and flirt. But I didn't know you were still in touch."

"We were debating, not bickering."

"And sneaking around after I went to sleep, apparently."

Zoe took a swallow of her drink and shook her head. "No. We didn't really get involved until after I went back to Colorado. It took me a while to decide if I could deal with his blockheadedness."

"At least you seem to know him pretty well. So why aren't you out there acting like an idiot with him?" He motioned toward Cooper, who was currently bringing up the tail end of the conga line. He did his damnedest not to look, yet again, at Nadia, who he knew was sandwiched between two of Joe's stepbrothers.

Zoe watched Coop, her eyes sparkling, and it was evident she was either in deep or on her way to being in deep. Though his first instinct upon seeing her on Coop's arm earlier was to beat up his roommate for taking advantage of his sister, Penn was starting to come around. Starting to think maybe the two of them were a perfect match, after all. Maybe they would balance each other out. And if Zoe was as happy in six months as she looked now, then so be it. He wished them well.

"I have a general anti-conga-line rule," she said.

The song ended and the noisy line of half-drunk, happy revelers dispersed, most of them re-gathering to dance to the next cheesy disco song.

Nadia caught his eye and she came over to

them. "Everything okay?" she asked, breathing hard from dancing.

"Just fine," Penn said. "You better get back out there, party girl."

She looked torn for a moment. "I wish you could join us."

So the hell did he. Then he wouldn't be fixated on which guy was touching her where.

"Go on. It appears you can dance for both of us."

"I'll be back soon," she said, and returned to the middle of the pack, between Faith and Mercedes.

"I'm surprised she didn't stay here with you," Zoe said matter-of-factly.

"She hung out with the crippled guy earlier. Brought me a straight-back chair and everything." He wasn't hiding his self-disgust well, he realized. "She's gone far beyond the call of duty."

"I suspect you're not a 'duty' to her."

If he wasn't yet, he should be. He sure as hell wasn't much of a date.

Penn checked his watch, wondering how much longer the party would go on. Surely the bride and groom would want to get a good night's sleep before their big day.

Zoe turned her attention to Penn, becoming serious. "Before I forget, I wanted to ask you something."

"Am I in trouble?"

"Well, probably, but that's not what I was going to talk about. I wanted to ask you to come home for a visit."

"To Colorado?"

"Where else?"

"My home is here now. Has been for years."

Zoe rolled her eyes. "Yeah, yeah, I get that. You know what I mean. You haven't been to Boulder for years."

He hadn't had any desire to go to Boulder. However, maybe it was time. The idea didn't make him want to poke his eyes out with a needle as it once had. "What would I do in Boulder?" he asked.

"Hang out. Visit your family." She took another sip of wine. "I know we said maybe Christmas but there's something coming up sooner. Mom has this thing in a couple weeks. The environmental group she's been doing pro bono work for is honoring her with some big award and they're presenting it at a formal banquet. She tries not to show it but she is so thrilled with the honor. I was thinking it would be nice for both of us to be there."

Penn ran over the objections that came naturally to mind. He was surprised to realize he didn't mind the idea so much. Getting out of town might be what he needed. "Maybe," he said. "I'll look into airfares."

Zoe gave him a wide-eyed look of astonishment. "Really? I was all poised to do battle and was even willing to stoop to guilting you into it."

"Don't know about guilt but if you want to try bribery, I'm open to it."

"Ha. You showed your cards too early."

The song ended and another one started. Cooper came over and put his arm around Zoe.

"Get your own woman," Coop said to Penn. "Speaking of, where's Nadia?"

Penn pointed her out easily, having been unable to stop tracking her in spite of his efforts. "Right in the middle of the groom's brothers."

"They behaving themselves or do I need to go kick some ass?" Coop asked, laughing.

"They're fine." Penn had trouble working up any good humor about the situation. "It'd be different if her date could actually move."

"I'm going after some dessert. You guys need any?" Coop asked.

"Some more strawberries, please." Zoe grinned at him, probably knowing full well how Cooper would react.

"I'll grab you a couple cheesecake bars, too."

She shook her head and waved him on his way.

"You don't seem to be enjoying yourself," she said once Cooper left.

"I'm not." Penn shoved his hands in his pockets, gritting his teeth. The truth was that Nadia should be here with someone who could dance with her. Someone who could have helped her move the buffet table down when she needed it. Hell, someone who could drive her home when the party was over.

"I'm sure it's not easy watching all those guys having fun with your girl."

No. It wasn't goddamn easy. He trusted Nadia. Joe's brothers were probably fine, too. But that didn't make it any bcttcr.

"I'm going for a walk, Zo. If Nadia wonders where I am, tell her I'll be back before the party's over."

Without waiting for his sister to reply, Penn stormed off into the darkness, wishing he could find a way to accept his situation because, frankly, being pissed off all the time was getting old.

CHAPTER THIRTY-THREE

PENN WOULD HAVE LIKED to be able to say that waking up with Nadia by his side the morning after the rehearsal party made everything right in his world.

It didn't, though.

Far from it.

At 6:42 a.m. he gave up on getting any more sleep. If he didn't get upright in the next thirty seconds, he swore he'd take a double dose of pain pills—pills he'd had to resort to for the first time in days just last night.

After staying with Nadia at the Silver Sands most of the past week, they'd come home to get his pills and decided they were too tired to go back. That'd been a mistake. Sharing his twin bed had apparently been the wrong decision. In spite of his being cautious, he'd managed to twist wrong, sleep wrong, God only knew what else wrong, and he felt as though he'd been compressed into a too-small box all night long. The physical aches had seeped into his mind and put him in a foul mood even before he was fully awake.

He eased away from Nadia, who'd curled her backside into him and was still sound asleep facing the wall. Sitting on the side of the mattress should have been a relief but it did nothing to ease his discomfort—physical or otherwise.

Nadia shifted as he watched her, rolling on her stomach and turning her head in his direction. He waited for her eyes to open, but she slept on.

The sheet, twisted around her, went only partway up her torso and he admired the curve of her breast, spilling out from under her. The skin of her back looked as silky smooth as it felt. Blond curls fell over her cheek and he had to rein in the urge to brush them back.

He didn't want to wake her. She'd likely slept as poorly as he had last night, thanks to his endless tossing and turning in search of a comfortable position. She had a marathon schedule today, the day of her best friend's wedding. The alarm was set to go off soon but he'd let her sleep for as long as possible.

Penn pulled on a pair of shorts and left the room as quietly as he could. The condo was silent, so Cooper and Zoe hadn't returned from the hotel room they'd splurged on last night.

He headed to the kitchen, deciding he'd make Nadia breakfast so she could get her hectic day started out right.

Fifteen minutes later, he was regretting that decision.

Maybe it was lack of sleep but his reactions seemed to be off. Everything he did was clumsy. He'd burned his hand on the pan when he was frying hash-brown potatoes. Knocked over the entire container of salt and had to sweep half the contents into the sink to get rid of it.

He hated his damn nonfunctioning body.

A minute after seven-thirty, when Nadia's alarm had been set to go off, he heard the shower in the bathroom turn on. Egg time. Imagining her smile when she found breakfast waiting for her lightened his mood considerably.

Unfortunately, that lightness seemed to fly out the window in no time at all.

Penn took out three eggs to use for an omelet. Proving he was the clumsiest idiot this side of the Gulf of Mexico, he somehow knocked his arm on the counter. Two of the eggs flew out of his hand and cracked on the floor in front of the stove. He managed to hold on to the third—too tightly. That one cracked right in his hand.

Dammit all!

NADIA REGRETFULLY PULLED on the clothes she'd worn to the party last night. It would have been more fun to meet Penn with nothing more than a towel around her, but she was pressed for time. She followed her nose toward the kitchen.

The aroma of food had wafted to her as she'd woken up and her stomach had been growling ever since. Now, however, it smelled as if something was starting to burn. She wondered if Penn had stepped out or something.

She rounded the corner into the kitchen and all her questions were answered simultaneously. As she watched helplessly, Penn slipped on something and went down, his leg not moving in time to stop his fall. She rushed forward.

"Penn!"

He landed on one knee. It wouldn't have been a bad fall for the average person, but with Penn's injuries it could do all kinds of further damage.

He yelled out in pain and pushed himself fully to the floor, leaning his back against the cabinets. "Dammit!" He rammed his elbow purposely into the cabinet door behind him.

"Are you okay?"

"Do I look okay?" he snapped, his teeth gritted.

"What can I do to help?"

"Just…leave me alone."

She stared at him, racking her brain for what to do. Looking next to them, she discovered the puddle of egg goop that Penn had slipped on. Without a word, she stood and went for the roll of paper towels. Penn's eyes were closed as she began mopping up the mess.

"Leave it," he said when he finally realized what she was doing. "I can do it."

It was on the tip of her tongue to point out he could barely get off the floor, but she stopped herself in time. Without saying anything, she continued to clean.

When the egg mess was just about under control, Penn still hadn't moved. Nadia began to wonder if he'd reinjured himself.

"Do you need help getting up, Penn?"

Before he could answer, the smoke detector started beeping. She noticed heavy smoke floating above them and she jumped up in alarm.

"The pan's on fire, Penn!" she yelled.

He swore and tried to get up. "Get the lid," he said. "And an oven mitt, in here." He moved to the side and indicated a drawer.

Doing her best not to panic, Nadia picked up the lid from the counter. She located the mitt and put it on.

"Use the lid to cover it and turn off the heat," Penn yelled over the racket.

She did as he said, terrified that her arm would catch fire as she got the lid in place. As the lid fit over the pan, the flames died down. Nadia exhaled in relief and reassured herself the element was turned off.

"What now?" she asked, shaking from the inside out.

Penn stood several feet from her, his arms braced on the counter, his face contorted. She could feel anger coming off him in waves from where she stood.

"Penn? What do I need to do?"

"Nothing." He answered without looking at her. "Just go."

"Quit it, Penn. Everything is fine." Taking another deep breath, she calmed herself, realizing he was probably embarrassed on a dozen different levels.

"There's no reason to beat yourself up. The fire is out. Eggs are cleaned. You can apparently stand, right? Is there any other damage?"

Instead of answering, he picked up the oven mitt and threw it across the room.

"Penn, stop it. Stuff like this happens to everybody—"

"How many times do I have to ask you to leave, Nadia?"

She glanced at the clock on the microwave, biting down on her frustration. "I'm going to be late. You're sure you're okay?"

He narrowed his eyes and answered in a low voice. "I'm just peachy as hell."

Nadia stared at him helplessly. "I have to go.

I'll see you at the wedding tonight, Penn. You'll feel better by then and everything will be fine."

She rushed out of the room before he could snap at her again, trying to believe her own words.

CHAPTER THIRTY-FOUR

"WHAT ARE YOU DOING here at this hour, Nadia?"

Crap. Nadia hadn't expected her mom to be in this part of the hotel this early on a Saturday morning. If she had, she would have made a point of closing the door.

"Just double-checking things for Faith's reception." She replaced a white flameless candle into the Red Hots candies at the bottom of the hurricane vase after testing to make sure the battery was good.

"That's pretty," her mom said.

"Faith wanted a firefighter theme without being overt. And Joe refused to have real candles anywhere besides the unity candle," she explained in as indifferent a tone as she could muster.

They hadn't yet cleared the air after the hotel-sale conversation. Truth be told, Nadia had kept out of her mom's path as much as she could. It hadn't been difficult, since in addition to her usual workload, she'd been meeting with Faith and Mercedes almost every evening to take care of last-minute wedding details. Thursday night, for instance, they'd worked on the table center-pieces and the favors until three in the morning. Add in the time she'd been spending with Penn, which was almost every night, and she'd barely had a moment to eat, let alone argue.

The thought of Penn tightened the knot in her stomach and she promised herself she'd make sure things with him were okay later.

"Makes perfect sense. What doesn't make sense is that you're here doing something the wedding planner or our staff should be doing."

"You're here, too," Nadia said defensively.

"I was just passing through."

Nadia moved to the next table, took the candle out, tested the battery and put it back in. She leveled out the candy and stood back to make sure it looked okay. "It's Faith's wedding. I want it to be perfect."

Her mom chuckled unconvincingly. "We have a very capable events staff to do that."

"Yes. And they've done well. But these are battery-operated. I'm making sure they haven't died yet."

Her mom looked around the ballroom at the round tables and chairs. "It does look perfect. Faith will be thrilled with it all, I'm sure. I imagine she'd even forgive you if one of the faux flames didn't light up."

"Probably. But it would bug *me*."

Still taking in the setting, Joyce shook her head, then she went to the next table and picked up the centerpiece. "You're just checking the batteries on these, then turning it back off?"

"Right," Nadia said.

Her mom got busy checking, moving systematically down the row of tables. Nadia started on the next row over and they worked in silence for several minutes.

When they were at adjacent tables, her mom spoke. "So who's the lucky man you've had in your room here at the hotel almost every night the past week?"

Nadia faltered for a moment, ridiculously forgetting she was an adult who could have a guy overnight if she wanted to. She laughed at herself. Narrowed her eyes at her mother, curious. "Who told you?"

"I'll never reveal my sources," her mom said smugly.

Nadia finished one centerpiece. Walked to the next table and checked another. "It's Penn. The firefighter with the back injury."

"Oh? And am I ever going to meet Penn, the firefighter with the back injury?"

"I'll introduce you at the wedding."

"I can't wait. Is this serious?"

Nadia shrugged. "I like him. A lot. But…I don't

know." She didn't feel like going into the nuances of their relationship with her mother.

Her mom had stopped a few tables down the row and was staring at her with a half grin. "I'm happy for you, Nadia. I meant what I said about living more, and if Penn helps you do that, I'm all for it."

At the mention of their last discussion, Nadia tensed and focused on her task.

"Incidentally," Joyce said, "after thinking about it all week, I've decided to tell Hennington we're not interested in selling right now."

Nadia swung her gaze to her mother. "Really?"

"You were right. This is our place and I'm not ready to let it go yet. I don't think I ever truly was, but sometimes you have to look into your options...."

Nadia felt as if she could breathe freely after more than a week of being underwater.

"I'm sorry I didn't talk to you beforehand," her mom continued. "Things have been off between us lately and maybe that was my way of lashing out. I don't know. At any rate, it was the wrong thing to do."

"It's okay. Some good actually came of it, I think. You made me realize how badly I needed to find more balance in my life."

"That sounds promising, honey. We both do."

They went through a couple more rows without

talking. Nadia just wanted to get done. She was supposed to meet Faith and Mercedes to start the marathon day of wedding activities soon.

"So tell me more about Penn. What don't you know?"

"We go a few days and get along so well and I start to think…maybe he's it." She thought of the nights they'd spent together, the conversations they'd had. There'd been moments when she was able to forget all of the bad stuff, times when he seemed to act more like the pre-accident Penn. Her throat swelled with emotion and she tried to swallow it down. "I think I'm in love with him."

The second the words were out, she became more sure. Nodded. "I do love him." Warmth spread through her and she realized she was smiling.

"Color me not surprised," her mom said with a sappy grin on her face. "Any man who manages to drag my workaholic daughter away from her job a few evenings a week… He must feel the same about you."

Nadia set the last centerpiece down and sighed. "I don't know. We have some things to work through." The lump in her throat had turned acidic with fear. While the past week had been amazing, they'd been avoiding issues. Namely, his anger. She'd tried so many times to help him work through it, tried to suggest ways for him to move beyond it, beyond the accident, but he didn't seem to *want* to move on.

"If it's important to you both, you'll get through them," her mom said.

Nadia nodded. It was important enough to her, but the jury was out regarding Penn.

She turned around and surveyed the room as a whole. The red-and-white theme was simple and beautiful. The centerpieces looked perfect.

Her mom walked up to her and hugged her. "Love you, honey. I hate when we disagree."

Nadia leaned into her mom. "Me, too, Mom."

There was nothing in the world like a mom hug. She held on for extra seconds, wishing she could take this comfort and cling to it for the rest of the day, until she saw Penn again.

PENN WAS NOWHERE to be found.

Nadia had held out hope through the chaos of the ceremony, pictures, the dinner, the toasts and all the official bits that she just hadn't looked hard enough. They'd agreed to meet at the reception since she had ridden to the hotel with the wedding party.

But no.

He'd stood her up.

After everything they'd been through, after the progress they'd made, he'd let this morning's anger get the best of him. And she could admit it—it was getting the best of her, as well.

As far as Faith knew, everything about the evening had turned out perfectly. All the faux candles had stayed on at dinner—and yes, Nadia had checked them—the unity candle had lit on their first try. Faith looked absolutely beautiful. Joe was killer handsome in his dress blues, and when they stood together, so undeniably happy as they posed for pictures at every turn, Nadia could easily imagine a little one joining them. A gorgeous little one with his or her mama's eyes and daddy's olive complexion.

Nadia stood against the wall, watching people dance but no longer really seeing anything. When one of Joe's stepbrothers asked her to dance, she tried to smile and shook her head. Then she decided to find a better place to wait out the rest of the party.

She couldn't, absolutely *would not,* leave her best friend's wedding early, but at the first opportunity, she was going to have a word with Penn.

CHAPTER THIRTY-FIVE

PENN REALIZED HIS MISTAKE when he saw Nadia approaching his front door from his spot by the window: he should have left the condo. That or locked the door.

When she knocked, he didn't move from his trusty straight-back chair. He continued to stare from the dark living room out toward the deserted swimming pool.

She knocked two more times, then tried the knob and, of course, came on in.

"Penn?" She hollered loudly enough it was evident she couldn't see him sitting there six feet away. She walked into the hallway and flipped on the light. He watched her reflection as she continued toward his room and said his name again.

After verifying that he wasn't in his room, she turned in his direction. The second she noticed him, she stopped and put her hand to her chest.

"What are you doing?" Anger was evident in her voice.

She came to the doorway of the living room

and stopped. Leaned against the wall, one arm to her side, the other gripping her own forearm.

He still hadn't stirred, instead watching her reflection in the window. She wore a fire-engine-red dress that hugged her body like a second skin. Thin straps gave way to a deep vee that revealed captivating cleavage. He'd explored that part of her body countless times and still had trouble pulling his gaze from it.

Below the narrow waist, the skirt flared out to highlight her hips and ended just below her knees in front, slightly lower in the back. Killer red stilettos finished off the look that made him almost regret not going to the wedding.

Almost.

Had he shown up, it would have been more of the same: avoiding the dance floor, feeling out of place, wishing he could be more of a date for Nadia.

"You don't have anything to say?" Nadia asked. "Nothing?"

"What do you want me to say, Nadia?"

She scoffed. "'Sorry' would be a decent place to start, but only if you really are." She paused. Waited for him to speak. "Well, there's one answer for me."

"Turned out I wasn't in the mood for a party."

Before he could register what she was doing, she rushed toward him and kicked his chair.

"Dammit, Penn! You can't even look at me while we have this discussion?"

"What discussion is that?"

She was fuming next to him, staring down at him. And son of a bitch that he was, he received a small amount of gratification that someone besides him was finally pissed off.

Penn stood up and turned to face her.

Nadia shook her head, slowly, deliberately, with a coldness in her eyes he hadn't seen before. "I can't do this, Penn. You've pushed and pushed and I've taken every last bit of it. I've been on the receiving end of your blame and anger for weeks."

"Probably all true," he said much more calmly than he felt. His heart hammered in his chest and, once again, he wanted to lash out.

"As long as you have such resentment about everything you've lost, you're going to hold the accident against me. I've played your guilt game. I've had bone-deep guilt eating me alive ever since I first saw you lying in that hospital room."

He flinched inwardly and then thought how screwed up that was.

"I can't live with that," she said. "I won't."

"Okay." Who could blame her? If their roles were reversed, he would have hit the road long ago.

"I've tried to help you get past this, to see that

you can build a good life, but as long as you sit there and refuse to move on, you're not going to be happy, Penn."

He clenched his jaw so tight his teeth nearly cracked. "You can't be my savior, Nadia. You can't begin to know what I'm going through, what it's like to lose everything—"

"No," she yelled. "I can't. Not when you're too scared to even talk about it."

"Who said I was scared?"

"I've done everything I can think of," she went on, ignoring him. "All you've done is sit there and be angry. You can do that all you want, but you're not taking me down with you."

Again, she stared at him as if she expected him to deny her accusations. He didn't.

"I'm done, Penn. Have a nice life."

She pivoted and walked out. The door slammed after her and the contrast of the silence was deafening.

Penn stood there, stunned, like a bird that had flown into a window. Except unlike the bird, he was pissed off to no end at the window.

He stormed to his room and dug out a duffel bag from his closet.

To hell with Nadia. She could be done all she wanted. He was out of here.

He sent his sister a text.

Flying out with you tomorrow. Will meet you at the airport.

Without waiting around for a reply, he stuffed what he'd need for the next week in his bag. He had no idea if Zoe and Cooper planned to come home tonight, but he didn't want to be here if they did. He wasn't in the mood to talk to anyone.

When his bag was packed, he switched off the light in the hallway, grabbed his keys from the kitchen and went out to his Jeep, paying no heed to the fact that his doctor hadn't approved driving yet. It was close enough.

He got behind the wheel and headed to the mainland, relishing the thought of spending the night alone in the airport.

IN TIMES OF UPSET, Nadia had always turned to work.

Tonight was no different. She left Penn's and drove directly to the hotel, telling herself she needed to make sure the reception had been wrapped up properly. When she reached the ballroom the only sign of the party that had ended just an hour ago was the custodial staff members cleaning the floors. Nadia ducked out of the doorway before they could spot her, acknowledging she wasn't up for cheery small talk, and that was exactly what the hotel's employees had come to expect from her.

On autopilot, she walked toward her office, taking the least populated route. When she got there, she did something she rarely did—she closed her door. Sat down at her desk and booted her laptop. Without thought, she clicked on the events and marketing budget master file.

The numbers blurred. The words meant nothing. When a tear dropped onto the keyboard, she shut the file with a shaky inhale.

She picked up the layout proof copy of the new sales brochure from her in-box and tried to check it for errors.

This was not working. She couldn't manage to submerge herself in anything to do with her job.

Rubbing a hand over her tear-dampened face, she opened her email program and typed in her mom's address.

Mom, Not coming into work on Sunday. Talk to you soon. Love, N.

What she was doing Sunday, she had no idea, but it didn't include the hotel, and it didn't include Penn. It might not even include getting out of bed.

Still wearing the red dress and heels, she went to her hotel room, ensured the Do Not Disturb sign was in place and shut herself in.

CHAPTER THIRTY-SIX

"IF YOU'RE GOING to waste yet another night of your life in front of the television, you should at least turn it on." Zoe sauntered into the family room of the Griffin home carrying a section of the newspaper and a mug of hot tea. She set both on the coffee table and curled up on the couch.

"Hadn't gotten around to it yet," Penn said. "What am I missing?" Not that he cared. He wasn't a big TV person, beyond sports shows. And yet, as Zoe said, he'd pissed away hours in front of it every day since he'd been in Boulder. In this very chair. A straight-back, cushioned one from the dining room table, of course.

"There's always a high quality reality show on somewhere." She picked up her tea and stirred it, the rhythmic clink of the spoon against the ceramic mug somehow soothing. "Thanks for cooking again. Mom and I may not let you leave. You're spoiling us."

"You've been spoiled since the day you were born," he said with a ghost of a smile. "The flank steak came out pretty decent, didn't it?"

"Everything you've made since you've been here has been 'pretty decent.' You're showing me up, you know. If I didn't get to eat what you cooked, I'd kind of hate you."

"Eh, you kind of hate me, anyway."

She sipped tea from her spoon, then put the mug back on the table. "I kind of hate the way you're basically drifting through your days, now that you mention it."

Penn held his cell phone in his hand, even though the screen had gone to sleep a few minutes ago. Though he had no reason to think Nadia would contact him, he'd kept his phone with him at all times as if it was a link to home. To her. Just in case.

Not surprisingly, in the eight days he'd been in Colorado, he hadn't heard a word from her.

"I hate it, too," he admitted uncomfortably. "But I don't know what to do about it."

Zoe leaned forward, picked up the newspaper she'd brought in and tossed it on his lap, opened to a specific page. "I thought you might want to read that story."

Biting down on the annoyance that had become so second nature to him, he picked up the newspaper and scanned the headlines, trying to guess which one she thought was going to change his life.

He didn't have to ask.

Local Firefighter Killed in Collapse.

Damn.

Penn forgot his sister was in the room as he read every word of the article. He could see the described situation in his head, imagine the guy going down when the apartment roof, weakened by fire, fell in.

When he finished reading, he studied the photo of the firefighter. He looked like the average twentysomething guy. He could be any one of Penn's brothers in the San Amaro Island Fire Department. Penn was choked up as if he was.

He noted the time and location of the funeral services and tossed the newspaper to the table. Zoe was absently stirring her tea again, the sound joining the ticking of the handcrafted wooden clock that'd hung on the wall even when Penn had lived here.

"You're trying to tell me I'm better off than him," Penn said.

"I know better than to try to tell you anything. I just thought you'd want to read it."

He nodded slowly, feeling as if he'd lost a friend or a brother, even though he didn't know the guy from Adam. "Thanks." When a couple more minutes had passed, he acknowledged, "I *am* lucky. I just don't know what to do about it."

"What do you want to do? Besides firefighting, of course."

"I got this email today," Penn said sadly, picking up his phone again. "From the arson investigator in San Amaro." He felt Zoe studying him, though he didn't look at her. "I shadowed him on part of an investigation a couple of weeks ago."

"That sounds interesting," Zoe said carefully.

"He forwarded me a letter from the mother of the victim in that fire. She'd written to him to thank him for doing his job so well and for solving the crime. Apparently they've got a guy in custody—the victim's ex-boyfriend—and though he hasn't gone to trial yet, the evidence is pretty compelling. She said she was able to sleep better knowing her daughter's murderer was going to pay for what he did. She said it had brought peace during the most horrible time of her life."

"He sent it to you because you were in on the investigation?"

"Guess so. I helped him find some of the evidence."

His sister didn't respond so he glanced at her. She was staring at him with that thoughtful, know-it-all look, nodding her head.

"Whatever it is, say it," Penn said.

"You're interested in that kind of job, aren't you?"

Penn stood and expelled a loud breath. "I don't know. It'd keep me in the same line of work, or close to it. Beats the hell out of anything else I've thought of, but…"

"But what?"

He shook his head as he tried to put his thoughts into words. "It'd be starting over from scratch. I don't know if I have it in me to be the new guy again. To spend months in classes, learning a new career. Studying, taking tests, trying to get back into that groove after all these years." It'd been tough enough to do the school part of firefighter preparation, not because he was dumb but because he and sitting at a desk didn't go together very well.

"What's your alternative?" Zoe asked. "You either start over with something new or…what?"

"There are jobs out there that don't require schooling. Food service, bartending, furniture-selling." Just listing them made him feel sick. But then so did the thought of going back to school.

"That's exactly it. Those are *jobs,* Penn. This would be a career. It's scary, but I guess you have to decide which one you want."

"Guess so," he muttered.

He wasn't going to admit it out loud, but he was scared as hell of the future.

If someone had told him before his injury that fear would have him paralyzed, he likely would've either laughed at them or punched them.

He wouldn't have liked it then, and he sure as

hell didn't like it now, but he had to figure out how to get over it.

One thing was certain. After sitting in his mom's house for eight days straight, he was tired of being stagnant. Even more tired of feeling sorry for himself. And unwilling to accept that fear was getting the best of him.

"I CAN'T BELIEVE YOU TWO are coming with me to this." Nell Griffin squeezed Penn's forearm nervously as they walked into the conference center where she would be honored this evening.

"Why wouldn't we, Mom?" Zoe said. "We're not complete heathen offspring."

"Most days," Penn added.

"It's just…for you two to take time out of your busy lives—and to dress up so nicely— Thank you."

"I don't wear a suit for just anybody. As for a busy life…my most pressing commitments are therapy and dinner."

"For now," his sister said. She leaned forward to shoot him a meaningful look but he pretended he didn't notice.

"Explain to me what you're getting an award for tonight?" Penn asked.

"I've been doing pro bono work for this organization to get legislation passed to protect ranch land. It's been a two-year project and we finally succeeded. A lot of people's well-beings were tied up with it."

"That's great, Mom. I had no idea you've been working on anything like that."

"That'll teach you to call your mother more often." She smirked at him as they entered the hall.

A half an hour later, Penn suspected he had a semi-permanent look of shock on his face. The first part of the gathering offered an opportunity for people to roam around the room to mingle and network. Penn had assumed his mom would hurry off to talk to everyone she knew in the room—which turned out to be almost all of them—and leave him and Zoe to their own devices. Instead, Nell had dragged them around with her. She'd always been proud of Zoe for her academic achievements and her doctorate studies and never made a secret of it. This time, she also gushed over Penn. She'd proudly introduced him as her son, the firefighter.

That was a first.

After the first couple of times, Penn had mentioned to her in private that he wasn't a firefighter anymore. She'd said something along the lines of "once a firefighter, always a firefighter, at least in spirit." He'd been about to argue but Zoe had stopped him. Shushed him, as a matter of fact, the way only a sister could do.

He'd been mulling his mom's statement ever since, in between smiling, shaking hands and being honest-to-God touched by his mom's undeniable pride.

Dinner had been served and the waitstaff was currently distributing raspberry cheesecake and chocolate layer cake while the organization's president addressed the group. Penn tuned out most of it, caught up in his own thoughts, until the guy started introducing Nell.

As he listened to the accolades, Penn began to view his mom in a different light. She was well respected, which he'd always known, but these people seemed to genuinely love her for what she'd worked with them to accomplish.

The president finally invited her up to the stage to receive her award. Penn was moved by the standing ovation she received, but it turned out that had nothing on her acceptance speech.

She went on and on, thanking countless people, telling enough amusing anecdotes about them to keep it interesting even though he didn't know any of them. She thanked Zoe for being an understanding "roommate" and for leaving meals in the fridge for her when she'd worked late into the evenings on the project.

"And last but not least…" Nell paused and breathed in, seeming a little nervous. "Thank you to my son, Penn. I hadn't expected him to be here this evening when I made my notes, but he's visiting from Texas and conspired with my daughter to surprise me. So forgive me if I stumble a little."

Again, she stopped and collected herself. Penn shot a questioning look at Zoe, who shrugged.

"I owe Penn my greatest thanks because, well, he inspires me."

Penn's eyes widened.

"He and I haven't always seen eye to eye, and because of that, he may be surprised to hear all this." She sought him out then, taking a moment to connect with him from the stage and smiling almost shyly.

"Penn is a firefighter. He was recently injured and won't be able to return to his career, but that's beside the point. Years ago, Penn was on the road to becoming another academically inclined college student. Mind you, he wasn't given a whole lot of choice about this, thanks to his high-strung mother." She paused while people chuckled. "So I can only imagine his struggle when he realized he'd much rather become a firefighter.

"When he eventually broke the news to me, I can admit, I didn't exactly take it well."

Penn laughed at the understatement along with the other two hundred people in the banquet hall.

"I refused to help him financially because, really, throwing away a quality education to learn how to run into burning buildings?" She waved her hand as if the idea was crazy.

"He did it all himself. Put himself through community college and became a firefighter. It couldn't have been easy, but that was never his concern. His priority was being true to himself. Sounds simple enough, doesn't it?"

There were nods and murmured agreements throughout the room.

"But Penn, he never wavered. Even when I was so ticked off I couldn't see straight, I had to admit, my boy had courage."

Penn cleared his throat as quietly as possible, her words *getting* him with a capital *G*.

"I have a good job, but I wouldn't say it's doing what I burn to do. This…" She gestured around to the large group of people. "This is what I burn to do. And I don't know if I ever would have had the guts to do it if I hadn't watched my son follow his own path."

The audience broke out in applause and a lump swelled in Penn's throat. He couldn't bring himself to meet Zoe's eyes at that moment because he was afraid he'd do something stupid, like tear up, if he did.

"So thank you, Penn Griffin, for being someone who goes after what's important to him, who has courage in freaking spades and is the bravest man I've ever known. And thank you all for this award. It means more to me than I can say."

Again, the audience stood and continued clapping as she smiled at them for several seconds and then made her way down the stairs to her table. She wrapped her arms around Penn, stood on her toes and kissed him.

"I don't know what to say besides thanks, Mom," he said into her ear.

She smiled and dabbed at one of her eyes, careful not to smear her makeup. "I meant every word I said."

As they took their seats again, the president went back on stage to go through some business, but Penn tuned it out. His mom's words had hit him like nothing had since the career-ending chunk of roof in the hurricane. Since then, he hadn't thought of himself as being brave or courageous or anything positive.

But he was the same guy inside. His fall in the storm may have taken some of his physical ability away but it didn't have to take any of the other stuff. Not unless he let it.

He absolutely wouldn't let it.

Ever since his conversation with Zoe the other night, he'd done a lot of thinking. Had started making some decisions. It was time, beyond time, to take action. Time to be the person his mom thought he was—the person he knew he was—and work on building a future.

CHAPTER THIRTY-SEVEN

PENN NEVER WOULD HAVE believed that something as cliché as returning to his roots would help him get his head screwed back on.

Well, semi-screwed back on, anyway.

He leaned his forehead against the airplane window, watching for the lights of Corpus Christi to come into sight. It'd been nearly three weeks since he'd flown out of Texas, but he felt a life-time away from the self-pity he'd been stuck in when he'd driven his Jeep to the airport that Sunday.

There was a saying, something about always needing your mom, even when you were half a foot taller than her and had been on your own for a dozen years. Or if there wasn't, there should be. Before this trip he would have claimed he was the exception to that rule, but now he could acknowledge that maybe there was some truth in it.

His mom's speech, along with attending the firefighter's funeral, had provided the kick in the butt he'd needed.

And of course, Zoe had been hanging around

to hammer the point into his head some more whenever his courage waned.

He loved those two crazy women who were his family. Zoe had been amazing when he'd decided to take the plunge and find an online program to start studying arson investigation. After collaborating on what their mom had declared the best meal she'd ever had, the two of them had researched until the wee hours for the past three nights. Penn knew more about the career now, and knew without any doubts it was what he wanted to do.

His future was looking brighter than he'd thought possible even a week ago. He was beginning to have faith in it and himself. He just had one more crucial part of it to take care of.

NADIA SPREAD AN EXTRA thick towel on one of the wooden benches and stretched out on her stomach.

When she and Penn had been together, it'd been easier for her to drag herself from work for a few hours a day, to begin to find some semblance of balance. Without him, she'd had to find other reasons to walk away from her desk. Her favorite so far was her 5:00 p.m. date with the sauna. Every day.

She almost always had it to herself, so when the door now creaked slowly open, she lifted her head to see who on earth was interrupting her Nadia time.

It was a good thing she was lying down, otherwise she might have fallen over from shock.

Penn, dressed in his standard shorts, tee and shoes, ducked his head and walked through the door, letting it close behind him.

While acting casual would have been Nadia's first choice, it was impossible. Not after she'd spent weeks feeling as if she was grieving. The intensity of her sadness after walking away from him had surprised her and concerned her mother. They'd been together such a short time, but Nadia's feelings for Penn had been stronger even than she'd realized.

A reality she pushed out of her mind now as she hid her face in her arms and tried to stop her heart from racing. She counted to five as she inhaled deeply.

"What are you doing here, Penn?"

"Getting ready to sweat, it appears. Damn, it's hot."

"It's a sauna," she said, daring to turn her head to look at him. "How'd you find me?"

"Your mom clued me in. I'd like to talk to you, Nadia. Is there any way we could take it out of here?"

She studied him for a hint of what he wanted to discuss but his face showed nothing. Apparently she wasn't over her anger because she said, "I'll be done in fifteen minutes."

He stared at her, disbelief in his eyes. He opened the door and she relaxed a degree—until she realized he was only grabbing a towel from the stack by the door so he could join her.

Penn sat on the bench at a ninety-degree angle from hers, leaned forward a little and pulled his shirt over his head.

Whatever the game was he so wasn't playing fair.

She bit her tongue and cradled her face out of his sight again before she could get sucked in to staring at his chest. Hearing him out anywhere else would have been a better option, she realized too late. Now she'd doomed herself to sitting with a shirtless Penn for the next fifteen minutes.

"Are you going to hide like that while I set my man card aside and bare my soul?"

She blinked a few times, trying to absorb his words.

Baring his soul?

She eased herself up and sat against the wall. He stared at her the whole time.

"Nice suit," he said, nodding appreciatively at her body.

Instead of the black one-piece, she wore her red vintage-style bikini that sat low on her hips and had a halter-style top. Thankfully not overly revealing—for a swimsuit—but still, she felt exposed.

"Red is one of my favorite colors on you," Penn said.

Her eyes immediately veered to his to judge his sincerity, then she looked away quickly and used her hand towel to wipe perspiration off her face, trying to hide how the simple compliment unnerved her.

"You wanted to bare your soul about something?" she threw out, trying to volley the discomfort back to him.

He chuckled. "Hadn't planned to do it in a thousand degrees Fahrenheit but I can be flexible." He stood and paced three steps to the opposite side and back. Faced her. "I've been in Boulder the past three weeks. Staying with my mom and sister."

She bit down on the instinct to ask how they were. Somehow, she sensed that wasn't the point of the conversation.

"Long story short, I finally get it, Nadia."

"Get what?" she asked, wondering if it was possible to be wary and hopeful at the same time.

He moved to her bench, sat so close their legs and shoulders touched. She waited, but he didn't continue. His brow was furled as if he was struggling to think of what to say.

The suspense was killing her. "Are you going to tell me why you're here, Penn?"

He took her hand in his. "I'm here to tell you I love you."

She stopped breathing and maybe her heart stopped, too. Slowly, she turned her head toward him, looked him in the eyes. "You love me." She repeated it as a statement, but it was definitely a question.

He grinned like a shy little boy.

"Yeah. I love you, Nadia. And you were right. I was scared. I *am* scared. That sucks to admit out loud."

"You love me?" she asked yet again, not hearing anything else he said.

"I love you."

The heat climbed higher, becoming stifling. If she sat there for another second, she swore she was going to pass out. She jumped up, thrust open the door and headed straight for one of the open-stalled showers in the common area. She turned it to cool and sat on the tiny shower bench under the spray. Within thirty seconds, the fear that she was going to pass out dissipated but she didn't budge.

The sauna door opened again and Penn emerged. He came over to the opening of her stall and stared at her.

"I tell you I love you and you run away," he

said, frowning. "How much should I read into that?"

She smiled. "Don't take it personally." She stood and shut the water off.

"So." Nadia went to the stack of towels and grabbed a fresh one.

"So," Penn repeated.

"You think you can waltz in here and tell me you love me and everything will be fine, huh?" She smiled as she said it, but she was about 50 percent serious.

"Actually, no. If you'll recall, you ran away before the discussion was over."

"Okay, so there's more?" She squeezed her hair with the towel to get as much water out of it as she could, trying to occupy her mind with that task instead of letting it wander to the "more."

"Yes."

The spa area of the hotel's fitness center was not where she'd choose to have this conversation. "Give me two minutes to grab a cover-up and a hair band and we can take a walk."

He chuckled. "Even when it's my show, you have to take charge, don't you?"

"If I didn't, we'd still be broiling in the sauna."

"Point taken."

She went into the locker room, ran a pick through her hair and gathered it at her nape. From her locker, she took the plum-colored cover-up she rarely had use for and pulled it over her head. She tossed the pair of cheap flip-flops intended only for the beach to the floor and slipped them on. Glancing in the mirror was a mistake—her cheeks were pink and her hair frightening.

But he'd said he loved her.

If he loved her, he better love her both ugly and pretty.

Her pulse raced at the idea and she closed her locker, painfully curious about what else Penn had to say. She had to admit, he was off to a good start.

When she rejoined him, he'd grabbed his shirt from the sauna and put it on, which was both a relief and a disappointment.

"Ready?" he said, looking her over from head to toe.

"As ready as I can get anytime soon."

"You're beautiful. Care to walk on the beach?" He held out a hand to her.

She looked at his hand, glanced at his face and wove her fingers with his.

They didn't speak until they were off the hotel's property and well onto the beach, walking along the waterline.

"So where was I?" Penn asked.

"Something about a good stay in Colorado and you love me."

"We'll start with Colorado."

He told her the effect paying his respects to the firefighter he didn't know had had on him. Then he explained how his mother had bragged about him to her friends and colleagues. He paraphrased her award speech—or at least the part that was about him and, call her a sucker, but Nadia's eyes teared up as she imagined the moment. Because she agreed with his mom. He had so many admirable qualities, so much to love.

"The more I thought about what she said, the more it sank in," Penn said. "All that stuff she was saying about when I'd decided to become a firefighter and about being a firefighter—she made it sound like it's more than a label. That it's what's inside of me."

"It is," Nadia said simply.

"I don't know if she's right about all the praise, but it made me realize something. Probably something you've tried to tell me a dozen times. While my job title may have to change, I'm still the same guy inside. Everything that saw me through in the past is going to get me through now. Just with a different result."

Nadia closed her eyes, wanting to pump her fist in the air that he'd finally grasped it. "Yes! That is so absolutely what I've tried to tell you a dozen times. Guess I just wasn't saying it right."

"Or I wasn't listening." He squeezed her hand

affectionately. "But you weren't listening a few minutes ago when I said you were right."

She replayed their discussion. "You must have rushed that out after dropping the big L bomb so I wouldn't notice."

"I might be guilty of that."

"What was I right about?" She leaned into him as they walked, feeling lighter than she had in three weeks. Lighter and…bubbly. That was the only word she could come up with.

"I'm scared. Of the future, of starting over, of not knowing what's going to happen. But I know now that I'm also brave."

"Yes, you are," Nadia said.

"I wasn't acting brave. Wasn't facing my fear, or owning up to it, like you said."

"Now you are?"

He stopped walking and faced her. Nadia's heart was fluttering hummingbird-fast.

"Now I am." He grasped her other hand so he was holding both of them. "I enrolled for two courses online and talked to Dave Applbaum about maybe shadowing him on some investigations while I learn the ropes. He's on board to help me however he can."

"Good for you, Penn. I think you'll be amazing at it. You have a passion for firefighting and justice and…you'll be perfect."

"I don't know about perfect, but I know I can love it. I think I can do it."

"There's no doubt in my mind about that." She studied their entwined fingers, his large and calloused, hers winter-white and dainty in comparison.

"I've made headway on the anger," he said, hitting on the very question in her mind. "I won't say that it or my frustration are gone completely, but you were right about that, too. Moving forward feels a thousand times better. I'm starting to get excited about possibilities. I no longer blow up when my future is mentioned."

She laughed quietly. "You realize you just said the word *future* without freaking out?"

Penn grinned. "It's getting a lot easier to imagine. One day physical therapy will be over. I'll get through classes, get a job as an inspector... And if I play my cards right, I'm hoping for a chance at long-term access to Great-grandma Hamlin's chocolate chip cookies. And the girl who can give that."

"Hmm, those are pretty high stakes. How do I know you really want me and not just cookie access?"

"I'll do my best to convince you," Penn said, leaning down and kissing her, thoroughly, tenderly. As though he meant it.

When he finally ended the kiss, Nadia's head

was spinning. She stared up into his green eyes and knew she would remember what she saw there for the rest of her life. The moment was perfect, the sun starting to set, the sky full of color, and this beautiful, amazing man looked down at her with so much love.

"Are you convinced yet?" he asked, his voice husky.

"You're most persuasive."

He brushed her hair behind her shoulder, breathed his next words into her ear. "Excellent. So now what?"

"You said this was your show. It's your turn to take charge."

"Yeah?" He teased her earlobe with his teeth, nibbling lightly. "In that case, I think it's time we go usher in that future we were just talking about."

Side by side, hand in hand, they walked toward their future together.

* * * * *

LARGER-PRINT BOOKS!
GET 2 FREE LARGER-PRINT NOVELS PLUS
2 FREE GIFTS!

Harlequin

Super Romance

Exciting, emotional, unexpected!

YES! Please send me 2 FREE LARGER-PRINT Harlequin® Superromance® novels and my 2 FREE gifts (gifts are worth about $10). After receiving them, if I don't wish to receive any more books, I can return the shipping statement marked "cancel." If I don't cancel, I will receive 6 brand-new novels every month and be billed just $5.44 per book in the U.S. or $5.99 per book in Canada. That's a saving of at least 16% off the cover price! It's quite a bargain! Shipping and handling is just 50¢ per book in the U.S. or 75¢ per book in Canada.* I understand that accepting the 2 free books and gifts places me under no obligation to buy anything. I can always return a shipment and cancel at any time. Even if I never buy another book, the two free books and gifts are mine to keep forever.

139/339 HDN FEFF

Name _____ (PLEASE PRINT)

Address _____ Apt. #

City _____ State/Prov. _____ Zip/Postal Code

Signature (if under 18, a parent or guardian must sign)

Mail to the **Reader Service:**
IN U.S.A.: P.O. Box 1867, Buffalo, NY 14240-1867
IN CANADA: P.O. Box 609, Fort Erie, Ontario L2A 5X3

Not valid for current subscribers to Harlequin Superromance Larger-Print books.

Are you a current subscriber to Harlequin Superromance books and want to receive the larger-print edition?
Call 1-800-873-8635 today or visit www.ReaderService.com.

* Terms and prices subject to change without notice. Prices do not include applicable taxes. Sales tax applicable in N.Y. Canadian residents will be charged applicable taxes. Offer not valid in Quebec. This offer is limited to one order per household. All orders subject to credit approval. Credit or debit balances in a customer's account(s) may be offset by any other outstanding balance owed by or to the customer. Please allow 4 to 6 weeks for delivery. Offer available while quantities last.

Your Privacy—The Reader Service is committed to protecting your privacy. Our Privacy Policy is available online at www.ReaderService.com or upon request from the Reader Service.

We make a portion of our mailing list available to reputable third parties that offer products we believe may interest you. If you prefer that we not exchange your name with third parties, or if you wish to clarify or modify your communication preferences, please visit us at www.ReaderService.com/consumerschoice or write to us at Reader Service Preference Service, P.O. Box 9062, Buffalo, NY 14269. Include your complete name and address.

HSRLP11B

The series you love are now available in

LARGER PRINT!

The books are complete and unabridged—
printed in a larger type size to make it
easier on your eyes.

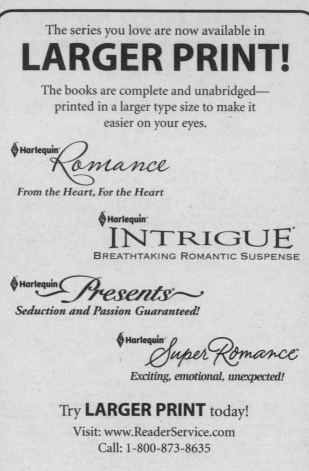

Harlequin *Romance*

From the Heart, For the Heart

Harlequin
INTRIGUE
BREATHTAKING ROMANTIC SUSPENSE

Harlequin *Presents*

Seduction and Passion Guaranteed!

Harlequin *Super Romance*

Exciting, emotional, unexpected!

Try **LARGER PRINT** today!

Visit: www.ReaderService.com
Call: 1-800-873-8635

Harlequin

A *Romance* FOR EVERY MOOD™

www.ReaderService.com

HLPDIR11

ReaderService.com

Manage your account online!

- Review your order history
- Manage your payments
- Update your address

> ## We've designed the Reader Service website just for you.

Enjoy all the features!

- Reader excerpts from any series
- Respond to mailings and special monthly offers
- Discover new series available to you
- Browse the Bonus Bucks catalogue
- Share your feedback

Visit us at:
ReaderService.com